WHERE THE BLOOD IS MADE

A SEBASTIEN GREY NOVEL

RYBURN DOBBS

PROLOGUE

The wary young woman scanned the classroom, watching her fellow students noisily settle in at their desks—chatting, shuffling, dropping backpacks, and setting out pencils for today's final exam.

But, unlike her, none of the others seemed particularly concerned with where they sat in the massive amphitheater-shaped lecture hall. She was fortunate, she felt, to once again find an open spot in the very back row, under the one burned-out light where it was just a little dimmer, a bit more shadowy. The phrase "dimness of anguish" came to her mind, although she couldn't place the source.

From her seat, she could barely make out the face of the teaching assistant who was standing behind the desk at the front and holding a large stack of papers. She had never seen him before. Maybe he was standing in for the regular TA—that frumpy girl with the massive glasses. Was he cute? Was he tall? She was too far back and too high up to tell. She could always move closer for a better look. *Better not risk it*, she told herself. And why would she do that anyway? She was in love. And he loved her. She knew that. At this point, she didn't have much choice. They were bound together now.

The TA split the tower of papers into smaller stacks then handed them to a few of the students in the front row, who began distributing them backward. The din of conversation dissipated as the test booklets spread through the rows.

Without looking, the greasy-haired young man in the seat directly in front of her threw a test booklet back over his left shoulder, which slapped her on the forehead as she bent over to retrieve a pencil from her backpack.

"Damn! Thanks a lot, jerk!" she growled sarcastically, almost to herself.

The offending student turned his head forty-five degrees and offered a dismissive "welcome."

After writing "Amber Harrison" in the uppermost right corner of the top page, she settled in as comfortably as she could and skimmed through the half-dozen or so pages of the test. She was looking specifically for things she had studied, things she thought might be on the exam. Thankfully, there was much she recognized—ATP synthesis, glycolysis, phospholipid bilayers. But a few of the questions—several actually—worried her. And what was even more worrisome was that none of the questions were multiple choice. She had been sure this would be a multiple-choice test.

She tucked some errant strands of golden hair behind her ear and looked to her left and right at her fellow back-row test takers. There was no more chatter about post-semester plans or frat-house parties. Heads were down, pencils were in various positions—from furious scribbling to suspended in confused stillness. A muted cough came from farther down the classroom to her right.

There was nothing left to do but get started. The first question was easy and gave her hope: "The alternate name for the citric acid cycle is_____." Her deep exhale lifted the edge of the test paper as she wrote in "Krebs." Question two was not so easy since she hadn't prepared for it: "Hemogenesis takes place primarily in the _____." She closed her eyes and bit the eraser end of her pencil in concentration, but the answer wouldn't come. Maybe she could reason it out. Hemo means blood. Genesis? Beginning, maybe? The beginning of blood? A shudder of doubt overcame her blank mind. It was true, what Brian had said. It didn't really matter how she did on the test, she reminded herself. But that seemed a whole lot truer when she thought—they both thought!—that the test would be multiple choice. She couldn't just leave a bunch of blank answers, could she? *Could she?*

Forty-five minutes later, she filled in the penultimate blank on the answer sheet and looked up from her work. A painful kink had developed in her neck somewhere around question thirty. She inclined her head deeply from side to side in an effort to stretch it out. The hall was about half-empty now. Just one more question. She hurriedly scribbled in an answer—God only knew if it was the correct one—and gathered up her belongings. The TA busily poked at his laptop as she approached him to place her completed test—upside down—on the growing and cockeyed stack on the corner of his desk. She turned quickly and headed for the exit door, not bothering to check the young man's height or his degree of handsomeness.

As she emerged from the science building, a young man lifted himself from the edge of the concrete border of the quad's large fountain. He was wearing tight black jeans and a yellow and black flannel shirt.

"Well, how'd it go?" he asked, standing as she approached.

"Okay, I guess. I think I did well enough."

He leaned in for a kiss, placing a hand gently on her neck.

"You didn't have to wait out here."

"I know," he replied. "But I feel bad, ya know? It hasn't been easy for you."

"Oh, that reminds me, the test was fill-in-the-blank and some short answers. Not a single multiple choice."

"Ouch. Sorry, babe. At least it's over with."

"Is it?" she asked dubiously.

"Well, just about. We'll be out of here soon."

The young woman swept her blond bangs from her eyes in an effort to read him a little better. He had expressed this sentiment before. Was he serious now?

"Where to? Where should we go?" she responded.

"Anywhere you want, babe. Somewhere warmer though, that's for sure. Maybe LA. You could be a model—like I told you. You would do great there."

She returned his embrace and the pair kissed once more.

"I love you for thinking that, but I don't believe it's true."

"You don't believe that I think you're beautiful?"

"No . . . I mean, yes. I believe you. I just doubt that I'm model material. I'm definitely not tall enough."

The young man gave her a firm two-handed squeeze over the back pockets of her jeans.

"You got a great body!"

"Oh, shut up! Let's go," she replied, looking around nervously.

The couple walked toward Student Parking Lot B. She had her backpack slung over her right shoulder, while he kept his right hand in her right back pocket. Perhaps they were too distracted by their affections to notice that behind them, beyond the opposite side of the fountain, an older man—a professor, perhaps?—hastily shoved the small book he had been reading into the pocket of his coat and started eastward against the wind in the direction of Student Parking Lot B.

Once they got in the car, the young lovers drove on. She stroked his nape-length hair from the passenger seat. They headed along the winding road, descending into the foothills.

"Are we really going to do this?" she asked.

"Why not? There's nothing for us here, except maybe trouble. You know it's for the best. A fresh start will change everything. Am I right?"

He was right, of course. This was one of the benefits of dating an older man. He was definitely more mature than college-aged guys—they weren't much better than the boys she dated in high school. They only wanted sex. Sex and beer, not love. At least she had that now.

"You're right."

She watched his lips purse as he mulled the next steps over in his mind. No, he was not impulsive and reckless like her last boyfriend. He was a planner. Wherever they went, he would take care of her. The thought of the future prompted her to reflexively look in the back seat at her suitcase and boxes, which contained almost all she possessed in this world. She gave away the handful of things that didn't fit, or that she no longer needed. None of those things mattered now. The semester was over, the tests completed. She was feeling optimistic about this fresh start.

"We've had a pretty good thing going. We made out okay. And I don't think anyone knows anything. Do you?"

She looked at him again, finding his face more serious now.

"No. At least, I don't think so."

"You're doing great too, by the way."

She smiled sweetly and squeezed his right shoulder.

"Thanks. But what do you mean?"

"I just mean . . . well, look, you can't blame me for wondering if you'd tell anyone. It would be natural if you did."

"I would never! Besides, what would I say? It's not like you're the only one . . ."

"I know. That's true. Oh, hey, before we head out, I need to make a stop. I got a guy who owes me some money. I don't want to leave town without getting it back, you know? We need all we can get."

~

NOT MORE THAN ten minutes later, a man—the same man who had been reading a cheap paperback under a tree in the university science quad—pulled off the highway and turned southward down a single-lane road.

A half a mile on, the pavement gave way to dirt. From here, he drove a couple of hundred feet farther, then made the prearranged left turn. He looked around just to make sure, but there were no other cars, no other people—no dog-walkers, no boondockers, no signs of anyone. Not even a deer among the brush.

The road made a gentle curve to the left, and it was not until he came out of that bend that the man saw the rear of a car parked off the road. A young man wearing a lurid yellow and black shirt emerged from the front of the car, jumping up and down, waving for him to stop. He resembled a bee, signaling for the queen.

"Well?"

"She ran off!"

"What do you mean, she ran off? Did you shoot her?" The older man pointed to the gun in the younger man's hand as he spoke.

"I tried . . . I missed."

"Oh, for hell's sake. Which way did she go?"

"That way."

"Wait here. And put the damn gun away before you shoot yourself."

There were no trails, but there wasn't much cover either. She couldn't go too far. And he realized, as he scanned ahead, that he held a distinct advantage.

"Come on, sweetheart. I'm a police officer. I'm here to take you home."

He stood still for a moment, straining to hear a reply, but only heard the wind.

"Police! You're safe now. We got here just in time. Your boyfriend is in custody. He can't hurt you now. Come on out so I can see you. That a girl. Come on out. Let's get you home."

A blond head rose up slowly from behind a lonely spruce, which had fallen into a patch of horsetail.

"There you go. It's all right now. You're safe."

The look of terror on the woman's head turned to relief when he waved her to him. She stood erect and began to approach, moving faster as she got closer. The dirt on her cheeks bore the tracks of tears, which caused a spark of pity to form in his mind. But he stifled it quickly. She was a few feet away when she opened her arms as if to grab on to this stranger-savior.

1

"You're out of your minds. Both of you."

Captain Roderick of the Custer County Coroner's Division pointed a hairy-knuckled finger across his desk, wagging it vertically. Lieutenant Breed of the Investigations Division and Coroner's Investigator Gerry Good Crow sat there silently on the business end of the digit.

"I mean, do you have any idea what you're suggesting?"

The question sounded rhetorical, and so it was.

"You think that human remains, which were found in September 2012, belong to a girl who went missing in January 2013. Ger, I know you well enough to know that you understand how the calendar works."

"Yes, I do, Captain. But remember, Amber Harrison did not go missing in January; she was *reported* missing in January. We technically don't know when she *actually* went missing."

"Don't we?" replied the captain.

The investigation's lieutenant took up the question.

"No, Gerry's right. We don't know. Our forensic anthropologist has looked at the remains, and he says they fit the profile of an experienced rock climber. Something about the spine, he said," added the lieutenant.

"Spine? We didn't recover a spine. Did we, Ger?"

The captain looked in Gerry's direction, hands suspended in frustration.

"No, sir, we did not."

Lieutenant Breed placed a file folder on the captain's desk and opened it.

"Captain, all we're asking is that we compare the DNA from the remains—which we already have—to the DNA from the missing Harrison girl, which we also have." A tap on the folder followed his statement.

"I am well aware of the process, Lieutenant."

Captain Roderick leaned back slightly in his chair, clasped his hands around his midsection, and rolled his eyes upward to the ceiling. His perfectly sculpted dark hair was reminiscent of the Bob's Big Boy statue, though no one would dare tell him.

"It's the ramifications that concern me, the idea that we have allowed a family—hell, a whole community—to assume a young woman left town willingly when her shoulder and arm bones were in our morgue freezer the whole time. It's actually unthinkable."

"I agree, Ted, but we can't ignore the possibility. We have no choice but to think about it. And, I hate to bring this up, but not everyone thought she merely left town."

Breed hoped the use of the captain's first name would soften him a bit, that it would appeal to the father in him and not the pencil-pushing, politicking drone that both he and his old friend Teddy Roderick had become when they got promoted to management.

"There was no spine found," reiterated the captain.

Gerry leaned forward in his chair as he responded. His dark features had a way of conveying a gentle wisdom when the circumstances called for it—all earnestness and sobriety.

"I know, boss, but this guy is good. He knows what he's doing. Maybe we don't exactly understand either, but Dr. Grey seems pretty sure about this."

"Lieutenant, what do you think?"

It would be a mistake to think Lt. Breed had not also considered the implications of this, the "ramifications" as Roderick had put it. He knew full well that public opinion on the Amber Harrison disappearance was deeply divided. Some believed the young woman ran off to California with a mystery man, while others believed—still believe—that the sheriff's office screwed this one up in a major way. It just didn't seem like the proper amount of resources had been committed to finding her. Once it was suggested that she had started a new life in Los Angeles, the matter lost its grip on people's attention.

AND THERE WAS SOMETHING ELSE. The public did not know a small amount of blood was found in the car that belonged to Harrison's mother, the car that was in Amber Harrison's possession before she disappeared. Was it enough to suspect foul play? Not necessarily at the time. Should it have been? Probably. But hindsight was twenty-twenty, as they say, and sometimes looking back can be dangerous, like it was for that lady in the Bible who turned into salt.

"I would hate for Dr. Grey to be right on this one, but I don't think we can ignore the possibility. And, like Gerry says, the guy has yet to be wrong."

Captain Roderick nodded as the lieutenant replied.

"I am aware of the contributions he's made over the last few months."

Breed continued, "So, yes, I do think we need to rule it out. It won't take long, and we don't need to announce it. I already spoke with Mindy over at the lab. She has room to knock it out and has agreed to fast track it. Forty-eight hours max."

"Does she know what case you—"

"Yes," interrupted Lieutenant Breed.

"I suppose that was inevitable. We'll be fine, but let's keep this as quiet as possible. And for goodness' sake, no one tell the sheriff until we know for sure. There's no point in bringing this up if it's not her. *Ever.* Can you imagine? Can you even imagine?"

"And in an election year," chuckled Gerry, as he rose from his chair and motioned to leave.

Lt. Breed likewise stood up giggling.

"You got a helluva sense of humor, Ger," hissed the captain. "You may want to consider keeping it to yourself this time."

To a regular resident of Custer, South Dakota, the precipitous drop in temperature, which is often yoked to the dreary advance of November, would hardly seem surprising. Nor would the few inches of watery snow that inevitably accumulated on Mt. Rushmore Avenue, only to be crushed into muddy ruts by passing cars. The wind too, biting through jackets and coats that were, just a few weeks previously, more than sufficient to keep one warm, would be a normal sign of the approaching holiday season to the folks who call the southern Black Hills their home.

But Sebastien Grey was not such a person. It was only a mere six or so weeks since he relocated from northern California to western South Dakota to be closer to both his family and the woman with whom he so recently came to regard as his saving grace. More than once he wondered if he would make it through his first honest-to-goodness winter. Tiffany had warned him, practically daring him to survive. But he was determined to endure, and he had many logs of motivation to stoke the fires of resolution.

Despite the aforementioned determination, Sebastien thought it best to endure this particularly frigid day from the comfort of his studio loft atop the Black Elk apartment building —an edifice he recently purchased. Comfortably installed on his leather sofa, Sebastien fixed his gaze through the large sliding window and surveyed the external goings-on. The sky outside was cauldron gray, and pedestrians were few and far between. One older man, waiting at the crosswalk on the opposite side of the street, caught Sebastien's eye. He drew attention not because he was fairly short; no, it was the man's tweed balmacaan covering his large frame and dark-brown bucket hat that set him apart from . . . well, from the entire scene, really. A handful of mental calculations put the coat at a few thousand dollars in Sebastien's estimation. *Damn*, he thought.

The traffic light changed, and Sebastien watched the man cross the street toward his building. Within a few seconds he was out of sight, obscured by the balcony lining the Black Elk's facade. Suddenly curious, Sebastien pulled up his phone and typed "balmacaan" into a search engine.

The buzzing of the doorbell sent Sebastien up from the sofa with a jolt, and Parsifal, his Cardigan Welsh corgi, gave a grunt of protest at being shifted from his owner's lap to the cool leather.

"Tiff! Tiffany! Did you hear that? Someone's at the door. Did you hear that?"

The whirring of a blow dryer ceased, and Tiffany Reese emerged from the bathroom on the far side of the loft.

"I'm sorry, Sebastien. Did you call me?"

"There's someone at the door. The doorbell. Did you hear it?"

"No."

"Are you expecting someone?"

"No."

"Well, who could it be?"

"How would I know? Just go down and answer it," she replied.

"Did you tell someone to come here?"

"Sebastien, what's your problem? No, I didn't invite anyone over. And who cares if I did? It's probably your brother anyway." Tiffany shook a tube-shaped hairbrush in his direction for emphasis. The ends of her brown hair were still damp enough to cling to her lithe neck. She wore a maroon Fair Isle sweater and blue jeans. Her oval face was plain and had yet to be accented with the light strokes of blush and shadow that were her style.

Sebastien descended the narrow stairway to the tiny entryway of the building while simultaneously searching his cerebral cortex for the names of people who knew where he lived or would have any reason to visit him. To his knowledge there were only two—Tiffany and his brother, Hank. Maybe his sister-in-law too, but that was it. A sense of alarm took hold as he realized the code of his solace had been cracked.

Sebastien opened the door just enough to peer through the crack.

"Dr. Grey? Dr. Sebastien grey?" A man with an egg-shaped head and fleshy, pink face removed a dark-brown bucket hat as he spoke.

"Who are you?"

"I'm sorry to have bothered you, Doctor. You are Dr. Grey, correct?"

The man, not receiving an answer, continued.

"I'm Milo Crane. I was wondering, er . . . *hoping* you would have a few moments to discuss an urgent matter. My client is in need of assistance, and I believe you can offer it."

Sebastien opened the door farther and examined the visitor's proffered business card. *Milo J. Crane, Esq. Attorney at Law.*

"How did you find me?" Sebastien asked before realizing it was a stupid question to ask an attorney.

"Public records, Dr. Grey. It's difficult to avoid leaving a trace in today's world."

Sebastien scanned the man's card once more.

"It's a pretty long way from Rapid City for an unscheduled visit, Mr. Crane. You're lucky to have caught me at home."

"Oh, I knew you were home, Dr. Grey. And the drive was unavoidable. There is no one with your particular set of skills any closer to town."

The man's canny use of flattery could not extinguish Sebastien's sense of paranoia. Was he being watched? Followed?

"Look, Doctor, I really do hate to impose, but it's rather chilly out here, and I can assure you that what I have to convey will be very interesting. May we discuss this inside?"

Milo Crane gestured, hat in hand, toward the entry.

"Sebastien, who is it?" called Tiffany from the top of the stairs.

"Ah, good, Detective Reese is here as well."

"How did . . ."

The visitor squeezed through the door, past Sebastien, and headed up the stairs.

Sebastien stepped out onto the sidewalk and looked east and west down the street before heading up to the loft himself. Just what he was looking for, he did not know.

"I'm a jazz man myself, Dr Grey. I never understood the appeal of musical theater."

Milo was looking up at the huge playbill that hung in the entry hall.

"It's not musical theater. It's opera. That playbill is a hundred and fifty years old."

"Ah, the latest releases, then."

Tiffany smiled at this and returned Milo's handshake.

"And you must be Detective Reese! I've heard great things about you."

"How?" insisted Sebastien. "How do you know about us?"

"I think he was referring more to me, Sebastien."

"I love your sense of humor, Detective Reese! But you're right, Dr. Grey. It's your twin reputations that precede you. I have it on good authority that the sheriff has put you both on some rather difficult cases."

"How would you know that?"

"Oh, lighten up, Sebastien. I'm sure Mr. Crane just read it in the paper. You aren't some sort of spy, are you, Mr. Crane?"

Two of the three laughed audibly at this. Sebastien grimaced.

"I can assure you I'm not. No, no. But I do donate somewhat generously to the Sheriff's Activities League and the charity golf tournament. I suppose that affords me some inside information. Oh, and speaking of that, I understand you've been tasked with the Amber Harrison case. I heard something about DNA?"

"That's far more than we know, Mr. Crane," answered Sebastien.

Milo threw Sebastien a knowing look and tapped his right nostril.

"I hear you loud and clear, Dr. Grey. But for what it's worth, I am fairly well connected here and in Pennington County. I would be happy to be of assistance in any way I can."

"Is that why you're here? Do you have information about Amber Harrison?" asked Tiffany.

"Not that it would matter to us, Mr. Crane. Like I told you, we don't know anything about that investigation."

There was something about Milo Crane that evoked a dissonant chord within Sebastien. Maybe it was the man's smugness or possibly his use of overly formal language that unsettled him.

"No, ma'am." Milo looked at Tiffany then at Sebastien. "Dr. Grey, I'm actually here on behalf of my employer. Your impressive skills are needed."

"Please have a seat." Tiffany gestured to the couch.

"May I?" Milo mimed removing his coat.

"Of course. Make yourself comfortable. Would you like

coffee or water? We have bottled." Tiffany turned toward the loft's kitchen.

"No, my dear, but thank you. Dr. Grey, I'm sure you are familiar with NAGPRA."

Sebastien lowered himself onto one of two wingback chairs situated perpendicular to the sofa. Tiffany remained standing behind him, her right hand resting on Sebastien's shoulder. Milo Crane, his expensive coat now draped over the back of the sofa, patted the curious corgi on the head.

"Of course," returned Sebastien. "The Native American Graves Protection and Repatriation Act."

"What is that?" asked Tiffany.

Sebastien looked up at her.

"It's a federal law, passed in the early nineties. Essentially, it forbids the taking of Native American remains or artifacts from archaeological sites, including their burials. Or, if leaving the remains in place is not an option, because of a need to make way for a road or building, the items need to be repatriated."

"Repatriated to whom exactly?"

Milo answered Tiffany with an innocent smile. "Given back to the tribal authorities, whomever they may be."

"Sounds pretty reasonable to me," she replied.

Sebastien agreed, though he was still too preoccupied with this unwanted visitor to express this sentiment. NAGPRA was a relatively contentious subject among scientists, though the controversy was somewhat ironic. On the one hand, anthropologists and archaeologists liked to claim a large degree of cultural sensitivity and respect for diverse peoples, past and present. On the other hand, massive amounts of historic and scientific understanding have come from the excavation and study of native artifacts and remains. The formulae for reconstructing height from various bones, for example, were mostly derived from large-scale studies of living and dead Native Americans, among other groups. The tug of war between scientific curiosity and respect for already heavily exploited cultures was now waning, with the latter team claiming victory. Sebastien, for his part, was fine with this. A large portion of his past "forensic" cases turned out to be ancient native graves that were inadvertently disturbed or, just as often, washed up from the delta silt during the rainy season. In those instances, he would instruct the coroner to notify the Native American Heritage Commission and leave the scene unbothered. It was all the same to him.

Milo waited in vain, once again, for a reply from Sebastien before continuing his narrative.

"You see, Dr. Grey, I represent a real estate developer— Fortunatas LLC—and they are in the process of improving a site northeast of Rapid City. It is to be a medical office complex."

Milo laid a brown leather briefcase on the coffee table and slid the brass latches. The lid sprung open, and the man fished inside for something.

"How's the thyroid these days, Mr. Crane?" Sebastien pointed to the man's hands, still in the briefcase.

"Very perceptive, Doctor. I recently switched medications. The swelling is not as bad as it was a few weeks ago."

Tiffany gave Sebastien's shoulder a squeeze.

"Forgive my friend, Mr. Crane. Tact is not his strong suit."

Sebastien nearly fell into one of his pre-sulk states. Milo unwittingly pulled him out.

"Tact isn't the service that Fortunatas needs from the doctor. It's those skills of observation, the ones you so ably just demonstrated. But let me get to the point, Dr. Grey. Fortunatas, who I represent . . ."

"So you said," interrupted Sebastien, prompting the lawyer to speak a little more directly.

"Fortunatas cleared the site for the building and were in the process of trenching the water main when they came upon a bone. A piece of human skull, actually."

Tiffany took the chair next to Sebastien and asked, "Native?"

"That seems to be the consensus. Naturally, representatives of the local tribe were called in. They took possession of the bone and excavated in the immediate area, but despite finding nothing, they feel the site is likely a larger burial complex and requested that work be stopped so that another complete survey and excavation could be completed. This delay, while perfectly understandable, could potentially cost Fortunatas millions of dollars—tens of millions if the project is canceled altogether."

"Okay. Sounds about right to me," replied Sebastien. "That's how these things go. I don't see how I can help here."

"Dr. Grey, what I'm about to tell you must be kept in strict confidence." Milo pulled a large multi-folded sheet from his briefcase and opened it onto the coffee table.

"Look," began Sebastien, trying to contain his exasperation for Tiffany's sake, "before you try to rope me into whatever this is, I repeat, this is not my area. At all."

It was Milo's turn to ignore Sebastien.

"This is the initial phase one survey of the site. It was done the summer before last by a CRM company out of Lincoln, Nebraska."

"CRM?" asked Tiffany, scooting forward in her chair to look at the survey map.

"Cultural Resource Management," explained Sebastien. "It's basically an archaeological company that surveys the site to make sure there are no remains or artifacts before construction begins."

"Yes, and as you can see here," Milo brushed a hand gently across the sheet, "nothing was found. No graves, no artifacts, no signs of prehistoric structures."

"And where was the bone found?"

"Up on the northeast side of the site. Here."

Sebastien and Tiffany followed Milo's pudgy index finger as it traced a line from the center of the map to the upper-right corner.

"I'm no expert in archaeology. I really just dabble, so to speak. But if you are correct, then I would say you have a potential case for a lawsuit. I hope the CRM company has errors and omissions insurance."

"We don't think it will come to that, Dr. Grey. You see, we feel very good about resolving this issue without any trouble."

"What do you mean?" asked Tiffany.

"Detective Reese, we believe strongly that the lack of any other archaeological evidence is highly indicative that the bone is simply an anomaly. We are of the opinion that it is just as likely the bone was brought in along with fill dirt, rather than being part of a deliberate burial. Would you not agree, Dr. Grey?"

"I do agree. In the absence of any other artifacts or remains, it is certainly possible."

Milo clapped his hands together and exposed his coffee-stained teeth in satisfaction. It was as if he'd hit the double-zeros on the roulette table.

"Excellent, Doctor! Then I will get right to the point. If we can obtain an expert opinion validating the strong possibility that the bone is not from the site, we believe we can convince the authorities that no further digging is necessary. As you pointed out, there is no evidence to suggest otherwise." Milo gestured to the survey map.

"And that's what you need me for," asked Sebastien, "to rubber stamp your theory?"

"I don't know if I would put it that way, Dr. Grey. You did agree with our premise, didn't you?"

"I did, but I like to consider all possibilities."

"Doctor, you have seen the survey for yourself. There is no

evidence of any more artifacts. The bone must have been part of the backfill."

Sebastien sat back in his chair and picked at the sparse growth of his new beard.

"Sebastien, what are you thinking? I know that look," Tiffany prompted.

"What if the bone was planted there? What if somebody put the bone in the ground after the survey?"

"Oh! Dr. Grey, you do have quite an imagination!"

"Who in the world would do that?"

"I don't know, Tiffany. Do you know, Mr. Crane? Is there anyone you can think of who would tamper with your site?"

"Really, Dr. Grey. All we need, all we are asking, is for you to validate the possibility that the bone was in the fill dirt. That would give us the greatest chance of getting our crews back to work in the spring. Barring that, we are looking at possibly a year from then to begin the work, if we do at all."

"Look, no offense, Mr. Crane—"

"Call me Milo. Please."

"Fine. No offense, Milo, but in my world things are seldom that simple, and a healthy suspicion pays off. Can you think of anyone who might have planted the bone?"

Milo Crane pulled an envelope from his briefcase and tossed it onto the coffee table. "Here," he stated, latching the case closed and standing. "I'm afraid I've wasted your time. That will hopefully make up for it."

"Mr. Crane, you're leaving?" Tiffany asked.

"Yes, my dear. It is not my employer's intention to make this needlessly complicated, as it seems Dr. Grey is determined to do."

Sebastien betrayed no intention of stopping the man from leaving. Tiffany caught his eyes and gave him a look of remonstration.

"I'm sorry, Mr. Crane. Sebastien has a tendency to be suspicious."

"Am I ever wrong?" spat out Sebastien bitterly.

"Yes, in fact, you *are* sometimes wrong." Tiffany turned her back to Milo and gave Sebastien a *stop it!* look.

"Fine. Fine. I think I can offer an endorsement of your theory, Mr. Crane."

"Excellent! There's more than that if you do." Milo nodded toward the envelope on the coffee table as he straightened the high, stiff collar on his balmacaan.

"That is, on one condition."

"What is that, Dr. Grey?"

"I need to visit the site and examine the bone. Okay, that's two conditions."

"Absolutely. That would be the natural next step, would it not?"

"It would. So, do you have the bone, or has it been handed over to the Native American authorities—as the law dictates."

"We abide by the law, Dr. Grey. The Tribal Commission has the bone but are willing to have it examined briefly. I will make the arrangements and be in touch. On behalf of my client, I cannot thank you enough. Oh, one last thing, if it would not be too much of an imposition . . ."

"What's that, Milo?"

Milo set the briefcase back down on the coffee table and opened it.

"We must insist on complete confidentiality in this matter. We ask that you tell no one. That goes for you as well, Detective Reese. Here. Please read and sign these non-disclosure agreements. I'm sure you can sympathize with the sensitivity of the matter."

"I'm sorry, Milo, but I do not plan on assisting with this. I'm afraid it might interfere with my regular duties as a sworn officer."

"I understand completely, Detective Reese. Nevertheless, we won't be able to employ the good doctor without both of your signatures."

"What do you think, Sebastien?" Tiffany asked.

"What if I find something illegal, Milo? Something I should report?"

The lawyer let out a belly laugh.

"Very amusing, Doctor. But I'm afraid real estate development is far more boring than your regular fare. What an exciting world you must live in. It's corporate competition that concerns us."

"That does kind of make sense, Sebastien," agreed Tiffany.

Sebastien shrugged and took one of the sheets from Milo. Tiffany took the other. Before they could hunt for pens, Milo produced two from his briefcase. He offered them, smiling widely.

"Here, I'll walk you down." Tiffany motioned Milo to the door of the stairwell.

"Thank you, Detective. Say, I don't suppose you are single?"

Milo turned and looked at Tiffany with one raised eyebrow.

"Excuse me?"

"I have a grandson. And you are quite a lovely young lady."

"We're engaged!"

Milo and Tiffany both made sudden turns from the open door and gaped at Sebastien, who had shot up out of his chair.

2

"This thing makes no sense," declared Sebastien as he watched Milo Crane, Esquire, cross to the opposite side of the street, clutching his coat collar against the wind. "That guy's client, Fortune Development . . ."

"Fortunatas Development, Dr. Details," Tiffany interrupted snarkily.

"Whatever. Fortunatas thinks all they need is my opinion to stop the Feds and get the tribal authorities to look the other way."

"You didn't say no though. And you didn't give him back that envelope full of cash, I noticed." Tiffany pointed with her hairbrush to Sebastien's hand.

"Looks like a couple of grand in here."

"Whoa, nice! And he promised there'd be more if you can convince the government to allow the construction to resume."

"I don't need the money."

"Oh, really? Engagement rings are very pricey, Doctor. My standards are ridiculously high."

"Yeah, sorry about that. I was just trying to get him to back . . . wait. What? Are you saying . . ."

"Calm down, loverboy. I'm just kidding too."

Sebastien could feel his heart rate jump. His lips parted as if to speak, but his thoughts collided at the intersection of possibilities. He turned back to the window as if to look for Milo. But that ghost was gone for the moment, replaced by a new one.

"Pretty interesting though. You have to admit that at least."

"Huh?"

"Milo. The case. The whole thing is . . . well, I don't know. You tell me. You're the expert. Is this kind of thing normal?"

"One hundred percent no. This is not right. And it makes me even more suspicious that he was ready to part with a few thousand dollars just to avoid answering my questions. And what about the NDAs?"

"The idea of planted native remains is pretty ridiculous."

"Yes, I know it is. But there's more to this, and I was hoping he would give something up if I gave him an opening."

"Well, he didn't. Better leave the interviewing to me next time."

Sebastien ignored the retort, picked up Parsifal, who had been staring up at him, and made his way back to his original spot on the sofa. The corgi gave him a few licks on the nose as Sebastien scratched the dog behind his ears.

Tiffany came up behind him and leaned over, kissing Sebastien on the crown of his head and running her hand down his chest. Sebastien leaned his head back and found her lips with his own.

"It must be nice to be in such high demand," she whispered into his ear. "I find it very sexy, to be honest. Too bad I have to go." She gave his left pec a squeeze.

"Wait, you're leaving?"

"I told you I'm having lunch with the girls today. I can't squirrel myself away from social obligations like some people."

Tiffany broke away and headed back toward the bathroom.

"Sure you can. You're just not trying hard enough," Sebastien called back.

With Tiffany gone, Sebastien's mind was clear to free fall down into the dark hole of self-recrimination. What a stupid thing to say: *We're engaged.* First of all, they weren't. Second of all, did she think that was a proposal? Did she think he was so inept as to try and turn a pointless meeting with an eccentric old man into a romantic and personal watershed? And what did she mean by "I'm just kidding too"? Did she think he would kid about that? Did she think marrying him would be a joke? Damn it, Sebastien! What did it all mean?

Sebastien closed his eyes and concentrated, trying to distract his mind, to stop the spiral. The Fortunatas case. He would think about the Fortunatas case. Maybe *case* was overstating things. It was just a simple request, validate the possibility that the skull fragment had been brought from outside of the site in a load of fill dirt. Just about anything was possible, after all.

But Tiffany *was* right. It was certainly interesting, if not absurdly simple. Though the simplicity of it gave him pause, and the fact that NAGPRA was at the heart of it. Anything to do with NAGPRA would be a political hot potato. There was far too much emotion built up on both the native and non-native sides—especially with money involved.

Sebastien recalled a time when he was in grad school spending a summer doing CRM archaeology for a large development company that was building multimillion-dollar mansions on the coast of Orange County. Several weeks into the dig they discovered human remains—Native American remains. Half of the development had to cease work for several weeks while the area was assessed and the burial removed for repatriation. And, during that time, whenever he and the rest of the archaeology team came to the site, they would be greeted by the curses, epithets, and middle fingers of men in hard hats atop their massive idling earth-moving machines. *Aren't you done yet, egg head? Yer holding up the damn job, Nancy! Time is money. Just dig the stupid thing up so we can get back to work, Indiana Jones!* He would have to keep his eyes open on this one.

A second and much more deliberate examination of the map didn't reveal anything new. The CRM crew did a great job of assessing the site, which Milo and Fortunatas obviously believed from their confidence in the work that had so far been done. The report, which Milo left along with the map, detailed a multi-modal approach to evaluating the land: ground penetrating radar, soil sampling, and numerous test pits. Geologically speaking, the soil on the site was a mix of sand and clay—loam, it was called. Clay was absolutely miserable for digging—Sebastien's own pernicious case of tennis elbow could attest to that. Clay, if it was compact, could also indicate that the soil was not trucked in.

The actual finding of the bone was one heck of a coincidence, to boot. The skull fragment happened to be lying right in the path of the connection to the water main. On a site that large, the probability must be infinitesimal. Sure, it could happen. Sebastien had been to plenty of complete human burials that were uncovered by utility work. In this case, however, a thirty-six-inch-wide, thirty-six-inch-deep trench cut through a six-hundred-and-fifty-foot-wide lot, which happened to uncover a solitary five-inch oblong of cranial bone . . . well, that would put a strain on any statistical calculator.

Probabilities aside, the bone fragment was found. Its existence was not to be argued. Like he used to tell his students in his Introduction to Physical Anthropology course, if human evolution was somehow an insult to their deeply entrenched belief systems, they were certainly free to ignore the evidence, the links in the fossil chain, or the genomic similarities. But what they couldn't do, if they were being honest, was say they didn't exist. Deal with them, or don't deal with them. Either way, there they were. If they chose to deal with them, the first logical question was "How did they get there?" In the case of the Fortunatas bone, Sebastien had an envelope full of hundred dollar bills that committed him to the possibility of its existence.

Despite his tennis elbow credentials, Sebastien was not an archaeologist. However, he knew enough about the discipline to understand that those who were archaeologists by choice were often geologists by necessity. The geology of the Fortunatas site would be—could be—important. Specifically, because bone was porous and absorbent, the mineral components of the soil should be reflected consistently in the bone itself. So, for example, if the soil contained measurable amounts of the element fluorine, or minerals that contain fluorine, the bone should have absorbed similar levels of fluorine. Sebastien wasn't at all sure if fluorine was to be found in the soil of the Upper Plains, but that was not the point. It was something to be checked, a lead to chase down.

In a similar vein, the bone could be analyzed for isotopes that reveal the dietary patterns of the individual who was buried. Diet reconstruction through stable isotope analysis was common in archaeological and paleontological contexts. An individual who subsisted largely on marine life would have a different ratio of nitrogen isotopes than a person who ate mostly terrestrial food sources. Similarly, carbon isotopes can help differentiate the types of plants a person ate. So, in theory, if it can be shown that the individual whose skull fragment was recovered on the Fortunatas site subsisted on food sources that were not native to the area, which could suggest it was accidentally brought in from another location far away and re-buried in western South Dakota. Of course, that type of analysis wouldn't help much if the fill dirt at the site was brought in from somewhere within the general region. This seemed more probable.

But what was he thinking? There would be no possibility of

performing lab work on the fragment of bone. Native groups were, understandably, opposed to having their ancestors subjected to the indignities of callous scientific analysis. As usual, Sebastien was letting his empirical mind lead him too far down the path. Even though human remains were involved, which happened to be his specialty, it did not mean every question needed to be answered. The universe owed him no resolutions simply by virtue of his chosen profession.

It may not matter, anyway. Macroscopic analysis of human bone was often sufficient to determine ancient versus modern remains, and in some cases just looking at a bone could give them an idea of diet and therefore the potential ecological region in which the person lived. Especially if the fragment was a piece of skull, as Milo had claimed was the case here.

Sebastien pulled a few books from the large bookcase, which took up nearly the entire back wall of the loft. There were a few things he needed to brush up on before seeing the bone for himself. In particular, what was the frequency of porotic hyperostosis or cribra orbitalia in native remains from this part of the country?

When an individual was deficient in iron, which could be due to congenital or dietary factors, their ability to produce red blood cells diminishes. The body compensates by creating more red-blood-cell-producing bone on either of the outside of the skull or on the upper wall of the eye orbit. The result was a layer of porous bone easily distinguished from the bone around it. These conditions were respectively called porotic hyperostosis and cribra orbitalia. Some ancient populations lacked access to the nutritional requirements necessary for red-blood-cell production and had a higher incidence of these malformations. Knowing this might come in handy when looking at the piece of skull found at the site.

As for Sebastien's own theory that the bone may have been planted—well, that was obviously both remote and ridiculous.

But Milo was being cagey. Something felt *off* to Sebastien. He had hoped to "tickle the lines," as they say in wire-tap cases—that meant doing or saying something to provoke more information. It clearly didn't work, but it was worth a try. Maybe Tiffany was right.

"Sebastien!"

"Huh? What?"

"I said I'm leaving."

Tiffany was standing at the door to the stairwell, her hand on the knob.

"Oh, yeah. Sorry. I was just thinking."

"Well, stop it and come give me a kiss. I'm late."

After seeing Tiffany off, Sebastien returned to his books. He didn't find much in the way of information on nutritional markers in native remains in the books in his library, which prompted him to recall that a student had borrowed, and never returned, one of his best volumes on the subject of paleopathology. So he replaced the books he'd been researching and began to organize the Fortunatas papers, stacking everything neatly on his desk and folding the map with care. As he did so, he noticed, on the bottom-right corner of the site survey, a physical address.

PARSIFAL LOOKED up at him ruefully, his quilted brown dog jacket wrapped tightly around his midsection making him look like a summer sausage. The dog had a disdain for both exercise and the cold, although to be fair he did not have much experience with hibernal extremes, having been dragged northeast from sunny California.

The dog stepped back and planted his square backside on the frozen ground in protest as Sebastien leaned down to fasten the leash.

"What? What is it, boy? You don't wanna go for a walk?"

Sebastien had parked just outside of the single metal barrier that blocked the dirt road to the construction site. A padlock held the barrier in place, which prevented him from swinging it open and driving the Rover onto the property. But there was nothing to keep him from walking to the side of the gate. The security measure was obviously installed with only vehicle traffic in mind.

Parsifal waddled reluctantly behind as Sebastien proceeded onto the construction site to better survey the area. The site itself was clearly identified from the surrounding open space. Tracks from various earthmovers and graders were visible in the flatted russet-colored earth. Wood stakes punctured the terrain at seemingly random intervals, flags of various high visibility colors tied to their tops, flapping in the wind.

Just ahead of them, in a straight line from the entrance road, sat a large yellow tractor facing southward to Sebastien's right. The tractor's long arm terminated at a narrow scoop. This must be where the trench for the water main was being dug, he considered, thinking back to the map of the site, which he inconveniently forgot to bring with him. Sebastien gently pulled the lead, and the pair made their way forward, trying to avoid the shallow puddles of icy water and patches of snow.

Sebastien lowered himself to his haunches and examined the walls of the depression carefully. He pulled from his back pocket a small trowel, then gently scraped the edges of the gap, allowing the frozen dirt to fall into his palm. It appeared to him that the color and consistency of the soil from the base to the surface was remarkably consistent.

"You coming or staying?"

Parsifal stood his ground near the trench and refused to follow his human to the south half of the site.

"Fine with me. Don't go running off anywhere."

Aside from the flagged stakes and scars from the tracks of

heavy machinery, there wasn't much to see at the rest of the site. He did notice a few areas where the soil looked to be disturbed. He supposed these were the remains of the test pits made by the CRM company. Finding what he thought was an untouched area, Sebastien tried to dig his own small hole with the point of his trowel, but the earth was too frozen. There was no way to tell if the dirt underneath his feet was consistent with the dirt of the trench, but it certainly looked the same.

The sound of a diesel engine coming from the direction of the gate caught his attention. He swung around and saw a man descend from his idling truck and approach the lock. Once inside, he headed straight for Sebastien.

"What are you doing here?" the man yelled to him from the lowered driver's window.

"Oh, I'm just out for a walk with my dog." Sebastien stashed the trowel in his back pocket, then motioned toward the trench and Parsifal, who was now lying on the ground.

"Out here? You're a little far from town, aren't you, son?"

The man was older, in his mid-sixties maybe. He wore a long-sleeved, dark-blue work shirt with a patch of the US flag on his left shoulder and the name "Bert" above the left breast pocket.

"Yeah, I guess so. I just wanted to stretch my legs. This seemed like a good spot."

The man looked in the direction of the corgi, then back at Sebastien.

"Your dog doesn't seem like much of a walker. Are you sure that's all you're doing? This is private property. You really shouldn't be out here."

"Oh, I'm sorry, I didn't think it would be a big problem." Sebastien tried to feign remorse. The fact was this encounter didn't surprise him all that much.

"I'm not saying it's a big problem. I'm just saying you

shouldn't be out here. This is a construction site. The owner wouldn't want anyone to get hurt. It's a liability," returned Bert.

"Who is the owner?" Sebastien asked.

Bert killed the engine of his truck without answering. Sebastien tried a different approach.

"Do you work for the construction company?"

The man pointed to the flag on his shoulder. "I'm security."

"Of course, the American flag should have told me that," Sebastien murmured to himself.

"What's that?"

"I said that I, uh, I should have seen that. I'll get my dog and get out of the way. Sorry for the hassle."

Security Guard Bert rested his left arm on the driver's door and leaned out the window.

"And who are you? What's your name? And what the hell kind of dog is that?" he asked, raising a finger.

"Oh, that's a Cardigan Welsh corgi. His name is Parsifal. My name is . . . uh . . . Sebastien."

"Percival, you say?"

"No . . . well . . . yes, actually. Kind of anyway."

"What?"

"That's right." Bert was clearly hard of hearing. Maybe the sound of his engine had taken a toll. "Say, there's not much construction going on around here. Is the site closed down for the winter?"

Sebastien focused on the security guard's face, attempting to assess whether his out-of-the-blue question raised any alarm.

"My grandkid, he's got one of those, what do you call 'em? King Cavaliers?"

Bert was still looking in Parsifal's direction. Maybe he was lonely. This could be an opportunity. Sebastien looked back as he answered.

"Cavalier King Charles, you mean? Those are pretty dogs.

I'm sure your grandson loves him. They make a good family dog, I've heard."

"Granddaughter."

"Oh. Sorry."

Bert descended from the truck, slamming the door behind him.

"Yeah, it's shut down but not for the winter though. Been shut down since last summer."

"Really? Why is that? Looks like a good spot to ground. What is it going to be, apartments?"

The security guard hiked up his dark-blue work pants and gestured toward the north side of the development.

"I'm not really sure. Some sort of office building, I think. See that trencher over there? That trench was the last bit of work they did before stopping. I'm not sure why. I just know I'm supposed to keep people out."

"That's interesting. Seems a little weird with real estate the way it is. What was this place before?"

"Been an empty lot for years. I think the previous owner was going to put in a big box store, but that never happened."

"How long have you been doing security here?"

The man squinted a little into Sebastien's eyes and tipped his head. Sebastien thought he could now detect a hint of caution in the man.

"Long enough. Now come on. Get your dog and follow me out of the gate. I'm afraid I'm going to have to ask you to leave."

"Sure thing. Oh, hey, mind if I ask you about dirt?"

Bert paused halfway into the cab of his truck.

"Dirt? What do you mean?"

"Looking at this place got me thinking. Do you think this construction company would be in the market for some dirt?"

Bert stepped back down looking confused. Sebastien continued.

"It's just . . . my . . . uh . . . my house is just east of here, and I'm digging a pool."

The man scratched his stubbled cheek.

"A pool? This time of year?"

"No. Not like right now. I . . . I started it in the fall. But the dirt, the dirt is piled up in my backyard. I'm looking to get rid of it. I just wondered if you knew if they needed any here."

"They don't need no dirt here."

"So, they brought all they needed, huh? Well, darn."

"They didn't bring in any dirt. The place is as flat as a pancake. Just look around. It's been that way for years."

A few minutes later, Sebastien and Parsifal were standing outside the locked gate watching the man sit in his idling truck, waiting for them to leave.

This sequence of events was both enlightening and concerning. Sebastien felt from the beginning that something was off with Milo's story, but now he had two points to corroborate his suspicion.

Certainly the site was real, and the trench was real. But, if Bert the security guard was to be relied upon, the story of finding a bone in the fill dirt did not make sense. No fill dirt was brought in, making it impossible for a partial human skull to be transported on to the site in that way. That said, it was very possible, and maybe even probable, that Bert didn't know what he was talking about. How much knowledge would a security guard have of the daily goings-on of the development? Quite a bit probably, concluded Sebastien. Contractors and subcontractors, and their attached workers, may come and go. But surely the person who oversaw the security of the construction site would have the best vantage point to observe its progress. Even if that observation was somewhat passive.

His second point very much supported the first. There was no evidence of multiple soil types from looking at the trench. One would expect to find different stratigraphic layers, if one type of soil was dumped on top of another. Or, at least, there would be a mixing of materials. But the walls of the trench appeared to be uniform in color and composition. No doubt a few trowel scrapings would not qualify as a comprehensive scientific analysis, but based on what Sebastien had seen for himself—and heard for himself—Milo and Fortunatas' version of things was not adding up. His visit to the site did nothing to quell the unsettled feeling that arose the moment he laid eyes on that man in the balmacaan.

3

Sergeant Hank LeGris ascended the stairs to the cold case office, being sure to make more noise than he usually would, just in case his star detective and little brother were up to something.

"Hank, you're here!"

"Of course I'm here. I work here, don't I? Oh, and it's sergeant, remember?"

Tiffany rose from her chair and gave the sergeant a loose embrace.

"I'm not your grandma's fine china, Reese."

"I know. How do you feel?"

"A lot better, thanks. After this experience I can recommend not getting shot, if you ever have the option, that is."

"Are you sure you're ready to come back to work?" asked Sebastien, still sitting at his desk.

"Yes, I'm sure, and my doctor agrees. You don't need to worry about your big brother, Dr. Grey."

It had been several weeks now since Sergeant Hank LeGris had taken a bullet to the right side while serving a search warrant. Fortunately, the round was deflected away from vital organs by Hank's body armor. But he still had some lead lodged in his back. It was too close to the spine to remove.

"You aren't in any pain?" Tiffany looked him up and down.

"A little. Really just a few aches. My physical therapist showed me how to stretch the muscles out, which helps."

"That's wonderful. So you're back at it. Good for us."

"I like what you've done with the place," Hank observed, looking round the large storage area above the crime lab, which Tiffany and Sebastien recently converted into their office.

"It is an improvement. Thanks for arranging for us to use it. It makes a huge difference not being so close to Patrol and all the distractions."

"And it keeps me out of the main building, which I think Lieutenant Breed appreciates," added Sebastien.

Earlier that fall, the investigations lieutenant banned Sebastien from the headquarters building to keep him away from the detectives, with whom Sebastien was butting heads. Hank almost replied by telling Sebastien that a few weeks ago may as well be a few years. Attitudes had changed, fences had been mended. Sebastien's work on the Boxwood Torso case and the Derek Manly homicide had all but swept the record clean. But Hank decided not to mention it. It might be better to leave things be. For now, anyway.

"You know what the place needs though?"

"What's that, Hank?"

"A chair for visitors."

"Here, take mine." Sebastien vacated his chair and pushed it toward Hank. "Really."

"I'll take you up on that. Chairs should be reserved for management anyway. So, what are you two up to? What's shakin' in the cold case business?"

"I'm just going through some of the John and Jane Does," replied Sebastien. "Some of these haven't been checked against the federal database yet. We may be able to clear some of them that way."

Hank nodded. "What about you, Reese? What's the next big thing?"

"I'm not sure. I've been looking through a case from the early nineties. A truck driver was beaten to death in the bathroom of a pizza place. Oh, and you know who the lead detective was on that? Our own Sheriff Castro."

"That's convenient."

"How so?" asked Tiffany.

"If the big man owned that case at one point, then he may be more invested in it—which translates to more resources if needed."

"Ah, gotcha."

"Did Breed tell you he got the lab to do the DNA comparison between Harrison and the remains that were found by the train tracks out near Fairburn?"

Hank asked this question in a bland way, as if it weren't monumental news. He didn't want to get their hopes up. He still had his doubts.

"No. No, he didn't. That's terrific! When?"

"They should be working on it downstairs as we speak. Lab says it will take a day or so. But Breed doesn't want us to say anything. Not until the lab is finished with their bit. And if they aren't a match, we are to never bring it up again. Capiche?"

"Capiche," echoed Tiffany.

"That goes for you too, little brother."

"Yeah, I get it. It's her though. I'm telling you it's her."

SEBASTIEN HEARD the door open and felt the cold breeze as he stood in the small entry of his building, looking through his mail. It was Tabitha Lee, one of his two downstairs tenants. To say Tabitha was an eccentric would be putting it mildly. She was an attractive woman in her early forties with long, dark hair streaked with strands of silver. She wore rings on most of her fingers—or maybe it was all of them. Tabitha was in the habit of speaking with her hands flailing animatedly to punctuate whatever point she was making, so it was difficult to count the turquoise, Black Hills gold, and silver that whizzed by during their relatively infrequent conversations. It seemed to Sebastien that the woman made her own clothes, which often hung loosely on her slim frame and featured animal prints, feathers, or some other nature motif. As Sebastien stepped aside to allow her entry, he couldn't help but notice she was mixing things up a bit today with purple snowflake-print leggings tucked into black cowboy boots and a puffy yellow down jacket.

Tabitha was the proprietor of Tabitha's Art and Jewelry, which stood not more than one hundred feet to the east of the Black Elk. Sebastien had only been in the establishment one time, and that was upon Tabitha's insistence that he "come feel the place." The invitation caused him significant reticence, yet he powered through, determining to be less of an awkward hermit in his newly adopted hometown. Tabitha's store, he came to discover, was about seventy percent bohemian sanctuary and thirty percent high-end art gallery. The place smelled of patchouli incense and vanilla. Dream catchers hung from the ceiling. Glass cabinets lined either side of the space and featured crystals, CBD, essential oils, bundles of sage, and other similar paraphernalia. On the wall hung several paintings, most of which were Native American or wildlife themed. One particular glass-mounted photograph of a massive bison breathing white vapor into a snowy background caught Sebastien's eye. It was titled *"Winter Thunder"* and priced at four thousand dollars. He recalled Tabitha's earnest efforts to talk him into buying it.

"Hello, Sebastien. Not too cold today. Better than yesterday."

Sebastien nodded and resumed looking through his mail in

an effort to avoid eye contact. From his periphery he could discern she was staring at him.

"Yes, it is," he turned and replied. "How are things in the store?"

"Slow. Damn slow. But it always is this time of year, isn't it? Oh, I'm sorry. I guess you wouldn't know. The southern part of the hills doesn't get as many winter tourists as up by Deadwood and Lead. They have the skiers."

Tabitha pointed toward the entry door with her left hand and made a downward undulating motion with her right.

"I'm sorry to hear that," Sebastien offered, wondering just how sorry he could end up being.

"Oh, thank you, Sebastien. It's okay. It's part of business around here. Oh, speaking of which, *Winter Thunder* is still available. I *could* go thirty-five on that, but just for you and don't tell anyone."

Sebastien ignored the wink and turned for the stairs.

"Oh, and don't you worry, Doctor. Your music isn't bothering me."

Once he entered his apartment, Sebastien threw his coat over the back of the couch and put his bag on the coffee table before reaching down to greet Parsifal. The dog was looking positively uninterested the last few days, which Sebastien attributed to a seasonal torpor. His usual excited wag upon seeing his human counterpart was absent, replaced by barely a tinge of recognition. And such was the case on this afternoon. Maybe it went beyond some canine seasonal affective disorder; maybe it was the move. Perhaps Parsifal missed California. But what could the poor pooch be missing? The Japanese lilacs planted along First Street, which became a favorite urinary target during the daily walks? Or, for similar reasons, the verdant lawns that fronted the homes along Third Street? Maybe Parsifal was pining for Mrs. Kimble, the neighbor who visited him regularly and always had a treat in her pocket. A spring of guilt began to bubble up in the back of Sebastien's mind. He didn't consider all of the effects of the move to South Dakota on his dog. Parsifal had no choice in the matter, did he?

"Come on, buddy. Let's get our walk done. Then how about something nice for dinner? Maybe a steak?"

It was nearly an hour later when Sebastien and Parsifal returned. The dog could evidently smell the ribeye wrapped in butcher paper; his tail had been wagging ever since Sebastien emerged from the market. It felt a little silly—cooking a steak for his dog. But who would know? And who cared anyway? One of the benefits of living alone was that he could do whatever he wanted, whenever he wanted, without judging eyes or recriminations—other than his own.

With Parsifal happily attacking a bowl full of chopped meat, Sebastien changed into wool pajamas and slid his feet into his Ralph Lauren slippers—an online impulse purchase that had seen little use prior to the last few weeks—and began to settle in. It was still early but, again, he could do whatever he wanted. He checked his phone, just to make sure he hadn't missed a call from Tiffany—and he hadn't. This might be a good opportunity to organize his thoughts. A quick scroll through the playlists on his phone produced a sonic match to his proposed mental labors. Ancient percussion, modern brass, and darkly fluid vocals filled his studio in an aural cloud. Norwegian ambient folk music had become a recent obsession.

Unlike Tiffany, and Hank for that matter, Sebastien found himself burdened with not but two cases. Okay, to be fair, the Fortunatas case was only urgent to Milo and his employers and could in no way be compared to a murdered woman. But Sebastien had agreed to help them, and once he promised to do something, the thought of not doing it, of not living up to his word, filled him with anxiety. It just so happened that his over-active amygdala was taking voltage from two directions now, in addition to the day-in-day-out buzz of fear and uncertainty that had become the status-quo scenario of his anxiety-plagued existence.

Supine on the sofa, Sebastien tried to mentally separate the points of interest in the two cases. They were becoming intertwined in his mind. Absence of evidence (in the Amber Harrison case) and evidence of absence (in the case of the Fortunatas skeleton) figured prominently in the affairs. As did the need for a well-considered approach and discrete interviews of select individuals—if they could be found. The multiple permutations were beginning to overwhelm, so Sebastien decided to lay the Harrison case aside for the time being. There would be ample discussion of that once the DNA came back a match. And it would.

In isolation, the Fortunatas case now seemed a bit more digestible. The facts, bullet pointed in his mind, lined up as follows: A buried fragment of human skull was uncovered within a construction site, which Fortunatas Development was in the process of turning into a medical complex. Eighteen months ago, that selfsame acreage yielded no indication of said remains when it was searched by archaeologists and geologists. Their report, coupled with their schematic of the site, was ample proof of that, although confirmation would have to be made with the involved parties. It wouldn't do to take for granted the veracity of the story, as laid out by Milo. Especially now that contradicting facts were beginning to emerge. He would need to find the workers who were digging the trench. And it wouldn't hurt to make contact with the archaeologists and geologists who did the survey. Investigations, forensic or otherwise, were reductive processes. It was always better to start off with too much information then whittle that down through analysis, interviews, deduction, etc. Whatever facts were left standing should form the shape of an answer. The corollary to this was that, by necessity, some time was going to be wasted, some work all for naught. But there was really no other way.

As for the fragment of skull, the coroner's report, photographs, and ultimate assessment of the Native American Heritage Commission should testify convincingly of its ancient and tribal affiliation. But it wouldn't hurt to take a look at things for himself, and Sebastien was relieved to know he would have an opportunity to do just that. As with the construction site, the bone could reveal important clues, despite already having been examined by so-called "experts."

Sebastien's mind began to drift backward. He couldn't help but wonder about his own offhand suggestion that the remains might have been planted. In other words, did the bigwigs at Fortunatas just assume the bone had been introduced in fill dirt because they had no other logical explanation? Maybe they had no idea about the actual specifics of the site's improvement. It would be perfectly reasonable for them to assume that fill dirt was used at the location—especially from their practical and intellectual distance. How many C-suite types actually participated in the construction and would thus know anything about the soil profile, ground stability, leveling, etc.? And, without any firsthand knowledge or expertise, it would make sense to assume that a bone found *after* the archaeological survey was deposited there *after* a mysterious load of fill. This being the case, Sebastien may be accidentally correct about the bone being a plant. What was that word used by archaeologists? Ah, yes. *Manuport*. Something carried in to the site by hand.

Just as Sebastien reached for the notebook in his bag, he heard his phone vibrate against the coffee table. It was Tiffany.

"Hey, Doctor. Whatcha up to?"

She sounded happy. But then, she almost always sounded happy.

"Just thinking about our cases—I mean, our one case and my job for Fortunatas. I'm just about done. How about coming over for dinner? I bought some steaks. Parsifal's had his, but I haven't eaten yet."

"You give your dog steak?"

Sebastien sat up on the sofa and leaned forward to get a glance at Parsifal, who was fast asleep in his basket on the kitchen floor.

"Not always. But he's been a bit down lately. I thought a fancy meal might cheer him up."

"That's nice, I guess. *Did* it cheer him up?"

"I really can't tell."

"Poor doggo. I'm sorry, Sebastien. I can't come by tonight. I need to stay in and get caught up on things. You understand, don't you?"

"Sure. Of course I do."

"I just wanted to say goodnight. That's all. I'll see you at work tomorrow, right?"

"Yes, for sure."

"Great. Goodnight, Sebastien."

"Goodnight, Tiffany . . . oh, wait . . ."

"What is it?"

Sebastien's chest began to tighten, the words he wanted to speak got lost on the way out of his mouth. There was just too much risk in bringing up the subject of engagement.

"I just . . . I love you."

"I love you too. Give Parsifal a pat for me."

Tiffany sat cross-legged on her couch with a glass of wine in her hand, her cat Mist at her side, and the Amber Harrison case file on her lap. Having decided it would be a wise move to review the case before a meeting with the sheriff, she politely turned down Sebastien's offer of dinner at his place and opted for a quiet night at home with her work—*if* there was going to be a meeting with the sheriff, that is. While she trusted Sebastien in his line of thinking, she had only skimmed through the files herself once at this point. And that was a few months ago, when they first started to work the cold cases. She had yet to bring herself up to speed on the entirety of the circumstances surrounding the disappearance, or the murder, of Amber Harrison.

In the file was a large cropped photograph of Amber and some others who were standing in front of a rock face. She was wearing a climbing harness over turquoise climbing pants and a blue tank top. Her hay-blond hair was pulled into a long pony-tail that hung over her shoulder. She was smiling into the sunlight, looking happy and confident. Tiffany wondered if the Amber Harrison in the picture had any idea what was about to befall her.

Amber was not reported missing until January 2013, and that report was made by her mother, who had been unable to get ahold of Amber since just before Christmas—Christmas Eve, in fact. That night Amber told her mother she was going to a party at a friend's house. Her mother had asked at the time which friend it was. Was it a boy? A boyfriend? Was it a girl from work? A girl from college recalled that Amber had been sheepish at the time and did not reveal too much information. In fact, her daughter had not revealed much information at all in the months leading up to her disappearance. *Distracted* was what her mother called it. Amber had been distracted. Not very talkative. Their texts had been short, and they had not spoken on the phone for several months. But Peggy Harrison had no indication that her daughter might be leaving town again, or that she might be in some sort of trouble.

Again?

Peggy reported that Amber had been issued a credit card— her mother had taken it out for her to help with basic needs or for unforeseen emergencies. That fall, most of Amber's card purchases were routine: meals at the university cafeteria, school supplies, gas, and of course, groceries. A few purchases stood out, however, and these had aroused Peggy's concern, even sparked contention between the mother and daughter. Most alarmingly were the purchases of airline tickets and hotels in Las Vegas and Tucson.

"I tried to get an explanation from her for why she left town. She knows I can't afford for her to be running up the cards for party trips with her friends. And she should be in school anyway."

There were other purchases too, Peggy lamented. There was the laptop—Amber already had a laptop, which her mother considered perfectly suitable for her school needs. Why purchase another one? Then there were the handful of cash advances—not many, but they totaled over eight hundred dollars. Plus some expensive clothes. It all seemed so irresponsible, so out of character for such a conscientious daughter and student.

And what was her explanation?

Peggy Harrison did try to have a conversation with Amber about her not getting permission for these expenses ahead of time, and to find out why she took those trips. Such approvals were part of the agreement when Amber was given the card. There was a limit on the credit, after all. But according to Peggy, Amber had been shockingly indifferent to her mother's protests. She didn't have time to explain. She was busy, she'd said. The semester had been a rough one. Her professors were pricks, the homework expectations ridiculous.

One of Amber's roommates, a young woman by the name of Barnadette Jacobs, was interviewed during the initial investigation. Jacobs said that Amber had been staying with a friend most of that semester. Evidently there was a new man in Amber's life and Barnadette did not see much of her. It was a secret, Amber had said. "Please don't tell anyone, especially my mother." Jacobs just assumed Amber was living with whoever this boy was—no, she did not know his name. Amber never told her. But there did not seem to be any cause for concern. She and Amber frequently exchanged texts. Everything seemed fine.

When the semester ended, Jacobs cleared out her belongings from the house she shared with Harrison and a third roommate —a young woman named Shelly Shields—and moved into on-campus housing. The rent for the house was too expensive, she had said. And Amber had become too unreliable with her share. There was no choice but to move out before the spring semester began.

The original detectives also asked Jacobs about Shields. Jacobs told them Shields had dropped out of school earlier that semester. And, as far as Jacobs knew, Shields had been in contact with Amber, speaking to her a couple of times a week and even meeting on campus for lunch. All these conversations were reportedly centered on their respective boyfriends, the drudgery of school, and in the case of Amber, a frightening pregnancy scare that took place sometime in October.

When asked what she thought happened to Amber, Jacobs offered something that was relayed to her by Shields after one of their lunches. Shields suggested their friend was planning on moving to Los Angeles with her new boyfriend. Something about becoming a model, she recalled. This, thought Tiffany, was where that Los Angeles version of the story must have started.

Also in the file was a list of Amber's professors. Some had been interviewed, but not all. There was even a transcript from that last semester that showed Amber had completed all of her classes and had earned, for the most part, decent grades. But how was this possible if Amber was dead and had been dead that whole semester?

Tiffany read through the interviews with professors. They all said essentially the same thing. Amber was shown to have attended class, done all of the work, and taken all of the tests. The records speak for themselves. Did any of them remember seeing Amber? Or talking to her face to face? Heck, did they even know what Amber looked like? It was a well-known fact of life in many universities that professors would seldom have much personal interaction with their students, and this seemed to be the case here. This was understandable. When Tiffany went to college, which was at about the same time as Amber, although in a different state, her classes were huge. She remembers personal interaction with a few of her professors a few times but not often. Nevertheless, they would need to run down the list of Amber's professors and other school contacts to interview them again.

The cold reality of Amber's school transcript sitting right there in the file—right in front of her in black and white—made Tiffany rethink the connection between Amber Harrison and the remains by the train tracks in east Custer County. It now did not seem possible, regardless of Sebastien's confidence, that those bones belonged to Harrison. She would have to let Sebastien know. Maybe she'd wait until the DNA analysis was done, just to be sure. Either way, it didn't look good for Sebastien's exciting new theory that Amber Harrison had been dead since December 2012 and her shoulder girdle had been in a cardboard box in the building across the street the whole time.

4

———————

"Whatcha got there?" asked Tiffany, as she closed the door behind her.

Sebastien looked up from the papers he'd been reading.

"My God, you look good."

"Oh, shut up," she replied, stopping mid-room and looking down at herself. "These uniforms are the worst. I swear, they think every deputy has the hips of a male. You would think in this day and age . . ."

"No, I'm serious. The uniform suits you. And your hair looks nice in a bun like that. What's the occasion?"

Tiffany approached Sebastien, put her hands on the armrests of his office chair, and leaned in for a kiss, thus breaking her own rule about keeping affection out of the workplace. Sebastien was not about to remind her.

"You are very kind," she said, before meeting his lips once more.

"Why are you smiling like that, Tiff? I know that smile."

"You and I, Doctor, have a date with the sheriff. Fifteen hundred sharp."

"You mean, *the sheriff?*"

"Yes, Doctor. Sheriff Michael Costa. The man himself. So try to keep your hands off of my beautiful class 'A's while we're there."

"Oh, ha . . . wait . . . you mean the DNA is back? It's a match, isn't it?"

Sebastien couldn't hide his excitement, not that he *tried* to hide it.

"Yes and yes. The DNA from the Fairburn skeleton matches the DNA of Amber Harrison. It *is* her. You were right. I must confess. I really thought you were off on this one. You'll need to explain how you figured it out to the sheriff. I certainly can't."

Sebastien nodded, his frown slight but perceptible.

"Don't worry. I have faith in you. Now tell me, whatcha reading?"

Sebastien swiveled around in his chair to once again face the desk. Tiffany took her seat next to him.

"This is the Pennington County coroner's report on the Native American remains found at the Fortunatas construction site," he said, holding up the report. "Gerry pulled some strings for me."

"Oh yeah, how's that going anyway?" Tiffany took the report from Sebastien and skimmed over the first page.

"Well, after looking through that report, I see why they determined the remains to be native. I can't fault the original analysis."

Tiffany's soft face moved slightly as she read, her bare lips opening and closing as she mouthed the words to herself. Her makeup was sparse today, Sebastien noticed. Just a faint brush of eye shadow and no mascara, though her cheeks bore their trademark sweep of blush—today it was coral pink—so softly applied one would think it had been left by a light breeze.

"This guy who found the remains, Bert Mabry, are you going to contact him? Maybe he can add some info. If the remains were so obviously native, I doubt the investigator asked very many pointed questions. You know what I mean?"

Tiffany had a good point, and Sebastien would be lying if he said he already thought of it. He would also be lying if he said he noticed the name of the person who reported the find. Could that be a coincidence?

"That's an excellent idea. You're right too. I've been called out to maybe a hundred native burial recoveries in my years of doing this, and I can testify that once the remains are ID'd as native, all the good questions stop. Understandably, of course."

"Of course," Tiffany agreed. "Except in instances like this where it would be good to have a little more context. I mean, this report is super sparse for a death investigation."

Sebastien shook his head. "That's the point though, isn't it? This was hardly a death investigation."

"What's next, then?"

"Well, I thought that . . ."

"And don't say 'we,'" Tiffany interjected with the wave of her right index finger.

"Really? I was hoping we could team up on this one."

"It's not a sheriff's case, Sebastien. Heck, it's not even a case! I just don't feel good about blurring the lines between my status as an official investigator for the sheriff's office and yours, a private citizen, conducting a corporate investigation."

Sebastien tried not to look as crestfallen as he felt. "That makes sense. I guess."

"It's all fine for you, Sebastien," Tiffany continued. "You're a contractor with the sheriff's office. I'm an employee. You and I have been in enough trouble with the lieutenant these last few months. We don't need to stick our collective head out of the hole. Don't you agree?"

And yes, Sebastien did agree. Except perhaps to note that their foreheads were already a few inches above the foxhole and, for the last few months, they had taken plenty of fire. First,

Sebastien's brother, Detective Sergeant Hank LeGris, brought in an anthropologist to help solve a number of baffling unidentified body cases without telling his boss, Lieutenant Breed, that the anthropologist in question was in fact Hank's estranged brother from California. And Hank still did not reveal their familial relationship when the lieutenant agreed to keep Sebastien on as long-term contractor to help work cold cases. Then, that same anthropologist begins secretly dating one of Hank's direct reports—the very detective who is also assigned to work cold cases. Of course, Lieutenant Breed, not being an idiot, figured this out all on his own. It was a minor miracle that the lieutenant did not run all three of them out of the sheriff's office and even out of town. Or maybe it was because the whole arrangement had been working out exceptionally well for him. With Sebastien on board, difficult cases were being solved, the media was eating it up, and the sheriff himself was happy. But there was no doubt that Tiffany had read the situation wisely. There was no point in rocking the boat at this point. Especially since Sebastien, much like the sheriff, found himself to be very happy indeed. And that had not been the case in . . . ever?

"You're right. I know you're right. I just like working with you."

"What are we talking about here? Are you using code words now?"

Sebastien smiled back at her. He felt better.

"And, by the way, the sheriff is probably about to unload a bunch of pressure on us to solve the Harrison case. You may have to back burner the Fortunatas caper anyway."

"Totally understandable," he assured her. "I'm not really looking forward to that case. Something is rotten in the state of Denmark."

"Whatever you say, Marcellus."

"How did . . . I didn't know you . . ."

"I was in drama club. Now, come on. Let's get going."

~

TIFFANY PAUSED to adjust her cap.

"Is this straight?" she asked him.

"Yeah, it looks great. You look great. Don't worry, next to me you look like a million bucks. I wish I would have known about this meeting. I would have dressed a little nicer myself."

Tiffany stepped back and looked Sebastien up and down.

"You look nice and fancy as per usual. Are those pants wool? I'm sorry, you probably call them trousers."

"Merino wool, actually."

"Of course they are. And custom made, I suppose. What'd you drop on those, three hundred? Don't worry, you look like a mannequin as usual. Turn around. Let me see your ass."

"Okay, okay."

Tiffany smirked to herself as she led the way down the hall to the executive suites.

"Hey, Becky, we're here to see the sheriff."

"Detective Reese, I'll let them know you're here."

The middle-aged woman at the desk picked up her phone and punched in some numbers. Tiffany took the opportunity to survey the large reception area while they waited. Pictures of former sheriffs and undersheriffs hung on the walls, including a portrait of her father—no females, she noticed; maybe she'd be the one to fix that —along with a large painting of Mount Rushmore and some prints of local lakes. Perched on a dark-stained console table against the wall was a miniature reproduction of the Crazy Horse monument.

"They'll be ready in a minute," announced Becky after hanging up the phone.

Tiffany nodded and smiled pleasantly but inwardly wondered why she and Sebastien weren't being ushered right in. What were they talking about?

"Oh, good, you're not in yet."

Tiffany turned to see Sgt. Hank LeGris walk into the reception area. He looked harried, frantically trying to complete a halfhearted Windsor knot with his uniform tie. His longish dark hair looked to be flattened against his head, as if his mother tried to smooth it with a spit-covered palm.

"Hey, boss, you look like hell."

"Thanks, Detective. I forgot my hat. Do they know we're here?"

"They know Sebastien and I are here."

Hank acknowledged his brother with a toss of his head, then said, "You got some schmutz on your face, little brother. Here, let me get that off for ya."

Sebastien barely dodged Hank's wet finger.

"Very funny! Stop it!"

"You kids behave," laughed Tiffany. "Don't make me turn this car around."

"I'm just messing with you, bro. It's coming in real nice. Pretty soon you'll be as handsome as me." Hank rubbed his brother's newborn beard and winked, his left hand still tinkering with his tie.

Tiffany turned back toward Becky, noticing the confused look on the poor woman's face. The dissonance snapped Tiffany back into her professional mode. Twisting around quickly, she gave her boss and his brother a warning glance. Hank stopped giggling. Sebastien tweaked the knot of Hank's tie into a more respectable shape.

The trio stood quietly and politely for several more minutes before Lieutenant Breed emerged from the sheriff's conference room.

"Come on in," he said.

Tiffany noticed the slightly worried look in the lieutenant's eyes. She took a deep breath.

"Oh, great, you're ready," said Hank as he rushed to be first in the door. "Detective Reese and Doctor Grey just got here. Perfect timing."

To Tiffany's surprise, the sheriff was not in uniform. But even in a rather plain dark-blue suit he looked august and commanding. The man was tall, perhaps six-foot-four, with a clean-shaven face. His dark hair had receded markedly in the seven years he'd been in office. His light-olive skin bore wrinkles and creases—especially along the forehead and at the outer corners of his eyes, which were brown and serious. Sheriff Costa was never known for affability, though all reports indicated he was a remarkable politician. But within the ranks, he could be cold and terrifying. Fortunately, Tiffany hadn't had any run-ins with the man. She shook his offered hand firmly and took a seat next to Lieutenant Breed on the near side of the conference table. Hank sat to her right. Captain Roderick of the coroner's division and Doctor Melinda Stark, the director of the crime lab, sat on the opposite side of the table.

Tiffany watched the sheriff greet Sebastien, who was the last to enter the room. It was impossible to hear what the polished law enforcement officer was saying to the insecure anthropologist, owing to the chatter of the others. But the sheriff looked to be conveying something serious. *Sebastien must be peeing himself*, she thought.

"Well, Mel, why don't you fill these guys in on our little situation? Although I have no doubt our Doctor Grey won't be surprised."

Our Doctor Grey, thought Tiffany. *Nice.*

Dr. Stark pushed her dark, round glasses up her long, narrow nose and consulted an open notebook that lay in front of her on the table.

"Yes, sir, Sheriff. A few days ago, Captain Roderick submitted three bones from coroner's case number 12-1023 to the lab for DNA analysis. These remains were recovered northeast of Fairburn, along some railroad tracks. The identity of the decedent was unknown, but the sex was estimated to be female based on the anthropology report from 2012. Cause of death for the individual could not be stated definitively based on what was recovered, but the shoulder blade displayed a defect that turned out to be a gunshot wound. So this is no doubt a homicide."

"Which we all knew," said Captain Roderick.

"I think you mean *suspected*," added Stark.

Tiffany watched Captain Roderick's face strain against a grimace.

"Anyway," continued Stark, "we were able to obtain a complete genetic profile of the victim. And, per the suggestion of the coroner's office, we compared the DNA profile to DNA recovered as part of the Amber Harrison investigation, which began in January of 2013."

"Which DNA from the Harrison investigation?" asked Hank. "I don't remember seeing any lab reports in the file."

"There was a small amount of blood recovered in Harrison's vehicle. A sample of that was kept in property. There was enough for us to analyze it."

"Her mother's vehicle," corrected Lieutenant Breed.

Dr. Stark ignored this latest correction.

"Anyway, a comparison between the two profiles reveals an eleven allele match, including some rare polymorphisms. I'm still crunching the numbers, but the statistics will be huge."

"It's her?" Sebastien asked, fingers over his lip.

"That's correct, Doctor Grey. The remains associated with 12-1023 belong to Amber Harrison."

"Hey, far be it from me to rain on the parade, but technically we don't know that."

"What are you saying, Ted?" asked the sheriff.

"All we know is that the body and the blood match. We would still need to test it against Harrison's family to make sure it's her."

"Actually, Captain Roderick, that's not technically the case."

Tiffany felt the tension level increase in the conference room. *Surely*, she thought, *Stark must have told him?*

The director of the crime lab continued, "It was Doctor Grey's suggestion, actually. You see, within the evidence for the Amber Harrison missing persons case was a hairbrush taken from her bedroom. That's pretty standard, I think. But the hair had never been analyzed for DNA. There was no reason to do so without more evidence that she might actually be dead."

"There wasn't much blood in the car, as I recall," added Breed. "So no real reason to suspect she was dead."

"Exactly. But my team was able to find root bulbs in the hair from the brush, which gave us a genetic profile. Again, it was the same eleven allele match as the blood and the shoulder girdle."

Roderick's face, which was beginning to turn red, suddenly became animated.

"Hey, that reminds me—and thanks for looping me in on the hair, by the way—"

"Calm down, Teddy," interrupted the sheriff. "Reminds you of what?"

Roderick looked across the table to Sebastien, unconsciously poking a finger in his direction.

"Your report mentioned the spine. You said the spine indicated the remains were Harrison's. We didn't recover the spine. Just the shoulder. What's that about?"

Sebastien sat up in his chair and shot a glance at Tiffany. She winked in return.

"I meant the scapular spine. That's the bony projection running medio-laterally on the dorsal surface of the scapula. It's the origination point for the deltoid muscles and the insertion point for the trapezius muscles."

Tiffany covered her smile with her left hand while the others stared wide-eyed in silence at Sebastien's anatomy lecture.

"Well, what I meant was, the scapular spine on 12-1023 is very pronounced, very robust. That tells me that that particular shoulder blade belonged to someone with very strong and large upper back and shoulder muscles. And that would indicate a great deal of either climbing or rowing, or at least those types of motions of the arms and shoulders. So, when Tiff . . . er, Detective Reese told me that Amber Harrison was a climbing pro . . . well, I guess I just felt it was worthwhile to check for a connection."

"Even though the shoulder was found before Harrison went missing?" asked Roderick.

"Was *reported* missing," said Hank, Tiffany, and Sebastien all in unison.

"So this is the situation we find ourselves in, ladies and gentleman." The sheriff tapped his gold pen against the table as he spoke. "How this happened, how we missed this back in 2012, or even in 2013 when the Harrison girl was reported missing, will be a PR nightmare. But it's that very timeline that's going to help us out, I think. Now, one of the questions I'm going to be asked is, why didn't we submit the DNA from the skeleton into the system immediately? And, secondly, why didn't we test the blood from the car for DNA immediately? Because folks are going to say that if we had done that, we would have found that they matched. What I would like to know from you experts, first of all, is whether that's true. I feel like that may be putting it a little too simply."

Doctor Stark nodded her agreement.

"That is correct, sir. There is no mandatory nationwide DNA database for John or Jane Does. There's the National Missing and Unidentified Persons Database, but only a fraction of agencies submit their unknown subjects and missing persons. Especially, I would say, on the missing persons end of things. The time and expense of DNA testing is not really justified for an adult who may have left voluntarily. The nation's crime labs are way too backed-up as it is."

"I agree," added Captain Roderick. "Even if we had uploaded the genetic profile from the bones at the time they were found, we would not have gotten a match—unless, that is, Amber Harrison's DNA was in CODIS for some reason. Which it would not have been, based on her lack of criminal history."

The sheriff lifted an eyebrow at this.

"Yes, we ran her records. Pretty standard in missing persons cases. Like I said, there would not have been a match in 2012. And as far as the following January when Harrison was reported missing, why would we even consider that the remains out at Fairburn belonged to her?"

"I'll tell you where we do have a PR problem."

Hank's preamble garnered a look of concern from Lieutenant Breed, but it didn't stop the sergeant from speaking his mind.

"There's a feeling out there that we mailed this one in. Sure, some people reported that Harrison left for California with a guy she met. But we didn't exactly run that into the ground, did we? So now we have to make an announcement that the remains in Fairburn match the blood from Harrison's car. Which we did not tell the public about in the first place. So people are going to say the blood should have lit a bigger fire under our asses. Pardon my French, Sheriff."

Tiffany puckered her lips. She hadn't thought of that. Leave it to Hank LeGris. Her boss came off as a little *aw shucks* sometimes, but he was one of the brightest in the department. And he was right about this one. This could get ugly very quickly.

"I appreciate your candor, Sergeant. But I advise you to tread carefully and remember that I own this department—the failures as well as the successes. I would appreciate you not accusing my staff of mailing anything in." Sheriff Castro's voice was much more pleasant than his message. His face was stony serious.

"Oh, no, sir. I didn't mean it that way. I just meant perceptions. I know our guys did all they could do. I'm just concerned that when the public finds out about the match to the blood in the car, they'll be wondering why it wasn't reported in the media. That's all I meant."

Tiffany felt a rush of sympathy and embarrassment on Hank's behalf. He'd been called out by the one person who could single-handedly ruin his career.

"Apology accepted, Sergeant. And in any case, we matched the remains based on DNA from the hairbrush, not the blood."

"Well, not initially, sir. It was the blood from the . . ."

Before Hank could finish his sentence, a low but abrupt "Sergeant!" came from Lt. Breed.

Tiffany watched Hank's face progress through shock, confusion, then finally understanding. She silently exhaled the breath she'd been keeping in for those few tense moments.

"Ah. Yes, sir. I see what you mean."

"Excellent. I'm glad we agree. Now, we owe it to Harrison's family, and to the people of this county, to find out what happened. We'll need to restore faith in this great institution and the best way to do that is to—how did you put it, Sergeant? Light a fire under our asses?"

Twist the knife, thought Tiffany as Hank looked sheepishly down at the table.

"We need to pay Harrison's family a visit as soon as possible. Breed?"

"Yes, sir, Sheriff. We'll get on that immediately."

"Um . . . excuse me." Tiffany tried to sound confident, but she'd be lying if she said she wasn't intimidated.

"Go ahead, Detective. What is it?"

"Thank you, Sheriff. I just wanted to point out that Amber Harrison's mother lives in Portland."

"Does she? Well, pack a raincoat, Reese. Should be warmer there than here at least. Now, what else? Lieutenant Breed?"

Tiffany scribbled "Portland" in her notebook, more to make herself look attentive than anything else. She appreciated the sheriff's use of her last name, sans her rank, though. That was a sign of respect with Castro.

Before Breed could answer the sheriff, Sebastien spoke up.

"I'm sorry, but if I may say so, I think the one thing we should be doing is checking the recovery scene for the rest of her remains. The family will be expecting that."

"And we would certainly do that in any case, Doctor Grey. We wouldn't just leave the rest out there!" exclaimed Captain Roderick.

"But you did, though, didn't you?"

Roderick's mouth fell open and his cheeks began to redden for the second time. Just as he was inhaling in preparation for a verbal assault on the smart-ass forensic consultant, Sheriff Castro spoke up.

"He's got you there, Ted. Doctor Grey, what exactly are we looking for?"

"All we have at the coroner's office is the left scapula, clavicle, and humerus."

Hank turned toward his brother and whispered, "Sebastien, laymen's terms here. You're killing me."

"Oh, I'm sorry. I mean the left shoulder blade, collarbone, and upper arm bone. So, there should be a lot to recover somewhere—although I don't think we should assume the rest of the body is where the shoulder girdle was found. The body parts could have been dumped in different locations. Or scavengers could have carried things off."

"That reminds me, nice work on the skull from Hell Canyon, Reese and Dr. Grey. I don't think I properly acknowledged you for that. Anyway, let me know how it goes. I want a team out there yesterday. Top priority. Let's hope the weather holds.

Lieutenant Breed, I want updates from you personally every morning and evening until this thing is buttoned up. I trust you will come up with a solid and effective investigative plan. I know this will be solved very soon. Now, I'm off to speak at the Rotary or the Elks, or . . ."

With that, the sheriff stood and headed for the door. Tiffany couldn't help but laugh when she heard, "Becky, where in the hell am I supposed to be?" from the reception area.

The three underlings followed the sheriff out of the room and past the receptionist's desk to the elevator. Hank elbowed the button for the first floor and the elevator door closed, leaving Tiffany, Hank, and Sebastien in momentary privacy. Tiffany took the opportunity to voice a concern that had been festering for the last several minutes.

"Sarge, do you think we could put the brakes on notifying Peggy Harrison?"

Hank was pulling at the knot of his tie like an escape artist wrestling off the chains.

"You trying to get me fired, Tiff? I think I made enough of a jerk of myself in there. You want me to disregard a direct order from the big man himself? You've been around my brother too much."

Sebastien didn't react to his name being brought in.

"I understand, Hank. I can go to Breed myself and leave you out of it, if that would be better. It's just that I think we need to do some initial interviews before the public knows Amber Harrison has been found—found dead, that is. I think witnesses and potential suspects would be more open to talking if we approached it from a missing persons matter."

Hank leaned back against the elevator wall and looked up at the metal grilling on the ceiling.

"No, I do not want you to go over my head. That won't make me look any better. But I do see your point. We need to lock some people into their stories before the news of her murder gets out. Okay, you guys get out of here. I'm going to go back up and see if I can catch the lieutenant. Let's meet at my place tonight and discuss a game plan. We're in the crosshairs now." Hank let out a sign of exasperation, which morphed into a slight chuckle. He put his arm around Sebastien and said, "You know, this job was a lot easier before you got to town."

Sebastien replied with a simple "I know" and a smile.

5

—————

"Where's Parsifal?"

"He's hiding from Mist."

Melissa LeGris paused clearing the table and pointed to a gray cat sitting in front of the fireplace, tail swaying slowly and green eyes looking up toward them. Tiffany's Nebelung cat was a frequent guest at the LeGris home. Hank and Melissa's six-year-old daughter, Kirby, insisted.

"Honey, let me get this. You sit."

Hank stood and gestured to his very pregnant wife to retake the chair she had occupied during dinner. She did so and blew a lock of wheat-blond hair out of her blue eyes before thanking him.

"How much longer, Melissa?" asked Tiffany.

"Three weeks, but I may not make it that far. Kirby was two weeks early, if that's any indication," she responded, referring to her and Hank's six-year-old daughter.

Hank looked back from carrying plates into the kitchen.

"Sebastien, why don't you help me clear so we have room to work?"

"Yeah, sure thing."

The Harrison case documents consisted of one two-inch binder, and the shoulder girdle from Fairburn required no more than a few handwritten report pages in a file folder. The effort to clear space wasn't necessary, but it did make room to divide things up and take the full measure of the known facts.

"Okay, here is a photograph of our victim, along with the original missing persons report." Hank pulled some stapled sheets out of the binder and handed them to Tiffany. "Tiff, you read through that. Sebastien, here is the forensic report from the search of her car and house."

Sebastien examined the photograph closely. She was a very pretty girl. Her face was narrow—leptoprosopic, though he would never say that out loud—with a long nose. Her squinting eyes concealed their color, but Sebastien would have guessed blue or green, even though the odds were genetically low. Her shoulders were muscular and round, and her collarbones bulged out from under her top. All of these features accorded perfectly with the bones in the morgue.

"We're already caught up on all this, Hank. Why don't . . ."

"Just do it, Detective. Don't question my process. You're learning from the best, after all."

"Oh, man. Is he always this difficult when he's working?" laughed Melissa.

"I have lots of stories," replied Tiffany with an exaggerated roll of her large brown eyes.

"Very funny. Just indulge me. And what about you, boy genius? Any complaints?"

"Hey, I didn't say anything," returned Sebastien.

"Thanks for having my back. Some boyfriend you are." Tiffany stuck two fingers in Sebastien's rib cage.

"Well, no . . . I just . . ."

"Oh, stop. I'm kidding. And what about you, Hank?"

"I'm going through these," Hank held up a stack of papers

about a quarter of an inch thick. "These are the follow-up interviews—Harrison's roommate, a few professors."

Sebastien knew what Hank was doing, and he appreciated his brother's approach. It was too easy to lose the trees for the forest, or overgeneralize when information was taken in mass form. Like a puzzle, it didn't help to know what the final picture was supposed to look like if they couldn't find the pieces that made up the sky, grass, or sun. Hank was making sure that didn't happen.

"Anything I can do to help?" asked Melissa.

Sebastien looked over at Hank, wondering if this would be awkward.

"Heck yeah, you can help. Here, read these interviews. This one is with Harrison's professor—chemistry or biology or some other useless science." Hank turned quickly toward Sebastien and said, "Don't even start, little brother. I'm kidding." Then he handed Melissa a few more sheets. "And this one is with her mother."

For the next thirty minutes, the table went relatively silent as the four read through their share of the case files. An occasional "hmmm" or loud sigh broke through the sounds of pages flipping and shuffling.

The forensic report was scant at best and revealed to Sebastien a lack of effort more than anything else. He would, of course, try to refrain from verbalizing that opinion—he was working on his tact. But on the positive end of things, what was not done at the time could be done now, and with better technology.

Harrison's car, which was technically not hers but was registered to her mother, was found in the driveway of the home she shared with two other women. When deputies arrived to take the initial missing persons report, they were given consent to search the house for clues as to where Harrison may have gone. The house didn't have much to reveal. There were no notes or diaries indicating self-harm, romantic entanglements, or planned trips to California or anywhere else. Her room was not in disarray or didn't seem to be. The bed was made, and her perfume and makeup stood undisturbed on her dresser along with a small white jewelry case containing assorted earrings, necklaces, and rings. None of it appeared too expensive, according to the report. The only thing taken from the bedroom by forensics was a hairbrush.

The car lacked much of interest to the investigation, with the significant exception of a small spot of blood on the interior panel of the front passenger door. The report contained a crude diagram of the door with a notation of the approximate size and location of the stain, which was subsequently excised and placed in evidence. There were no fingerprints found on the interior or exterior. One potentially noteworthy find was that the driver's seat of the car was adjusted significantly forward when it was parked in the driveway. Harrison was a tall woman —five-foot-nine, according to her driver's license. Some had speculated that a person of that height would not have fit behind the steering wheel with the seat in its current position. Others concluded the seat had likely been moved up in order to retrieve something from the rear of the vehicle.

The blood, though not enough to be conclusive evidence of death or major injury, did raise sufficient alarm to send the forensic team back into Harrison's apartment to look for more. The mattresses of all of the beds were lifted and checked, as was the carpet underneath the beds. There were no smells of bleach or other cleaners, nor any floors or walls that looked to be recently cleaned.

Sebastien tossed the report onto the table and shook his head in contempt. The motion of the papers caught Hank's eye.

"What, Sebastien? Nothing burger?"

"The only items taken for testing were the hairbrush and the blood stain from the car—both of which, as we know, were left untested until now."

"Let's not get too critical there, little brother. I mean, it was a missing persons case, not a homicide. And more importantly, the amount of blood in the car was relatively insignificant. What was the size of the stain? About a square inch?"

"It was roughly three by three-and-a-half centimeters."

"Okay, well, I don't know what that means in inches, but the point is it was a small stain. So even if they tested the blood and made the connection to Harrison's hair, it was still not enough to suspect foul play. And, by the way, you've seen our criminal-istics lab. It's tiny now and was even smaller back then. We need to prioritize. The public doesn't understand how that works, but I know you do."

Sebastien nearly provided the metric conversion for his brother but stopped himself.

"You're correct. It was a relatively small amount of blood— which is very bothersome, *dans ma vie*. And, if they knew back then that the blood belonged to Harrison, they would have found the location of the stain to be equally troubling. That may have affected the prioritization of things."

"Oh, for heaven's sake. If you're going to slip into French, I'll need a drink." Tiffany reached for the bottle of wine in the middle of the table.

Sebastien opened the forensic report to the diagram of the car seat and slid it in front of Hank.

"See here," he said, tapping the page. "Look at where they found the blood."

Tiffany strained to get a better look at what Sebastien was showing to Hank.

Hank lifted the page and brought it in front of his nose.

"Well, I'll be damned. It's her car. Why is it on the passenger door?"

"What, Hank? What?" demanded Tiffany.

Hank tossed the report over to Tiffany.

"Are you kidding me?"

"Nope," replied Sebastien.

"What is it?" Melissa asked.

Hank lifted the autopsy report from the Fairburn skeleton and turned to Melissa.

"You wouldn't have known this, sweetheart, but the autopsy of Harrison shows she was shot in the left shoulder."

"For the sake of accuracy," began Sebastien, "that was just a piece of her—her shoulder girdle."

"Well, imagine my embarrassment," Hank replied. "The autopsy of Harrison's left shoulder shows she was shot."

"Hey, I'm just being technical," exclaimed Sebastien.

"Wait, so what you're saying is that your victim, who had been shot in the left shoulder, bled onto the right front door of her own car?"

"We can't say for sure that the wound that left the blood in the car was the same wound caused by the gunshot. At least not without the rest of the body. Any no one bothered . . ."

Hank stuck a finger at Sebastien.

"I swear, dude, if you say it, I will punch you."

Melissa intervened once again.

"Sebastien, why does the amount of blood bother you? What are you saying?"

"Look, I'm no pathologist . . ."

"You sure act like one."

"Hank!" Melissa half-slapped Hank on the back of his head.

"It seems to me that the amount of blood on the passenger seat is insufficient given the likely wound track. There are several large arteries in the shoulder—axial, subscapular, and thoracoacrominal come to mind."

Tiffany motioned to the autopsy diagram with her glass, nearly causing the red liquid to spill.

"The blood didn't come from the wound?"

"Not directly. I'm suggesting it was transferred to the car by one of the killers."

"What do you mean by '*killers*'? You're going to pull a muscle jumping to these conclusions, Sebastien."

~

TIFFANY ALWAYS GOT a kick out of watching Sebastien and Hank go at it, even though at times, like tonight, Hank was a little too aggressive. As a rule, Sebastien was overly sensitive and prone to defensiveness, but he had gotten better since moving to South Dakota. Tiffany liked to think she was a big reason for that, though she could be deluding herself. Maybe she had grown used to his idiosyncrasies after spending so much time with him. But something was definitely off with Sebastien. He looked distracted and wasn't giving it back to Hank as much as usual. She wondered what it might be but was too wise to ask him in front of the others. She would bring it up later. Tiffany put her hand on Sebastien's left leg under the table and gave him a squeeze of reassurance.

"Honey, go easy on your brother," chided Melissa. "Sebastien, don't worry about my lug of a husband. He's just jealous of you. You are clearly way smarter than him."

"Better looking too," smiled Tiffany.

"Hey, hey! Come on, now. What is this, attack-poor-Hank night at the LeGris house? Ha, ha! I'm just joking with you, Sebastien. I love ya, little brother."

Hank put Sebastien in a headlock and gave the crown of his head a noisy smooch.

Tiffany and Melissa laughed out loud. Sebastien pushed Hank away angrily, but Tiffany could see his smile. She gave Melissa a wink of gratitude for breaking through the tension.

"Okay, Detective. Lay it on us."

Tiffany looked down at the open case file on the table in front of her.

"Not much. The original missing persons call was made by Harrison's mother, Peggy Harrison, on the evening of January 10, 2013. According to her mother, the last time she spoke with her daughter was on the afternoon of Christmas Eve. Harrison told Peggy she was planning to go to a party with some of her other friends that evening."

"And did she?"

"No. She never showed, according to Barnadette Jacobs, one of her roommates who was at the party. In fact, Amber and Barnadette had agreed to meet there. That's what Jacobs told Peggy Harrison, anyway."

"But she wasn't reported missing until two weeks after that. Seems strange to me," said Hank.

"Mrs. Harrison assumed her daughter was just too busy to talk. She tried to reach out a few times after Christmas Eve but got no responses. She had no real reason to believe that her daughter was not safe. But by January 10 she began to worry, so she called Jacobs, who said she likewise hadn't talked to her since Christmas Eve, when they discussed meeting up at the party. Although, they exchanged a few texts."

"Did her mother mention Amber having any plans to travel, or anything about a boyfriend?" Sebastien asked.

"No. Her mom was certain there was no long-term boyfriend. Evidently, since her parents were divorced, Amber and Peggy had been as close as girlfriends. Amber told her everything. She even told her mom about a one-night stand that resulted in a pregnancy scare. That's how close they were. But there was some talk of a potential new love interest, a boy from work."

Hank rubbed his chin pensively before asking, "What did her mom have to say about Amber's state of mind in the months prior? Anything unusual?"

"She mentioned it had been several months since she actually spoke with her daughter, but they texted almost every day. Amber seemed a little distant, she said. A little preoccupied."

"Did anyone check her social media? To get her frame of mind, I mean. What was she posting? What were her friends saying?" asked Melissa.

"No, they didn't. But that would have been a great idea," replied Tiffany. "Nowadays that would be standard. But ten years ago, not so much. So, what about her roommates?"

Hank patted the thin stack on the table in front of him.

"Barnadette Jacobs—she was also a student at the university —said that Amber was out of the house that entire semester. She only saw her a few times at school."

"But wait," interjected Melissa, "they were roommates. How is that possible? How could they have not seen each other for six months?"

"Jacobs said that, even though they were roommates, and they were splitting the rent with a third roommate, Amber was not living there. Evidently she met a boy at work that summer and moved in with him right away."

"But how does this Barnadette Jacobs know—"

Hank cut off Tiffany mid-sentence. "They were in communication via text. Jacobs specifically remembers that she and Amber were arguing over the rent. Amber, it seemed, had a spotty record of paying her share."

"When was the last time they texted?" asked Sebastien.

"Jacobs wasn't positive. Early January she thinks. She definitely remembers that much, at least."

"What are you writing, Sebastien?" Hank gestured to his brother.

"I'm keeping track of the lies and who's telling them. So far, that's numbers one and two. Amber Harrison had been dead for several months. Jacobs did not, could not, have expected to see her on Christmas Eve, nor could she have been in communication with her in the days after. She could not possibly have seen her at school either. That's actually three lies if you break it down."

"Maybe she didn't know she was dead?"

The rest of the table turned their focus to Melissa.

"What do you mean, hon?" prompted Hank.

"Well, the Jacobs girl said she saw Amber at school a few times. But what does that mean? Did she talk to her or see her up close? Or did she just believe that she saw her—you, know, from a distance? Unless I'm missing something."

"I don't think you are," Tiffany responded with a wide grin before turning to Hank. "Boss, I think you way outkicked the coverage when you married Melissa."

"What does that mean?" inquired Sebastien, looking confused.

"I'll explain it to you later," giggled Tiffany.

"I don't think so, Reese. I mean, yeah, I totally struck gold when I married my hot wife. But check this out. Jacobs mentioned in her interview that the third roommate, Shelly Shields, had *seen* Amber regularly when they met for lunch or coffee at the university. This is according to Shields, of course. Jacobs also reports it was during one of these lunches that Amber told Shields she was planning to leave town with her boyfriend at the end of the semester."

"Lie number four," Sebastien mumbled while continuing his list-making.

"So that's where that rumor started." Melissa nodded in understanding. "People were talking about her leaving for California."

"Oh, that's right, you would have been around for that," said Tiffany.

"Yes, we were," Melissa replied. "It was a really big deal at the time. And yes, half the town thought she ran off—although I don't recall there being any proof of that."

"There wasn't," replied Hank. "That's why things stalled."

"And I suppose this Shields person confirmed all this?" asked Sebastien. "What? Oh, for hell's sake. Don't tell me they didn't interview her."

"Calm down, Doctor. I haven't found that supplement yet. I'm sure there's an electronic copy in the system."

"That will be important."

"Well, thank you, Dr. Grey. I didn't realize that. It's good to get your expert clarification." Hank shook his head and turned to Melissa. "Anything interesting from the interview with her professors?"

Melissa drummed a naked fingernail against her assigned stack of reports.

"Not really. They interviewed her biology and math professors. Unfortunately both had huge classes and didn't know any of their students by face. The day-to-day classwork was handled by teaching assistants in both classes. But the detectives did get her transcripts from that semester—here." Melissa handed a photocopied sheet to Hank. "Amber Harrison was registered in five classes that term and completed them all."

"That's not possible. When did the semester start? September? And it ended in December, right?"

"That's right," Melissa affirmed.

"I saw that too when I was going through the files last night. It throws everything into question."

"There are no questions," Sebastien barked. "Amber Harrison was not taking any tests or going to any classes. As I keep reminding everyone, she was dead."

"It could be a bookkeeping error by the university. With all of those students to keep track of, it's inevitable that mistakes would be made," suggested Tiffany. "Maybe this has the wrong year or semester printed on it."

Sebastien reached over and took the transcript from his brother.

"Let me see that."

"Hey, Sebastien, why don't you go ahead and take that?"

"I swear it's like you're both still teenagers," remarked Melissa. "Growing up in your house must have been a nightmare."

Tiffany could swear she saw Hank and Sebastien lock eyes for a millisecond before Sebastien shifted his focus to the transcript. A nerve had been unwittingly struck.

Speculation and theory gave way to silence as Sebastien examined the transcript for an inordinate amount of time. His eyes followed his index finger as it traced the rows of classes with their respective section numbers, descriptions, professors, and final grades. After a few minutes, Tiffany reached over to Sebastien and, with two fingers under his stubbled chin, lifted his head up.

"What do you think about that, Sebastien? You were a college professor. Do you think those records could be wrong?"

Sebastien shook his head softly.

"Can't have it both ways, little bro. She can't be dead and going to school."

"And yet, that's how we have it." Sebastien's reply was short and directed at the table. He waved the transcript. "This indicates Harrison was in her third year. Do we have the transcripts from the semester before this?"

"You mean spring of 2012? Why the hell would we need that?" shot Hank.

"We have to get them." Sebastien ignored the question. "What about phone records?"

"Yes. Right here." Tiffany fished through the case binder and handed a few sheets to Sebastien. "But it doesn't look like anything was ever done with them. There's no mention of the records in the supplements I read."

"None in these either," offered Melissa.

"Why am I not surprised?"

Hank's face showed annoyance.

"Go easy, Sebastien. It was a different time, and Amber was an adult."

Tiffany pulled out her phone and began punching in a text.

"What's up, Tiff?"

"I'm texting Erin in Crime Analysis. She's an expert on cell phone stuff. She can help us go through these."

As surprising as it may have been to have the phone records go unanalyzed, it was not unheard of, especially a decade ago when deciphering the toll records and matching the calls and texts to cell tower listings was a bit of an arcane science. Tiffany knew well that, even in recent cases, search warrants were often written for the cell phone records more as a matter of custom and routine than for investigative purposes. There was a work-flow in major investigations that amounted to essentially a checklist of forensic possibilities: ballistics, fingerprints, DNA, cell phone records, etc. This was a supposed to be a reminder that such things not only needed to be collected, but they needed to be submitted to the lab with the proper paperwork. It was a two-step process: collect and submit. It wasn't so long ago that Tiffany and a colleague were cleaning out the desk of a recently retired detective only to find the buccal swab of a homicide suspect stuck in the back of the top drawer, still in its paper sleeve. At that point, of course, it may as well have been in the garbage can. These kinds of mistake were inevitable at a low frequency—detectives were human, after all. But in every case they made for embarrassing reports up the chain. Tiffany was beginning to feel bad for Lieutenant Breed, who was in for some uncomfortable briefings to the sheriff.

"So, to recap," began Hank, "Harrison was last seen alive in October, by Shields, according to Jacobs. We need to dig up Shields's interview, then pay visits to both roommates and get some clarification—especially from Jacobs, to Melissa's point. Did she really see Harrison at school, or could that be a mistake, like the transcript? And I want more details about Shields's interactions with Harrison too. The cell phone records should fill in the rest of the picture."

"We only have Harrison's records, so they won't fill in everything," added Tiffany.

Sebastien shook his head, frowning.

"The transcripts aren't a mistake. Those kinds of mistakes just don't happen. We're looking at this too narrowly, too discretely. And Shields wasn't interacting with Amber Harrison. No one was. Why are we pretending we don't know that?"

"I'm not—we're not. We're just looking back, trying to recreate how it went down. The investigators at the time didn't have reason to suspect that Harrison had been murdered."

"Actually, they did. It was in the coroner's . . ."

"Damn it, Sebastien! We get it. We screwed up. We all suck. Horrible investigators. Now can we let it go, please?"

Hank's face was bright red and aimed directly at his brother, accompanied by a histrionic finger poke.

"I'm sorry, Hank. I didn't mean . . ."

Hank didn't let his brother finish.

"You just need to hit the brakes on this sanctimonious attitude, Sebastien."

Tiffany drained her wine and saw through the bottom of the empty glass that Sebastien had fully folded into himself. This happened from time to time when he was upset, embarrassed, or particularly anxious. It was a form of catatonia, he once admitted. His mind would get stuck. She put down her glass and signaled at Hank with her eyes, who nodded in acknowledgment.

"All right, Sebastien. Sorry that I kind of overreacted there. It's just a touchy thing, you know? The sheriff's office is twisting in the wind on this one, and we're all a bit worked up."

Tiffany scanned Sebastien's face, looking for the telltale softening around the mouth and semi-lowering of the shoulders. She didn't see either.

"Sebastien, what did you mean when you said we're looking at the transcripts too discretely?" Tiffany hoped her question, which was genuine, would move them past the tension.

"It's not an either-or, is it?" replied Sebastien. "It's too simple to think she was either in class or she wasn't. Melissa just told us none of her professors knew Harrison by face. And it was the teaching assistants who managed the classes—big classes too. Remember? So, obviously, this presents a whole new question, in addition to the ones we already had."

The other three waited in silence for Sebastien to elaborate. When it became clear he wasn't going to, Tiffany prompted him.

"And that would be? Those would be?"

"Who was impersonating Harrison at school? Who was texting with her mom? Was it Shields or Jacobs, or someone else altogether? Also, she was obviously not working. What's the story there? Did anyone check with her job? And how many other people are involved? It seems to me like it would take one hell of an effort to make it appear as though she were still alive for six months or so after she was killed. And what's the motive for doing that?"

The warm feeling that began to fill Tiffany's chest was not due to the alcohol, she knew. It was just that one glass of wine, after all. No, it was gratitude for that quirky new man in her life —all their lives, really. And pride—pride in the closeness and intimacy they shared.

"So that's where we're going with this?" Hank looked around the table as he spoke.

"Unless there's some sort of major mistake or massive misunderstanding, I don't see the alternative."

"I didn't find a record of anyone talking to her manager at the gym, but that can't be true. God, I hope that's not true."

Tiffany began to feel sorry for her boss. This was different for him. There was more than just the truth on the line; politics and reputation were at stake as well.

"I know this is awkward, Hank. But think about it. We'll get to the bottom of it, and you will be the one who got us there. We can only win."

"Tiffany's right, honey. This was going to get cleared up some day. Wasn't it? Why not by you? Cheer up, sweetheart."

Hank kissed his wife's hand, which had been extended to rest on his own.

"I have more questions," announced Sebastien, ignoring the tenderness of the moment. "I would really like to know how public the Fairburn skeleton find was made. Is it likely the roommates knew Harrison's body was found? What was their reaction? What changed in their lives, if anything? Knowing this could help break an alibi, I feel."

Sebastien was coming out of his funk. Tiffany could see it in his eyes. The best way to take his mind off of his own insecurities was to put it to work on a case. She ran her hand along his thigh and smiled at him.

"Good points. So let's game plan." Hank sounded much more hopeful now. "Sebastien, you're needed out at the Fairburn site tomorrow. Is it safe to say you feel confident that the rest of Harrison is in that area?"

"I do," answered Sebastien. "Despite what I said in the sheriff's meeting, it's almost unheard of for a dismemberment to result in a complete shoulder girdle separated from the body. So I think that was the result of decomposition and scavenging or major trauma, rather than someone dumping those elements separately from the rest. I would think the rest of her is in that same location. And, of course, it would be completely skeletonized at this point."

"Perfect. You'll be out there, then. Tiffany, see if you can track down the roommates. Find out where they are as soon as possible. We need to lock them in a little tighter before we visit Peggy Harrison in Oregon and before Harrison's death is made public. The sheriff gave us until the day after tomorrow to do that.

"What about this?" Tiffany lifted the transcript. "We need to find out how this came to be."

"Yes, we do," agreed Hank. "I'll pay a visit to the university and see what I can find out."

"And how about the gym? Maybe someone there would have been around ten years ago and will remember the last time Amber Harrison was at work. We do need to actually pin down the time and date of her death, after all."

"True, Tiffany. Let us know how that goes." Hank's mischievous smile returned. "We've got to scramble. Now, get the hell out of my house. All of you. Not you, Melissa."

Melissa pushed against the top of the table and lifted herself from a sitting position with a grunt.

"You better watch it, old man. Tiffany, Sebastien, you all stay as long as you like. But I'm going to bed and taking Hank with me."

"That's all right, Melissa. I'm heading out. We have a long day tomorrow, and I need to call Erin first thing in the morning and follow-up on my text about the phone records. What about you, Sebastien?" Tiffany punctuated the question with a subtle squeeze to his thigh.

SEBASTIEN AWOKE to a pulsating pressure on his chest and a soft murmur. It was Mist, Tiffany's cat, kneading a comfortable spot into the duvet just below his manubrium. The sound of light snoring told him Tiffany was still there next to him. He extended his left arm for tactile confirmation, being careful not to move too much and thus disturb the cat, now comfortably curled up. His hand found Tiffany's right hip as she lay on her left side—the very hip where her pistol hung on most days; the hip that, paired with its left counterpart, formed the lower border of her somewhat rectangular yet athletic trunk. He traced his finger forward along what would be her iliac crest, just above her right buttock, searching for the anterior iliac spine. Her slim figure made the bony landmark easy to find. He rested his palm there, on her side, as she slept.

After working so many cases involving skeletons, decomposed bodies, or individuals' bones, Sebastien could not help but notice the bones beneath the skin in nearly all of those with whom he came in contact—living or dead. It was admittedly a quirk, and maybe even a ghoulish one at that. But he found it difficult to turn off. Where most people might see a pretty face, Sebastien imagined the musculature and skull that provided its shape and form; the way the cheekbones project forward, connecting to the lower eye orbit; the shape of the nasal aperture and its relationship to the length and width of the nose; and the small separations in the masseter muscles that most people call dimples.

And it went far beyond the face, though that was often the most apparent target for these mental exercises. For Sebastien, the shoulders of a shirt or straps of a bra were merely indications of the size of the coracoid processes that jutted forward from the shoulder blades. That inverted triangle at the lower back, sometimes exposed when low-cut pants were worn, revealed to him spinal segments that were misaligned, surely causing their owner lower-back pain. Less common, but just as evident, were the slightly misshapen heads that resulted from the various forms of craniosynostosis—the premature fusion of one or more sutures. Well did Sebastien identify with Dr. James Mortimer from Arthur Conan Doyle's *The Hound of the Baskervilles*: *"It is not my intention to be fulsome, but I confess that I covet your skull."*

Tiffany began to stir slightly, so Sebastien quickly pulled his hand back, then gave Mist a scratch on the neck. With his opposite hand, he felt for his phone on the nightstand, the screen emitting a sharp glow as he checked the time: 2:43. Rotating the phone, he trained the light on the corner of his bedroom and lifted his head slowly. Parsifal was in his oversized bed, eyes covered with a paw and left back leg jerking to a dream of some sort. Sebastien wondered if he was dreaming about running far away from this place, back to California.

He replaced his phone and focused on the sudden blackness of the ceiling, trying to take his mind off of the growing sensation of having to empty his bladder. His thoughts turned to the two cases currently absorbing his attention. The Amber Harrison homicide would certainly be cleared up in a matter of time and a few interviews. The cell phone records too would be critical. How interesting that will be. Certainly, barring the details—like motive, etc.—and excluding any unforeseen surprises, the bizarre matter should be resolved soon.

Speaking of bizarre, there was Milo Crane and the mysterious Fortunatas affair—that one was murky. Nothing straightforward about it, although he had his plan of approach. But there was something . . . something said tonight at Hank's that made him think of the Fortunatas matter. He closed his eyes and searched his mind, groping for a stillness to clear out the clutter of so many thoughts. He could feel Mist's heartbeat thumping ever so softly against the xiphoid process at the bottom of his sternum. Ah! There it was. He would have to remember to write it down first thing in the morning: "Call Melissa."

6

Sebastien zipped his coat up to his chin and repositioned the knit cap on his head, which had been knocked slightly askew when he emerged from the passenger seat of the coroner's van. Coroner's Investigator Gerry Good Crow exited the driver's seat and sidled up next to him.

"This is it?" asked Sebastien.

"According to the report," returned Gerry. "See where the train tracks cross the road, just there?" Gerry pointed about thirty feet down the road. "A surveyor slowed down as he approached the tracks in his truck. When he did, he spotted the bones in that shallow ditch running next to the railroad tracks."

"Did you work this case yourself? Back in 2012?"

"No, I had the pleasure of being on vacation. Alaska cruise. Ever done one?"

Sebastien considered the area in front of them. It was all fields, though his knowledge of plant science was insufficient to tell him what species of grass was being whipped furiously by the southerly wind. For some reason, he had expected the area to be a near-perfect representation of flatness. But the land undulated like a frozen wave, creating a series of small hillocks.

"No," Sebastien responded.

"You should. Maybe you and Tiffany—"

"You know about that?"

"Everybody does."

Gerry's reply was matter-of-fact, as flat as the terrain should have been. Sebastien turned toward him to see if it was accompanied by a smirk or wink, but the coroner's investigator kept his head straight, breathing a fog into the wind.

The sound of cars pulling in behind them and doors slamming broke the odd moment. The pair turned, and Gerry walked off, spotting someone.

"Hey, Trish. How do you want to do this?"

Gerry was approaching a woman wearing blue BDU pants and a thick blue jacket. She wore a gray trapper hat with a wool lining.

"Sebastien, have you met Trisha Curtis? She's with forensics."

Sebastien approached and looked in the direction of the woman's face, avoiding eye contact without trying. She seemed vaguely familiar; Sebastien had not met many African Americans in his new hometown yet.

"Dr. Grey, hello. We have met. Do you remember?"

He must have looked confused. The woman let out a half-chuckle.

"We met a few months ago at the house where that reporter got his brains blown out. You must remember. He was in his basement."

"Ah. Yes, I do remember that. Pretty bad scene."

"Anyway," began Gerry. "How do you want to work this, Trish?"

The woman pointed to where the train tracks ran across the road.

"Over here, right? This is where they found it?"

Gerry nodded. "Yes. And, back then, they did a line search out a hundred meters."

"Not a spiral search?" asked Trisha.

"Not a grid search?" asked Sebastien.

Gerry shrugged at them both.

"All right, then. How many people do we have?"

Trisha's question was evidently directed to herself, as she turned and poked a finger into the air, counting the men and women who had arrived and were waiting in a large group by the vehicles.

"We have thirty heads. Dr. Grey, any suggestions? Any idea where we might expect to find the rest of the body?"

Sebastien looked out through the density of his own breath and slowly turned in a full circle.

"What kind of animals do you have out here? Predators and scavengers, that is."

Trish and Gerry looked at each other for an answer. Neither had one. Gerry hailed one of the waiting searchers.

"Hal Greene, this is our anthropologist, Dr. Grey. You know Trish, of course."

The man nodded, then declared, "Hell of a day for a search. Freeze your plums off out here."

He was large and wore a red jacket that matched the color of his plump checks, one of which was distended by a wad of chewing tobacco.

"Hal here is a taxidermist. Hal, what kind of animals you think we got out here?"

Hal looked around, then thought for a moment. He spit a black glob onto the prairie grass and wiped his mouth with the back of his coat sleeve.

"I get quite a few deer in my shop. Mulies and some white-tail. Pronghorn, too. Seen some bighorn in my time. Those are higher up, of course."

"Meat eaters, Hal. We're talking meat eaters and scavengers. Ya know, 'cause of the body ..."

"Oh, yeah. Sure, Ger. Well, coyotes, for sure. I don't think mountain lions get down this far, but maybe. Lots of hawks too. Mice and prairie dogs are all over the place."

"What about snakes?" asked Trisha.

"I don't think a snake is going to carry off a corpse," replied Hal.

"No arms, you mean?" Trisha replied, swallowing a laugh.

Sebastien was feeling a bit dubious about Hal's wildlife expertise. He approached the spot pointed out by Gerry. Trisha followed.

"Here's what I suggest." Trisha stood like a scarecrow with her arms straight out to her sides, her dark fingers poking through fingerless wool gloves and terminating in light-blue nail polish. "Let's have half the team spread out in the direction of my right arm, facing east, and the other half to my left, facing west. How much rope do we have?"

"More than you'll ever need," called a voice from the group by the vehicles.

"Fine. We'll need a stake too."

"More than you'll ever—"

"Great. Drive it in right here between my feet. Tie two lengths of rope to it, both about a hundred and sixty meters long. Send one in the direction of my right hand and the other to my left. Spread each team out about ten meters apart, everyone holding the rope. Keep the rope tight as we move forward and search the ground. That will keep the radius at the max. If anyone spots anything, yell it out and we'll all stop."

The din of busyness replaced the low chatter of the searchers. Sounds of vehicle doors, trunks, and cargo gates opening punched through the air.

"We'll need to move the vehicles back too. They'll be in the way. Oh, and hold up a second while I call dispatch and have them contact the rail company. If a train comes through, it'll be our bodies they're looking for."

Sebastien, who had taken a few steps north along the train tracks, paused and turned.

"In which direction does the train go?" he asked.

Trisha lowered the radio mic from her lips and scanned the tracks. "Both, I assume."

"Can you ask?"

Sebastien didn't wait for an answer. He continued northward along the tracks. The sounds of the search party disappeared into the wind behind him, like the volume of a stereo being turned down. The ground crunched under his new Sorels. Isolated patches of shallow snow and frozen puddles made searching the ground for bones or other evidence wholly futile. This was a waste of effort, he figured. They were battling time, the elements, and a lack of information. Taphonomy—the study of how dead organisms were broken down and recycled into the biosphere—was difficult enough without nature getting a ten-year head start.

A squawking from up above and ahead split the sound of the wind in the grass. Something on the ground had caught the attention of a group of vultures, which were circling low in the sky. Sebastien got a momentary rush of excitement before reminding himself that if Amber Harrison's remains were out here somewhere, they would have lost the interest of scavengers a long time ago. Still, he traced an imaginary line from the birds to the ground and tried to force a view of their quarry through a squint. There was a patch of scrub about two hundred meters ahead and thirty meters west of the train tracks.

There was a slim chance that anything related to the Harrison case was in those bushes. But something was off. And why not check it out? Trisha and Gerry didn't need him. Sebastien was certain there was nothing to be found where they had set up the search. No, the answer was farther down—or up

—the train tracks. It wouldn't hurt to see what all of the avian fuss was about. It was a well-known and widely accepted aphorism among the forensics crowd that human remains were more likely to be found by accident, or coincidence, than by deliberate search. And wouldn't this just be one hell of a coincidence?

~

BARNADETTE JACOBS, DVM, tapped the woman's business card against the palm of her hand as she watched her walk out of the waiting area. Though about her own age, she seemed youngish for a detective, not to mention more attractive than she would have expected—*had* she been expecting her. Tiffany Reese reminded Barnadette of one of those pharmaceutical representatives who came into her practice a few times a month, recently out of grad school and dressed for persuasion. But there was an air of authenticity and confidence about the cop, and an absence of that small talk that normally preceded the sales pitch about the latest development in canine anti-virals or whatever. Detective Reese's directness unnerved her.

Yes, the visit was a surprise. But then again it wasn't really, was it? Barnadette had been expecting the police to come talk to her again, ever since she read the story in the papers about the sheriff's office taking another look at cold cases. She wondered at the time if that would include Amber's disappearance. It clearly did.

It was not like she had much more to say though. She told them everything she'd related back then. Amber Harrison had, for all practical purposes, ditched her roommates and her friends that fall semester. It was that boy, whoever he was, who took all of her attention. Barnadette reiterated that she and Amber had indeed been in contact only a few times during the course of that semester. *Was there any problem between you two?*

the detective had asked. No, Barnadette replied. There wasn't really much of a problem. Although, as she pointed out before, they were having some issues with the rent.

Again, she was pressed about the identity of Amber's new boyfriend. And again, Barnadette responded that she did not know who the boy was. She was certain he was no one who belonged within their circle of friends, no one she knew. Otherwise, she would have found out pretty quickly. There were few secrets in their tight group of college friends. At least, that was what she thought at the time. But what did she think now? Looking back, maybe there were nothing *but* secrets. Not that she would open that can of worms with the police.

"Amber's mother reported her daughter missing on January 10 of 2013. She said she had not heard from her daughter since Christmas Eve. Apparently, Amber told her mother about a party she was attending that night. Did you know anything about that party, Miss Jacobs?"

"That was a long time ago, Detective. I'm almost certain I was asked the question back then. Isn't that on your report?" Barnadette jabbed toward the detective's notepad for emphasis.

"I don't want to lead the witness, so to speak. Can you try to think back?"

Barnadette knew she was being disingenuous. Of course she recalled the Christmas Eve party. She was there, after all. She helped plan it too.

"So, this was a party you hosted? Was it at your house? The house you were renting?"

"No, Detective. I didn't host the party. I just helped plan it, like I said. It was at the home of one of our friends. A rich friend —his parents were rich, anyway. Still are, probably."

"And who was this friend?"

"Adam. Adam Ball. Or was it Bell?"

Detective Reese scribbled on her pad, then said, "Back to Christmas Eve. You didn't see Amber that evening?"

Barnadette once again recounted the events as faithfully as she did ten years ago, which was to say *somewhat* faithfully. No, Amber did not show up, despite promising to meet Barnadette and the rest of their friends there. Barnadette just figured that Amber had better things to do with her mysterious boyfriend. But she tried to think. Did she see Amber after that? No. She was very sure she had not. Like she said, she had not seen Amber very much since earlier that year.

"*Very much,*" the detective echoed inquiringly. "Can you tell me about the times you did see her? In your original statement, you said you saw her at school a few times. What does that mean, exactly? Do you mean to say you spoke with Amber? You met her at school? Or are you saying you just ran into her, or saw her in the crowd—something like that?"

"What difference does it make? I don't understand what your point is."

"Miss Jacobs, the difference is very important. I'm trying to figure out if you are simply mistaken or outright lying."

Barnadette's blood ran cold at this. A tingling sensation crawled upward from her shoulders through her neck. She hoped her discomfort wasn't in any way visible.

"Detective, I am certainly not lying. If you're asking whether I can remember a specific time I met Amber on campus . . . I suppose the answer is no. I'm sorry to be vague. And I do resent your accusation, by the way."

"I'm sorry to hear that. What about after Christmas Eve? Do you remember if you spoke with her after that? Did you ever ask her why she didn't show up for the party?"

"I honestly don't remember. Maybe? Probably? I mean, I was trying to get the rent out of her. And, in fact, now that I think about it, I was texting her around that time. Oh, yes, that's right. I was telling her I was going to move out. I let her know I gave my notice to the landlord. She would be the only one responsible for the rent. Shelly was out by then. But did I ask her about the party? No, I don't recall asking her about that. I really wasn't that worried. Amber is an adult."

The detective flipped her notepad to a fresh page and continued writing. Barnadette tried to get a look but could only make out a neat small cursive script with exaggerated loops.

"You're referring to Shelly Shields, correct?"

"That's right, Shelly Shields. Yes. But she moved out in October. Amber knew that. She knew the rent was on us. I recall being very frustrated."

"Miss Jacobs, do you think Amber ran off with her boyfriend? Or do you think something might've happened to her?"

"I have no clue. But she's an adult, right?"

"True," replied the detective.

"I mean, if she's still gone, still missing, then something must have happened. Do *you* have any idea what happened to her? Is that why you've come to talk to me again? Are there new developments? You seem to know something since you're so sure I'm a liar."

"No, ma'am. It's just about time that we took a fresh look at things. And I do apologize for implying that you aren't being honest."

Yes, it was about time, thought Barnadette. But she didn't believe for a minute that there wasn't something that prompted the reopening of the case. And it wasn't just a routine look through cold cases either. And no, apology not accepted.

"What about Shelly Shields? Are you still in touch with her? Any idea where I might find her?"

"Hill City Cemetery."

"I'm sorry, what do you mean?"

"Shelly is dead."

"Dead? What happened? When?"

"You didn't know? It was a hit and run. That's what we were

told. Shelly tried to run across the highway and got hit by a truck."

"Really? And what do you mean by, '*That's what we were told*'?"

Barnadette was enjoying the surprised look on the detective's face. Later on, she would almost feel bad about that. For Shelly's sake.

"Oh, I didn't mean it like that, like I don't believe it. I just mean that's what the state patrol said, that she was hit by a truck while crossing the highway."

"Where did this happen, Miss Jacobs? That wasn't here in Custer, was it?"

"No. Up by Spearfish, I think. I'm really surprised you didn't know. For some reason I thought that would have come up."

The look on the detective's face prompted Barnadette.

"I don't know what happened, exactly. I think she was hitchhiking. She used to do that a lot. That's pretty much how she got around if one of us couldn't give her a ride—and of course neither of us would have been able to give her a lift to Billings."

"She was trying to get to Billings when she was killed? Do you know why?"

"Her family is there. At least, I assumed that's where she was headed. Makes sense, right?"

"And when did you say this happened?"

"That's the bitch of it, isn't it? Shelly's accident happened a few weeks before the police came to see me about Amber, so . . . late December of 2012 or early January of 2013. I basically lost both of my friends at the same time."

"Lost? What do you mean by that, Miss Jacobs? You're talking about Amber Harrison, I assume. Are you saying you think Amber is dead? Like Shelly?"

Despite her earlier apology, the detective's tone continued to irritate Barnadette and made her feel like she was truly under some suspicion. For what, though?

"Well, she went missing, didn't she? And she hasn't turned up anywhere. So, yeah, I'd say I lost her. Wouldn't you?"

The detective paused to scribble some more before continuing.

"Of course. So that semester, you say Shelly was getting rides from Amber?"

"Yes. And her boyfriend too."

"You know this for a fact?"

"No, I know this because Shelly told me."

"In person? You spoke to Shelly about Amber in person?"

"Yes. Why is that so hard to believe? I lived with her most of the semester."

"Let me see if I have this right. You had heard from Amber that semester, and as far as you know, Shelly had also?"

"Yeah, that seems right."

"Was Shelly at school with you and Amber?"

"She was, but she dropped out in the middle of the semester. I think she just lost interest. She got involved in a rough crowd. They were more interested in partying than in school."

"I think that happens to a lot of people."

"Yes, I suppose it does, Detective Reese. But anyway, Shelly really did just kind of tune out. She changed that fall. It's really weird, you know? It seemed like both of my roommates, both of my friends just changed. I don't know what happened, but it was a very weird time."

"Was it drugs, do you think?"

"Shelly definitely partied hard. Not Amber though. A little drinking here and there on weekends was all."

"Miss Jacobs, let me try to get this right because, like I said, I just want to understand for myself—we're kind of starting from scratch here. You're saying that . . ."

"Go ahead, Detective."

"That fall semester, you, Amber, and Shelly Shields were in

school together. Did you have any classes together before Shelly dropped out?"

"No. No, we didn't. Amber and I were both biology majors, but I was a year ahead of her. Shelly was in marketing, I think—although . . . she really just partied and took easy classes, as I recall."

"Okay, so the three of you were in school but not together. You didn't see each other at school?"

Barnadette was trying not to get irritated at the repetitious nature of the detective's questions.

"No, that's not what I said. I *may* have seen Amber. And from what she told me, Shelly *did* see Amber."

Detective Reese did not seem surprised by Barnadette's clarification. It was obviously a trick question.

"This boy Amber met, how did she meet him?"

"At work, I think."

"The Black Hills Fitness and Climbing Club?"

"Something like that."

"Just a couple of final questions, if I may. Do you know anyone in either Tucson or Las Vegas? Any connections to those areas?"

"No, I do not."

"Do you know anyone who does? Or do you recall Amber talking about those places?"

"No, I'm sorry."

It was with relief that Barnadette watched Detective Reese stand.

"Thank you for your time, Miss Jacobs—oh, I'm sorry, it *is* miss, is it not? Or do you prefer to be called doctor?"

"I have a girlfriend. Are you going to write that down in your notebook too?"

"Oh, I don't think that's relevant. But . . . uh . . . what about back then? Were you attached then? What was your relationship like with Amber?"

Barnadette resented the probe into her private life, but she reflected that it was she, herself, who had created that opening.

"Like I told you—and told the police ten years ago—we were roommates. And Amber had a boyfriend."

"And your relationship with Shelly? What was that like?"

"Detective Reese, I don't appreciate being questioned like this. Everything I know is in your reports, or it should be. Now, if you'll excuse me, I have patients."

As Barnadette replayed this exchange in her mind, she considered that perhaps she had gotten a bit too touchy. After all, the police were only trying to help. And if Amber was still missing, if she was not found in LA doing whatever a person in LA does, well then she must have really gotten into trouble. Maybe she *was* dead? As dead as Shelly?

It occurred to Barnadette Jacobs later that afternoon, while cleaning out the ear canals of a Holland Lop named Chester, that perhaps she could have been a little more forthcoming with Detective Reese.

BY THE TIME her car left the parking lot, Tiffany had taken a mental inventory of the facts as she now knew them. Aside from the revelation about Shelly Shields's death, the interview with Jacobs revealed nothing new about Amber Harrison's murder. At least nothing in the way of direct information. But based on Jacobs's facial expressions and overall touchiness, Tiffany suspected she knew more than she was saying— although the statement she just gave aligned very well with her original one. This could be either suspicious or not, depending on how one looked at it. One thing was made very clear to Tiffany from the interview: Barnadette Jacobs did not know that Harrison was dead. At no point did Jacobs refer to Harrison in the past tense. "Amber *is* an adult." "I have no clue. But *she's* an adult, right?"

This business of Shelly Shields being killed in a hit-and-run accident at the very same time, or at least nearly the same time, as the disappearance of Amber Harrison, was almost too much to believe. And how did this elude the original investigators? Maybe the detectives back in 2013 never tried to make contact with Shields? Maybe they felt they had no reason to? Shelly had moved out of the house by the time Amber was reported missing. But why should that matter? Or maybe—and this was far more likely, Tiffany realized—maybe they tried to interview her but found out she was dead. Which made one think. Was Shelly's death a coincidence, or a convenience? *Jeez, Tiff. Now you're thinking like your boyfriend.* But it was true, wasn't it? With Shields dead, there would be no way to verify the claims that she had seen Amber several times during the period when it was now known that Harrison herself was dead. In other words, if that was Shields's claim, then she was lying. But there was no police report to document that. It was all based on hearsay from Barnadette Jacobs. Shelly would be providing no answers.

The more Tiffany thought about it, the less Shields's accident seemed like a coincidence. She was too integral to the disappearance—no, murder—of Amber Harrison. Tiffany was pretty sure her sergeant would be on the fence about that. But her boyfriend would not be. No way. Sebastien didn't believe in coincidences, but she knew he would need a little more information. She called in to dispatch and requested a phone call from Lawrence County. Within minutes she was on the phone with a woman someone in Lawrence County's Sheriff's Records Division. A very helpful woman.

It was in the dim light of dusk when a man, driving in the northbound lane of 14A near Lead, saw the semi-truck clip the young woman as she thumbed for a ride on the road's narrow shoulder. The impact sent the woman flying over the guardrail and down the steep ditch, her broken body landing on chunks of concrete.

The driver of the truck must have known he struck someone, the witness reasoned. He saw the truck's brake lights illuminate briefly before the driver of the massive double-trailer accelerated away. Though the witness pulled over at the scene, it was far too dark and treacherous for him to attempt a descent into the ditch and render first aid. But the man called 9-1-1 mere moments after the drama.

It was there on the side of the road (in the pulsating glow of the emergency lights and traffic being waved through a lane of flares, as Tiffany imagined it) that the driver of the witness vehicle expanded on his story. As it turned out, it was no surprise that such an accident occurred. The witness had been keeping a long distance between himself and the truck since making that left turn on 473 about four miles back. The driver appeared drunk or otherwise distracted, having crossed the middle line several times and even temporarily jumping the right-hand curb near the park in town.

No, he did not get a license plate or any description, other than that the truck was definitely pulling two belly dump trailers. Otherwise, there were no markings to indicate the truck's affiliation.

"And the witness was sure the victim was hitchhiking?" Tiffany had her phone on speaker as she drove back to HQ.

"That's what it says," replied the Lawrence County Sheriff's Office records clerk. "He seemed pretty sure."

"But you say this happened in the dark?"

"Dusk, it says. About four-twenty in the afternoon."

"And the truck was how far ahead of the witness vehicle?"

Tiffany heard the sound of pages flipping.

"Approximately two hundred yards. Would you like me to send you a copy of the accident report, Detective?"

. . .

JOHNATHAN SHIELDS, a lawyer and legislative aid in Helena, Montana, was happy to take Tiffany's phone call, although he offered his apologies. He would likely be of little help. Time had dulled his recollection, and the details of the accident were sketchy to begin with.

"What was Shelly like?" Tiffany inquired, after Johnathan more or less corroborated the official record of the accident.

Shelly had always been somewhat of a disappointment to the family. That notwithstanding, it did catch her parents off guard when she dropped out of school. Johnathan supposed it was the drugs, which had been an issue for Shelly in high school, but when Shelly eked her way into college, her parents felt sure the worst was over. It was all such a tragedy, to be sure. Just when she was starting to get on her feet in life, Shelly made the inexplicable decision to leave school. Before she could make that second great course correction, which her family had been zealously encouraging, she was tragically killed by a distracted motorist.

Tiffany hated to do it, but she really felt like she had no choice.

"Mr. Shields, you never had any suspicions about Shelly's accident, did you? Like something was not right?"

"Well . . ."

"Go on, Mr. Shields. Please."

"You know, I get the hitchhiking part of it. Shelly was known to hitchhike, and she was always a risk taker. I don't think anyone was surprised about the accident."

Tiffany pulled into the nearest parking lot and fished in her bag for her notebook and pen.

Johnathan continued, "But I never understood why Shelly was hitchhiking in that area. It wasn't exactly the quickest or most direct way to Billings from down there. You know what I mean?"

"You mean the interstate would have made more sense?"

"Sure. Wouldn't you think so? I mean, she would have been way more likely to find a ride at one of the truck stops off of I-90."

"So you can't think of a reason for her to be in Lead? No friends there? No business there?"

"No, not that she ever told me."

"And would she tell you, Mr. Shields? Were you two close?"

"I think she would have."

"What about her boyfriend?" Tiffany asked. "She had a boyfriend, correct?"

Johnathan confirmed there was a man in Shelly's life, a man who in all likelihood contributed to her dropping out of school.

"It was a Brian somebody. That's all she told me. I think that's all anyone knew."

7

There were only a handful of visitor parking lots on campus. Hank circumscribed the area looking for an open spot and found one, luckily, a few blocks away from the Natural and Biological Sciences Building on Prairie Street. The fall semester was in full swing at the University of Western South Dakota—the narrow streets were choked with cars parked along the curb, like arterial plaque, and the sidewalks were alive with students wrapped in heavy coats, carrying bags. Most cut through the dormant grass next to the dormant fountain to avoid patches of ice on the concrete. The tableau took Hank back to his own college days. All of the faces around him were young and determined, optimistic, naïve. A young woman passing by eyed him suspiciously as he emerged from the Tahoe and holstered his pistol beneath his heavy sheriff's jacket.

There were no chairs or benches in the hallway outside of the biology department office, so he stood there, as inconspicuous as an elephant, leaning against the wall. He was hoping to ambush Professor P. Belanger, who would not be expecting him, of course. He might not even be there, might be on sabbatical for all he knew. Maybe he should have called ahead. It's not like he was trying to get the jump on a suspect or anything. *Oh well,* he thought.

Hank noticed a plumpish woman approaching, her eyes fixed on him from behind oversized glasses. She looked to be in her mid-thirties. She wore jeans and a light-blue blazer over a white blouse, her ebony hair in a tight bob.

"Good afternoon," she said. "Are you waiting for someone in the biology department?"

Hank attempted a polite, disarming smile. "Yes, actually. I'm looking for Professor Belanger."

"Do you have an appointment?"

He knew she would ask this. "I, uh, no. I was just in the area. Is he here?"

The woman's eyes narrowed. "What is your name, please?"

"Sergeant Hank LeGris of the Custer County Sheriff's Office. I'd like to discuss an important matter with him."

The woman seemed to loosen a bit. Her lips curled into a slight smile. She eyed Hank vertically.

"Oh, well, let me check and see if she is here today. I'll be right back."

"Thank you."

She, eh? Well, that's good to know.

Hank turned to look out the window over the courtyard that circled the building while he waited. Two young men were sitting at a table with an umbrella, smoking and talking animatedly. They looked cold. A woman wearing a drab olive army jacket and brown crocheted cap walked by them through the cloud of cigarette smoke, using her left hand to hold a scarf against her mouth and nose. With her right hand, she pressed a phone against her ear. Hank reflexively checked his own phone for any texts or calls. There was just one text.

"Boss, I just left Barnadette Jacobs's clinic. She told me Shelly Shields is dead. She was in an accident about the same time

Harrison was reported missing. I got the report coming from Lawrence County, and I'm going to put in a call to Shields's brother. I'll have more details in a bit."

Hank reread the text to make sure he had it right. There was nothing in the case file that mentioned Shields's death—not that it necessarily *should* be mentioned in relation to Harrison's disappearance. Interesting? Maybe. Accidents happen all the time. But there must be more to it if Tiffany texted him specifically to let him know. Otherwise it would come up later in their debrief. Lawrence County though?

Hank began to punch in a reply when he felt a palm on his shoulder.

"Sorry, I hope I didn't startle you. Professor Belanger is finishing up with a student. If you could wait five minutes or so, she will be happy to meet with you."

"Oh, sure. That would be great. Thanks."

"But, please . . . we have chairs in the office area. Why don't you come sit and wait?"

The woman led Hank to a chair outside the professor's office, taking her own seat at the desk facing him. She smiled sweetly and ran her red fingernails through the thick hair at her temple.

"We don't get the police around here much," she offered.

"You don't? I'm surprised. You look like trouble."

The woman giggled, covering her mouth.

"I'm Heather Jensen, the departmental secretary."

"Good to meet ya, Heather. Sounds like you're in charge around here."

"You know I am, Sergeant Degrees. Are you going to want to interview me too?"

Heather leaned forward with an elbow on the desk and her chin in her palm. Her fingers tapped her face just under her nose.

Uh oh, Hank. You better turn it down a bit, you charmer.

"It's, uh, Sergeant LeGris. It means the *The Grey* in French."

"And is 'Hank' French too?"

"I'm sorry?"

"Your name. 'Hank.' What does it mean in French?"

Hank stifled the handful of smart-ass retorts that danced on the surface of his tongue.

"Actually, Heather, you might be able to help me with a few things."

"It would be my pleasure."

Her coy expression indicated she was clearly enjoying this byplay, and maybe a tad too much. In situations such as this, Hank would be inclined to drop a line about his wife. But he had some leverage and didn't want to spoil it just yet.

"Yeah, maybe. Hey, while I'm waiting, I don't suppose you keep records from previous years, do you? I'm talking about enrollment, attendance, grades. That kind of thing?"

"We keep grades and enrollment forever, of course. But attendance, it depends on the professor and how far back we're talking."

"The professor?"

"Some don't take roll. Or, if they do, they may not keep it for too long. It's up to them. I'm not sure about Phyllis, if that's why you're here."

Hank must have looked confused. Heather smiled and said, "Professor Belanger, I mean. So, I take it you're not a personal friend of hers?"

"No. Like I said, I'm just here on official business. Any chance I could get a particular student's enrollment information for 2012?" Hank asked hopefully.

"From me, you mean? Or just in general?"

"I guess I can go pay a visit to the registrar—if that's the right name for it. It's been a while since I've been in college. But I assume that would require me filling out a bunch of forms. It would probably take a while to get the information back, wouldn't it? Maybe you have the information I'm looking for on your computer." Hank winked as he gestured to the monitor on Heather's neat desk.

"Hmm . . . I don't know. I think you would need one of those subpoenas."

"You mean like the court issues? Oh, no, Heather, I'm not the court. Just a cop. I think you're thinking of something else."

Heather looked unsure, so Hank tossed in another wink for good measure.

Hank knew he was playing awfully fast and loose with the truth. Heather wasn't that far off, after all. *Search warrant* was the technical term for what she had referenced; she just didn't know it. And why would she? He was taking advantage of the woman's naïveté—and maybe a few other frailties. But, hey, Amber Harrison was dead—murdered, in fact. There was no harm in helping the department secretary make her own decision, if that's what it would take.

Heather's heavily mascaraed eyes searched the room, and she bit her bottom lip, both gestures signaling indecision to Hank's trained eye. As was his wont, he pondered the next step, realizing to his own agitation that if Heather agreed to help him, he would have to give her a name. He couldn't go through dozens of class lists looking for the name Amber Harrison. For one thing, it would take too long. And for another, if he didn't find her name anywhere, he would have no way of knowing if he had just had the secretary pull the wrong classes. If Heather Jensen knew of the mystery surrounding Harrison's disappearance, she would certainly be tipped off to the investigation. But was that a bad thing?

"Tell me, Heather—can I call you Heather? Or is it Mrs. Jensen?"

"It's Heather. I'm not married."

"Re-ally?" Hank knew he was being cruel, but he resolved to keep the manipulation brief and hopefully harmless. "I would not have guessed that. So tell me, how long have you worked at the university?"

Heather was blushing. She no longer had that unresolved look. Her mind had been flipped, he could tell.

"Three years, Hank. If I can call you Hank?"

"Of course you can! All my friends do. So, I tell ya what, Heather. I'm just going to jot down a name, and if you could take a look-see in that computer and tell me if this person was enrolled in classes in . . . let me think . . . let's say, spring of 2012 to spring of 2013 . . . I would really appreciate that."

Hank pulled a sticky note from the pad on the corner of Heather's desk and retrieved a pen from his breast pocket. As he was scribbling, he heard a door open and felt something collide with the outside of his right thigh, nearly knocking him out of his chair. A young man paused, gave a polite "sorry," and disappeared into the hallway.

"Officer, this is a surprise."

Hank looked up to his right and saw a woman standing over him, extending her hand. He stood up and took it.

"Professor Belanger, sorry to barge in like this. I'm Sergeant Hank LeGris from the sheriff's office. I just had a few quick questions if you have a minute."

"No problem at all. It's just the usual midterm circus. Come on in and have a seat. Tell me how I can help."

The biology professor, as it turned out, was not much help at all. Like most of her colleagues, her introductory and general requirement biology classes were huge, sometimes up to a hundred and twenty students. It was all but impossible to know each student by name, or by face for that matter. What was more, she rarely gave any lectures herself, instead relying on teaching assistants. As for keeping attendance, that was up to the TA.

"And I don't suppose . . ."

"I'd have to check my records. I usually have two or three

assistants each semester and, though I don't specifically remember their names from back in 2012, I can tell you they've all moved on to other things. That was a long time ago, you understand."

"So, you do have records, then?" Hank tried.

"I'm sorry, Sergeant. That was a figure of speech."

"But no trouble with any of your students, or TAs, back then? That you can recall, I mean."

"Sergeant, I'm afraid I don't know anything about Amber Harrison."

The declaration startled Hank. He hadn't mentioned any names yet.

"You were aware of her disappearance, then?"

"Everybody was. It was all over the news. And yes, I did speak with the police back then. I'm afraid I couldn't be of much assistance."

How sad, thought Hank. Belanger was so distanced from her students that she had to find out from the media that one of them was missing.

The small printer behind Heather's desk was noisily coughing out sheets of paper when Hank emerged from the office. This was a good sign.

Erin Morgan, senior crime analyst for the sheriff's office, preferred to stay close to her data. There were some among her colleagues, in her own agency and at other agencies, who were quite happy to employ whatever fancy computer program that was available when analyzing information. This was especially true of cell phone data, which could be difficult to decipher and varied depending on the phone carrier. Admittedly, it was much easier to load the records and let the computer do the work than to go line by line with a ruler and highlighter, identifying who called whom, when, and from where. But Erin had been burned by the easy method too many times, each more embarrassing and mortifying than the first.

It was early in 2007 when Erin—a somewhat new analyst at the Denver Police Department—was visited by a rookie homicide detective. The man entered her office looking dejected, even hopeless. He was carrying two large blue binders.

"What can I do for you, Jay?" Erin had asked. "Need me to run someone out?"

"I don't know what to do." The detective handed the binders to Erin, practically putting them in her lap. "I just got this case from Dennis. He promoted out to patrol. It's a double homicide, a drive-by. This thing is a mess. Do you suppose you could . . . I mean, if you don't mind, I could use your opinion."

The scenario had been played out many times before, but never from a homicide detective. That group was hard-core and loathe to admit to any weakness or lack of total omniscience. But Jay was a property crimes investigator before moving in to homicide. And he had leveraged Erin's talents many times for things like predicting the time and location of the next hit in a series, recognizing a particular MO as belonging to one villain versus another, and knowing which pawn shops took bent gold and which only bought the immediately resellable loot. Basically, Erin excelled at the nerd end of the investigative process, which was just fine with her and the burglary detail. But the homicide team, back then, was hermetically sealed against all outside "non-sworn" help.

Erin sent Jay away, promising to take a look at the contents of the binders and see if there was anything she might do to help—and she was happy to do it. This was her opportunity to convince Jay's counterparts what she could do.

Going through the binders, a couple of things stood out to

her. This Dennis, who had the case before Jay and with whom Erin had never worked or even met, must have possessed the organizational skills of a kindergartener. There was no order to the material. Crime scene photos, lab reports, and supplemental reports were scattered between both binders without rhyme or reason. Erin knew that in order to make sense of information, it must first be organized in a meaningful way. Otherwise things got lost, overlooked, or taken out of context or order. She removed all of the contents of both binders and separated it all into categories.

Next, she took the time to read through absolutely everything. There would be no way of knowing what was missing until she knew what they had. Unbeknownst to most laypeople, and unrecognized by many a detective, was the fact that a good crime analyst was trained to think like an investigator. This, coupled with their quantitative reasoning and critical thinking, made them highly valuable members of the investigative team and process.

It was no wonder that Jay felt lost on what to do next. All of the avenues of investigation had been taken, or so it seemed. The neighborhood was canvassed immediately after the scene was secured, but no one would talk. Nor did anyone have cameras on their houses. Moreover, doorbell cameras were not a thing back then. The slugs that were taken from the victim's bodies and from various places in the house indicated that the weapon was an AK-47. This firearm was not that common in street-level violence, so there was some optimism that informants could point investigators in the direction of who might be running around with a Russian-made assault rifle. But no luck there.

The next logical step, when gang shootings occur, was to find out who the rival gang members were, who had been "funking" with whom, and what incidents may have occurred that sparked the attack. The gang unit was consulted and, after they "shook the trees," they learned that one of the victims had gotten into an argument with a group of rivals at an all-you-can-eat buffet downtown. Whether it was over a girl, drugs, or just a general testosterone-slinging contest, no one knew. Regardless, two very strong suspects were identified. The only problem was a lack of evidence. One of the suspects had a strong alibi—his girlfriend said they were together down in Fort Collins when the house had been shot up. Neither Jay, nor the previous detective, were sure what to believe; both sides of the equation—alibi and implication—were strong. But which was the truth?

Erin noticed a thick stack of printouts stuck into the back pocket of the second binder. Each sheet had fifty or so lines of text, the headings of which included things like date, time, duration, number, direction, switch, tower, and sector. At the top of each sheet was a header that read, "Call Detail Record." This was Erin's first exposure to cell phone records.

She didn't recall seeing any analysis or interpretation of these cell phone records when she read through the documents, but she searched again through her categorical stacks just to be sure. There was nothing. If Jay was missing a piece to his double-homicide puzzle, this could very well be it. That she didn't know anything about analyzing the records did not stop her from figuring it out. In retrospect, learning how to interpret the information was something like an algebra problem: She used what she knew in order to calculate what she didn't know.

Looking back, that was something of a watershed moment for Erin. That case was her first foray into not only telephone toll analysis—the analyzing of cell phone records in criminal cases—but also major crimes. It turned out to be just the icebreaker she needed with the homicide squad. That's because the investigation turned out to be what's called a "cell phone case." The phone records showed that the subject's phones were not where they said they were. They were hitting off a tower about three-quarters of a mile from the homicide scene directly before and after dispatch received a report of multiple shots fired. Did that mean that someone else had their phones at the time? Sure, it could be argued that that was the case. But in reality, how often do people part with their phones? Certainly no one on the jury could relate.

The alibi witness—the girlfriend in this case—was lying. Not only that, the cell tower hits on one of the suspect's phones showed it to be in a remote and wooded area at two in the morning following the homicide. As part of a plea agreement, in which Suspect Two threw Suspect One under the bus, the investigators were taken to where the AK-47 was recovered, not far from that remote tower. Since that first case, Erin had worked dozens more homicides and testified in probably half of them.

Not so much at Custer County though. Ever since she moved north with her husband, the cell phone work had slowed quite a bit. But the principles of telephone toll analysis stuck, as did her insistence on doing things the same way she had done them when she started. That was with pen, paper, spreadsheets, and Google Earth. There was no budget for expensive software packages back then, nor did she even know those things existed. She had to learn the hard way: trial, error, and experimentation. The method served her well and held up in probably a dozen trials.

Fifteen years later and a few hundred miles farther north, Erin found herself running through her now familiar order of operations. Amber Harrison's printed cell phone records were not in electronic form, so they could not be opened as a spreadsheet. She could always transcribe the records onto an Excel sheet, but that would introduce the distinct possibility of data corruption via human error. Transposing just a few numbers in all that data could change the entire picture and create reasonable doubt at trial if it came to that.

The other thing lacking in the Harrison file was the complementary cell tower listing that is necessary to determine the location of the cell towers referenced in the call record detail. As a rule, these are included in the search warrant. But that had been overlooked apparently. Erin would have to let Tiffany know. Unless they wrote a search warrant for the 2012 version of the tower listing—if it still existed—there would be no way to map the location of Amber Harrison's phone in the weeks before she went missing. They could find out what numbers the phone had been calling and receiving calls from, but, to add a level of difficulty, those numbers may no longer belong to the same people they did so long ago. *This one is going to be fun*, she thought sarcastically.

8

The vultures began to squawk and dive as Sebastien closed the distance toward the brush. He wondered to himself about the term for a group of vultures before stopping to look up. This arcane bit of trivia had once come up in a search for remains when he was in grad school. Was it a kettle? A committee? A wake? Perhaps it was all three, as he couldn't really remember. Maybe it depended on whether the birds were flying or on the ground. With his nose in the air, Sebastien caught the familiar scent of putrescine coming from just ahead. The vultures were on to something.

The birds dispersed, landing on the ground about forty meters north to watch the interloper. Sebastien stood at the edge of the brush and took a quick look southward, toward the search area. He was alone, several hundred meters down the tracks from the rest of the group. If there was anything dangerous, poised to attack him from behind the woody blind, his calls might not be heard. He took a deep breath and steeled himself before parting the branches just enough to get a look. He saw it immediately. The carcass of what looked to be a deer, or maybe a pronghorn, lay there, the spine exposed at intervals, the head reduced to a greasy pink skull, and the limbs missing.

Based on the state of decomposition and the current temperature, it was clear the animal had died when the weather was a bit warmer—maybe a few months ago. There was some evidence of insect activity on the exposed viscera, mainly in the form of pupae cases. But the temperature was far too low for maggots now, unless they were under the remaining patches of hide—where it might be a bit warmer. Using a stick, he pushed to reposition the carcass and poked a few holes in it to get a better look. He saw no maggots squirming about, a fact that made him wish he had a probe thermometer so he could measure the core temperature of the dead animal – more out of professional curiosity than morbid fascination.

Feeling reasonably assured it was safe, he stepped into the copse and probed the vegetation for a right shoulder girdle, or skull, or anything else attributable to Amber Harrison. He wasn't expecting to find anything, to be sure. But the vultures and the rotting ungulate had him overthinking things. This was a good place to hide a body—but no, it was just a dead animal. A mid-morning meal for the kettle, committee, or wake.

After several minutes, he picked his way through the brush back onto prairie grass. The vultures had moved in a little closer, staring at him through darting eyes, hopping and calling. *It's all yours*, he thought, before heading eastward back toward the tracks. This side trip into the brush took him farther westward, by twenty meters or so. He reproved himself for being distracted. He should have kept walking along the tracks. They were the key, after all. He knew it. Yes, Amber Harrison was shot, but there was a theory incubating in his mind. If he was correct, she survived that injury for a period of time. Regardless, he was sure it was the train that tore through Amber Harrison, ripping off her left arm. The rest of her must be out here. Just follow the tracks. But which direction?

Sebastien crossed over the tracks to the other side and began to make his way back in the direction of the searchers, paying special attention to the ground in front of him. Once again he encountered only shallow snow and frozen puddles. This was the wrong time of year to do this.

The faint sound of yelling prompted him to look up. A figure was hurriedly coming toward him, arms waving. He waved back.

"What are you doing all the way up here?" Gerry panted.

"I don't know. I was just walking the tracks. I don't think you'll find the rest of her back there."

Gerry pulled Sebastien by the elbow gently and said, "You're right. She wasn't there."

"What do you mean? Did you find her?"

"I'm not sure it's *her*, but I think so. One of the volunteers found a sock south of the search zone."

Sebastien's eyes widened. "A sock?"

"Yep. A sock. And there's something in it."

"What kind of sock is it? Like, a lady's sock?"

"It's hard to say. It's pretty degraded. Very dirty too, and looks like it could have been chewed up by an animal. Come on, let's go have a look. The team is waiting for you before they open it up."

Sebastien broke his way through the party of searchers, who were standing in a half-circle behind one of the pick-up trucks. Laying on the open tailgate was a patch of fabric, brown from the dirt and stiff from the cold.

"What do you think it is? Could it be hers?"

"Can somebody bring me gloves?"

Sebastien took a pen out of his jacket pocket and used it to poke around at the sock, turning it over and scrutinizing it from the outside.

"Here, here, give these to the doc."

Sebastien put the nitrile gloves on and opened the sock carefully, reaching in with one hand.

"Ah," he muttered.

"What is it, Doc?"

The contents of the sock were tactilely unmistakable. The bones of the foot and ankle were irregular and each distinct from their neighbor—at least, they were to their trained observer. Sebastien rolled the various elements between his fingers, taking mental inventory: several phalanges, three metatarsals, two of the cuneiform bones, the navicular, the calcaneus, and the talus—maybe half of the foot bones altogether. Sebastien pulled his hand out of the sock and turned to face the others, presenting his find.

"Foot bones." Sebastien pointed with his left index finger as he spoke. "These long ones are metatarsals, the bones in the middle of the foot. These shorter ones are from the toes. And these here are from the ankle. This big one is the heel." Sebastien picked up the calcaneus and handed it to a woman in the front of the crowd, who received it with a horrified expression. "Pass that one around, in case anyone wants a better look."

"Is it human?" someone asked.

"No, a bobcat was wearing that sock," replied someone else.

Gerry Good Crow made his way to the front of the group and held out his hand for a turn.

"So this could be her?" Gerry asked.

"Sure, I don't see why not. There's no way to tell sex or age from just looking at these bones, but it seems rather probable. Even if it isn't Amber Harrison, the fact is that a human foot still wearing a sock was left out here to decompose—whether that foot was connected to anything, I mean *anyone*, is academic. This is a death scene. Where exactly was this found?"

The woman at the front stood a little more erect.

"I found it. I was at the end of the search line on the south radius when I saw it. It was twenty feet or so away."

"You have great eyesight," offered Sebastien. "Near the tracks?"

"Yes," the woman said. "About fifteen feet from the tracks on the east side."

"And there was nothing else there?"

"I didn't see anything," she replied.

"Show me."

The woman led Sebastien and the rest of the group southward.

"There. Just under that little bush. It was caught in there."

"How the hell did you see it?" asked Trisha, shaking her head.

"It just sort of stuck out. I don't know. Maybe it was luck."

Sebastien pointed to the ground and ordered, "Somebody put a stake right there. Do the spiral search again but from right here."

Gerry looked over to Trisha with a grin. She shrugged in return. This was no longer her crime scene.

As the rest of the party set up the spiral search, Sebastien approached the tracks and got down on all fours. He was too busy examining the rails and the ties to feel the cold dampness penetrate his knees.

"I take it you think she was hit by a train," Gerry said from above.

"We don't know that the sock belonged to her, but it belongs to someone." Sebastien looked up momentarily. "What do you think, Gerry? I admit, I've never done a train fatality before, so I'm not sure what the trauma pattern would entail. I assume it would be massive disarticulation and blunt force though."

Gerry nodded. "We get our fair share around here. Most of the cases involve vehicles, so obviously that would be different, but the pedestrian cases vary."

"Based on what?"

"Let me think . . . okay, like for example, was it an accident or a suicide? What position was the victim in when the train hit? Were they standing there waiting for it? Did they throw themselves under the train as it went by? Did they get caught by surprise? Were they looking in a different direction, bending over or whatever? Those are just some factors that will determine if the body will be thrown down the tracks, or away from the tracks, or get caught under the train, etc. But yes, in all cases it is major trauma—including dismemberment."

"Disarticulation, you mean."

"Sure. Disarticulation."

"It's important though, isn't it?" Sebastien paused once again and looked up at Gerry. "Dismemberment involves removing the limbs or head with a sharp instrument. It's intentional. However, in the process of decomposition, soft tissue will disappear, allowing the joints to separate. Animals will help that process too. Larger scavengers tend to grab on to whatever they can and take it back to their den to be consumed. That's why legs and arms are seldom recovered in exactly the same spot as the trunk—and then rodents and smaller animals carry off things like hand and foot bones. A train hitting someone would also be an environmental process, rather than intentional. That's disarticulation."

"Dr. Grey, it's cold as hell out here. With all respect, can we skip the semantics and get to your point?"

"I do think Amber Harrison got hit by a train. I believe her body got dragged down the tracks and disarticulated that way."

"But you said she was shot. The autopsy said so too."

"Yes. She was shot."

"We can't have both, Doctor."

"Really? Why not? And why does everyone say that?"

As if on cue, Hal the taxidermist, who had taken his place on the rope, called over to them.

"What do you think happened to her, Doc? I heard she was

shot, but now it looks like she was hit by the train. I mean, if the toe bones next to the track are hers."

Sebastien turned as if to answer the man and noticed that most of the searchers stood at their respective spots on the rope, also eagerly awaiting a reply. But all Sebastien offered was a dry, "Yes," before turning to Trisha. "You think it's possible to find blood or tissue on the tracks?"

"From 2012? I highly doubt it. And even if we did, the DNA would be degraded. We wouldn't know who the blood belonged to."

"Any other fatal train accidents in this area, Gerry?"

"No, Doc, I can't think of any."

Sebastien shifted his focus from Gerry back to Trisha, who looked at him resignedly.

"I'll get a couple more techs out here to walk the tracks. We need to get some portable toilets out here too. You're killing me though, Doc. You know that?"

BERT MABRY BROUGHT the driver's window down, then cut the truck's ignition, causing the diesel engine to sputter and choke its way into silence.

"What's that?"

"I said, did you check the south side?"

"South side?"

"Yes, Bert. The south side of the property by the highway. When I pulled off I could see beer cans by the 'no trespassing' sign. I think we got homeless down there."

Bert tried to reconcile the notion of a homeless encampment on an open and empty construction site in light of the twenty-degree weather. But he was in no position to argue with the construction supervisor.

"Oh, right. Homeless. I'll check it on my way out."

"Good. And I got a crew coming to pull that trencher out of here. I'll need you to open the gate."

Bert glanced at the large piece of machinery along the north edge by the vacant field.

"Sure thing. And when is that?"

The supervisor took his phone from his back pocket and fumbled through the screen.

"Five-thirty-ish."

Bert checked his watch: one-forty-eight. *Damn.* He was hoping to get off early. He still had the other two properties to patrol, after which he was going to rush home, change, and meet the fellas for a beer and the game.

"Ah, heck, Chuck, are you sure you need me for that? I, uh, have an appointment."

"Yes, I do. I would do it myself, but I don't wanna miss the start of the game. There's playoff implications, and Denver's on the bubble. Again."

Bert searched his mind for a way out, for an excuse to avoid missing the game. The answer he came up with was much simpler than he thought.

"How about this, boss. How about we leave the gate unlocked, then I'll come back after the ga . . . after my appointment and lock her up? It's not like there's anything to steal, especially once the trencher is gone. You know?"

His supervisor's face looked thoughtful. Bert was growing more optimistic by the second.

"I suppose that's okay. Just make sure you clear out those beer cans on your way out."

You mean the ones that got blown there by the wind, you dumbass? Homeless! What an idiot.

"Thanks, Chuck! I'll do that. Oh, by the way, some fella came by the other day asking about dirt."

"What do you mean, dirt? This guy wasn't from the county, was he?"

"No. Just some younger guy walking his dog. He asked if you needed more dirt on the site. He said he's got dirt left over from digging a pool. He's trying to get rid of it, I guess."

"Do I look like I need dirt?" The supervisor pivoted and pointed to his left and right to accentuate his sarcasm.

"No. And that's what I told him. I just thought I'd mention it."

"What was the guy's name?"

"It was Sebastien something. I didn't get his last name."

"So what if I told you I did need dirt, Bert? How would I get ahold of this guy?"

Bert took a deep breath, trying to resist the temptation to descend from the cab and pound Chuck into the ground. He needed this job.

"I knew you didn't need any dirt. That's why I didn't ask for his last name."

"You're a helluva security guard, Bert. Tell me, what exactly did this guy look like?"

9

The young man at the front desk of the Black Hills Athletic and Climbing Club greeted Tiffany with a beaming smile. His arms were massive, as were his shoulders, pecs, and neck muscles. His nipples poked out from behind a tight black nylon golf shirt as he not-so-subtly pulled his shoulders back, like a horny ape showing his size to the competition. Tiffany knew she was going to break his heart when he found out she was not a potential new client and source of commission.

The man himself being far too young to have any memory of what was going on at the gym nearly ten years ago, Tiffany asked to see the manager or someone who might have been around at that time. She was led into a small office where another man, in his early forties, sat on an exercise ball at a desk.

"Hey, Lance, this lady wants to talk to you."

Lance turned on the ball and looked at Tiffany, instantly forming his mouth into a fake smile. *It must be part of the job*, she considered.

"Hey there, what can I do for you? Are you interested in the

122

yearly program? What are you looking to do? Weight loss? Strength training?"

Weight loss? What the hell?

Tiffany pulled back her wool coat, revealing the gold-colored badge fixed to her waist, which also, conveniently, showed her flat abdomen against her tight black sheriff's polo.

"I'm not here to sign up, Mister . . ."

"Oh, damn. Sorry. It's Madison. Lance Madison."

"Mr. Madison, I'm Detective Reese with the sheriff's office. I was wondering if I could ask you a few questions."

"Oh, sure. Am I in trouble?"

"Did you kill someone?" Tiffany was still not over the weight loss remark.

"No. No, I swear!"

"I'm just playing with you, Mr. Madison. No, I'm only looking for information about anyone who might have worked here back in 2012 to 2013, that time frame. Specifically, I'd like to see time sheets or shift schedules, if you have them."

"I wasn't here then, but there might be records somewhere."

"Wonderful. Is there somewhere I can sit while you go look?"

Lance stared at her for a moment, frozen, as if not sure what to do next.

"Mr. Madison?"

"Oh, sure, sure. Let me, um . . . let me check for you. I'm afraid there's no other chair in here though."

"The ball will be fine."

Ten minutes later, Lance returned, cradling a load of rubber-banded cards in both hands.

"I was able to find these," he declared with a tone of pride as he dropped the load onto his desk. "Nowadays everyone clocks in on the computer. But back in the day you had to fill in a time card by hand."

Tiffany picked up one of the bound stacks and examined the topmost card.

"Well, that's very helpful. Did all the employees have to fill out a card?"

"Oh, sure. Except the GM. That's the only salaried position at the club."

Tiffany put down the single stack and gestured to the pile on the desk.

"What am I looking at here, Lance?"

"Each stack is a month's worth of cards. I have 2012 and '13. Is there something specific you're looking for?"

"I would love to see the time cards for the climbing leaders, if that's what the position was called."

"We call those people *group facilitators*."

Lance took a stack and fanned through the top edge, like it was a pack of playing cards.

"Here's one. See this? Next to *Position*, this employee wrote *GF*. That's what you're looking for."

"And what's the name on that one?"

"A. Harrison. Oh . . ." Lance's face suddenly lost color. "Is that why you're here? Do you want me to help? I can look through them with you."

Tiffany thought it best not to confirm or deny Lance's insinuation.

"No, that's okay. You can get back to whatever you were doing. I'll take a look at these. I appreciate the offer though."

Lance lingered in the door, looking lost.

"Oh. So you're just going to . . . you're gonna look through those now? Here?"

"Thanks, Lance. That would be great." Tiffany winked.

It didn't take too long to get through the stacks, although she didn't trust the job codes entirely. Eventually, Tiffany ended up with about thirty smaller piles, separated by the employee's name. Sure enough, Tiffany was able to find more time cards for Amber Harrison, the last being from the end of October 2012. S. Shields was written on several cards as well, the most recent from December 5, 2012. Tiffany put the Shields and Harrison stacks in her bag and left, leaving the rest on the desk.

"Thanks so much for your help, Mr. Madison," said Tiffany as she passed the front desk on the way out.

"Oh, sure, sure. Did you find what you were looking for?"

"Yes, in fact I did. Just a few cards. I'm going to take them back to my office and make copies. You don't mind, do you . . . Lance?"

"Well . . . I'm not sure. I guess it . . ."

"Thanks, Lance. I appreciate it. Oh, by the way, I do have one question."

Lance, still undecided, replied, "Sure, um, what is it?"

"If the job title on a time card says *SMD*, what does that mean?"

Lance thought a minute, trying to come up with an answer. A young woman wearing yoga pants and a half shirt, standing next to him behind the reception desk, offered what sounded like a reasonable assumption.

"*Shift Manager Day*. I think that's what it means. Probably, anyway."

Lance glanced at the woman with a hint of contempt, then turned back toward Tiffany.

"Oh, yeah. That's what that means. We don't use those titles anymore, but yeah, that makes sense.

"So," Tiffany began, "you're saying that the shift manager would be someone in charge? Someone who takes care of the place? Makes schedules and keeps track of things?"

"For sure. In fact, that's what I am. Like Lindsey here said, they don't call them that anymore. It's assistant manager now."

Tiffany nodded a thank you and exited into the parking lot, feeling like that had perhaps been the most fruitful part of an exhausting day.

~

SEBASTIEN REMOVED his clothes and deposited them in the laundry hamper before turning toward the bathroom mirror. The jury was still out on the beard. Tiffany said she liked it; she liked scratching, pulling, and kissing at the hairs protruding from the dimple in his chin –

that genetically determined separation in the mentalis muscle. Hank had that dimple too, and he looked good with a beard. Was that the look he was going for? Was he trying to be more masculine and roguish? To be more like his brother? If so, he would need to hold out a few more weeks for the length to be just right.

Running his hands down his chest, Sebastien felt for any incipient softening of his mid-section. This too was a trait noticeable in his brother. But he had been fortunate, thus far. Never one for exercise, save the short but frequent walks with Parsifal, Sebastien's metabolism had been his friend, but surely that could not last forever. And what of the soreness in his hip flexors, thighs, and calves he was now feeling as a result of tramping through the soggy soil of East County? Was it time for a gym membership? If so, should it be weight training, cardio, or both? Tiffany would certainly have opinions on that, being a devotee of most fitness regimens.

By the time Sebastien emerged from the shower, he reconsidered the shift to a more active lifestyle. The warm water running down his body, the release of tension, made him think, as it often did, of Tiffany—which in turn led him to realize that in all likelihood, he could not keep up with whatever fitness challenges she would inevitably arrange for him. It was dangerous ground, a sure path to embarrassment. One more thing to avoid.

Sebastien slipped under the sheets and pulled the thick duvet up to his chest. He retrieved a leather journal from the nightstand, its lined pages empty save for the first two, a testament to numerous thwarted attempts to follow his therapist's advice and journal the positive experiences in his life. This, she said, would help him refocus his attention on all of the good that surrounded him and help him uncover his own role in that goodness, thus reinforcing his self-worth. "Positivity journaling is most effective when it's done consistently," she reminded him during their last virtual session. Had he been consistent? No. He had failed. But every day was a clean slate, she assured him. The important thing was to try. Write just a little bit every day. That was all it would take.

Partly out of hope in the cure, but mostly to stave off the inevitable guilt he would feel during his next session, Sebastien put pen to paper for the first time in months.

The other day, I was reading about the role that neurochemicals play in regulating our emotions—I know, it's not what most people would do in their free time. But I'm not most people, hence the problem (speaking of dopamine, I suppose I could develop a taste for video games. Would that be more acceptable or less?). It seems to me that a more rational understanding of the biological processes underlying my anxiety could just about get me to normal. Or maybe not. But as an exercise in positivity, I am grateful for the ability to think rationally and understand what's happening inside my brain on an intellectual level. Does that make me sound arrogant? I don't think so. In fact, I will choose to discredit that explanation. Let us just say I am an over-analyzer. I think everyone who knows me knows this. And why not flip that weakness on its head, turn it into a strength? If I can think of my moods in terms of neurological chain reactions, thereby depersonalizing things and removing self-blame, I may be able to block that inevitable spiral into a familiar catatonic melancholy. I am resolved to try this.

Tiffany is wonderful, beautiful, and terrifying (forgive me, Dr. Lucas. It can't all be positive). Each day I am with her, I can't help but wait for the other shoe to drop, like Hoffmann discovering that the beautiful Olympia is nothing but an automaton—although, in my version, I play the role of Olympia. When will Tiffany-Hoffmann see me fall to pieces and realize that, all along, I was nothing but a robot?

Okay, that probably wasn't helpful or in the spirit of the exercise. I need to work on that. I know Tiffany loves me. Yes! I know it! How do I know? She's told me. But why should I believe it? Well, why shouldn't I? How's that for a serotonin-inducing positive?

These cases, the two I'm working now—there's no point in rehashing the details here—are contradictions of one another. The Amber Harrison murder is as straightforward as can be, except perhaps for motive. But motive is far less important than most people make it out to be. Why does everyone obsess over motive? It's a distraction from the facts. And the fact is her roommate killed her.

On the other side of the scale, the Fortunatas matter has me concerned, even anxious. I feel something is acutely wrong. It's too simple, yet too absurd. The few facts I have are not jibing. What about motive in this case? It's incredibly tempting to get distracted into wondering why I'm being paid two thousand dollars to offer a simple conjecture, no strings attached. But again, whatever the motive, I need to be careful.

"I TALKED to Hank a few minutes ago."

"Oh, yeah. What did he have to say?"

Tiffany could tell she was on speaker. She heard drawers opening and closing, and it sounded like Sebastien was speaking from across the room.

"Sebastien, what are you doing?"

"I'm putting my clothes on."

"You're naked?"

"I was naked. I just got out of the shower."

"You don't have to get dressed to talk to me."

Tiffany giggled, trying to picture Sebastien hurriedly throwing on his silk boxers for the sake of a phone call.

"I'm not. I always get dressed after a shower. Don't you?"

"I would say that's a personal question, but you already know the answer. Anyway, tell me when you're decent and I'll continue."

"Go ahead. I'm ready."

"Good. So Hank tracked down one of Amber Harrison's professors at the university today. She didn't know anything. In fact, she didn't even know Harrison was missing until she saw it on the news."

"I'm not surprised."

"Me either. But you might be surprised to learn that he managed to get Harrison's transcripts from the previous two semesters, just like you suggested."

"I didn't think he was listening."

"He pays more attention than you realize—especially to you, I might add."

"What did they say? The earlier transcripts, I mean."

Tiffany noted the lack of acknowledgment of the subtle compliment.

"I think I now see what you were going for there. In Harrison's first two semesters, she earned a three-point-eight grade point average."

"I bet it was much lower in the fall of 2012."

"Two-point-seven, which seems very out of character."

"I've told you, it wasn't her."

"I know you say that, Sebastien . . ."

"You agree with me."

"I do. But how do we prove it?"

"We don't need to prove it. It's axiomatic. A dead girl is not taking tests. What about the teaching assistants? Has Hank tracked them down?"

"He did, actually. One of them. He didn't remember Amber

at all. He never even heard of her disappearance. But Hank was able to get the roster for the biology class she was in. I think he bribed someone at the school or something. Anyway, watch out. Your brother is very proud of himself. I swear he's in full peacock mode."

"Sounds to me like he should be."

"He'll be happy to hear you said that. What about the search today? How did things go out there? Did you find anything?"

"We found a sock with some foot bones and a left fibula. But that's all."

"Fibula? Is that the shin bone?"

"No, it's the one next to it. Touch the outside of your ankle. Feel that bump? That's the bottom of the fibula connecting to the talus bone, the upper ankle."

Whether or not Sebastien was being rhetorical, Tiffany ran her fingertips down the side of her lower right leg out of genuine interest.

"Ah, yeah. There it is. You think the foot and leg are from Amber Harrison? Got to be, right?"

"Technically, no, they don't have to be, but that makes the most sense. And I measured the leg bone. Fibula length is not a sure-fire way to determine sex, but this one is below the sectioning point."

"Sectioning point?"

"That's right. The formula is a discriminant function."

"Sebastien, if you keep talking sexy like this, *my* clothes will be off."

"Sorry. I mean if the length of the bone is below a certain point, then it is estimated to be female. The measurement is used to discriminate between the sexes."

"Thank you. So, likely female. What about the foot bones?"

"Impossible to say. Not much has been done with osteometrics on the tarsals."

"Sebastien, you know I love you, right?"

"Oh, my . . . yes. Yes. And I love you too."

"Great. Now, please talk to me like a normal person."

"Sorry. I keep doing that. I can't tell sex from the ankle bones, but the fib—leg bone was found about fifteen meters from the sock, so it should be a match. DNA will tell us for certain if it's her."

"Great. And thank you. Are you going back out there tomorrow?"

"Yes, we are. We're going to move the search site farther west, I think. What about you? Wanna come?"

"That sounds super tempting, what with the freezing cold and snow in the forecast. But Hank and I are going to Portland to visit Amber's mother tomorrow."

"Oh, that's right. Snow? Crap."

"Yep. You may want to call Trisha and reschedule that. I'm sure the sheriff will understand."

"Good idea. What about you? How was your day?"

"Well, thanks for asking, darlin'." Tiffany affected her best Dolly Parton accent.

Sebastien laughed loudly through the phone. Mist looked up from her warm spot on the hearth, concerned at the sudden burst of noise.

"Ha! Now I know how to make you laugh. That should come in handy."

"You always make me laugh."

"I'm going to mark that down as flattery, Doctor. My day was good—very busy, which I know you can relate to. I managed to visit Barnadette Jacobs and the club where Harrison worked before she was murdered. Oh! I can't believe I nearly forgot to tell you. You remember Shelly Shields? She's the third roommate, the one who moved out shortly before the end of the semester."

"Sure. What about her?"

"She's dead! That's what about her! She was killed while

hitchhiking the same week Amber's mother reported Amber missing. Isn't that a crazy coincidence?"

"You think it's a coincidence?"

"I knew you would say that! And, no, I don't. I talked to Shields's brother, and he confirmed she was a hitchhiker. That's how she got around when not bumming a ride from friends. But the accident was near Lead, which is on the north end of the Hills, and he couldn't think of any reason for her to be there. Neither could Barnadette Jacobs."

"Pretty handy, isn't it?" replied Sebastien. "We don't have a statement from Shields but, if I recall correctly, she was supposedly an eyewitness to Harrison being alive after the time we know her to have been killed. Without Shields there's no way to circle back on that."

Tiffany beamed in pride for knowing exactly where Sebastien would go with this. Too bad he couldn't see her smile through the phone.

"You do recall that correctly. And convenient is the word I would use. This also explains why there was no supplement for an interview with Shields in the case file. She was dead. Aside from that, my visit with Jacobs didn't give me anything new—except that she's a veterinarian now and she lives alone, but I don't see how that's relevant."

There was a long pause on the other end of the line.

"Sebastien? What is it? Do *you* think that plays into this somehow?"

"No, I don't."

"What's on your mind, then? What is it?"

"You don't happen to know what kinds of animals Jacobs treats, do you? Does she work with household pets, or is she more of an agricultural vet kind of thing?"

"It's funny how you have a knack for big words, but have trouble with the small ones."

"What do you mean?"

"Never mind. Jacobs is a small animal veterinarian—cats, dogs, birds, rabbits probably."

"You don't happen to have the address of her clinic, do you?"

"Sebastien, there are plenty of vets close to town. You can find someone else for Parsifal."

"It's not Parsifal I'm thinking about. Well, not entirely. Jacobs is the closest living witness to what happened. And who knows, she might be in danger."

$\sim$

IT WAS A LITTLE HAREBRAINED, considered Tiffany as she packed a small bag for her trip to Portland. Just because both of her roommates died tragically ten years ago, it didn't mean that Barnadette Jacobs witnessed any of it. Nor did it mean she was being targeted by whoever killed Harrison.

Sebastien had been cagey when pressed about his reasoning. Tiffany assumed this was because he realized he jumped the gun a bit. There was no evidence, just emotional reaction. Fortunately, she was able to convince him to stand down. Going by Jacobs's clinic and stirring things up would only complicate things. And in no case would Sebastien go alone if such a step were to be taken. That was against the rules of the cold case protocol laid out by Lieutenant Breed. Sebastien was a non-sworn consultant and, as such, would not be undertaking interviews without Tiffany or Hank present. Would he?

10

This was too early for Milo Crane. Too *damn* early. It was freezing cold out for one thing, the sun wasn't even thinking of shining, and he hadn't had his coffee yet. But he didn't even have time to make his coffee, did he? It wasn't exactly instant, was it? He only drank the good stuff his son-in-law brought back from Costa Rica. Whole beans. Had to grind it himself, didn't he?

"Milo, we need you."

At four in the morning? Who calls a person at four in the morning? Lawyers don't work at four in the morning! Why the hell do you think they became lawyers! It wasn't to get up with the bakers and garbage men!

"What? Now? What do you need?"

"Just get over here. We're all waiting. We got a problem."

Milo backed his Mercedes out of the garage slowly, squinting into his rearview mirror so as to avoid that one patch of ice where the driveway met the street, that one spot that never seems to dry and often sends his car careening to the left when he puts it in drive and hits the gas.

What kind of problem could there be that required a pre-dawn sortie, he wondered. After all, he was a corporate law guy, an expert in real estate litigation. He was no mafia lawyer like in those documentaries on TV—although . . .

"But not the usual place," he'd been told. "I'll text you the address."

Very strange.

Milo headed west out of the driveway, catching his right tire on the ice patch, as per usual. After regaining control of the Mercedes, he drove fifty or so yards farther to the stop sign before looking down at his phone. He didn't recognize the address.

Very strange, indeed.

With the heat cranked up and his phone's GPS directing him, Milo headed into the blackness. There was absolutely no one on the road at this time of the morning, so that was good. *Look on the bright side*, he reminded himself. *There's always a silver lining.* All things considered, and with the car warming up, Milo realized things were not too bad. Yes, being at the beck and call of others was an annoyance and sometimes hurt his pride. But his salary—which nearly kissed the mid-six-figure mark—was more than ample remuneration for the eccentricities of his working life.

The coffee at the gas station at the bottom of Old State Highway 40 was as horrible as anticipated—a consequence of being used to the good stuff, he knew. But the injection of caffeine further improved his attitude. He remembered that today was the day of the week, the dreaded day, when they were supposed to visit Edith's mother. He smiled to himself as he waited in line to pay for his coffee and a fresh donut. *No trip to the mother-in-law today. Oh well!* Edith would be resentful, of course, but her Escalade wasn't free and neither was their large house in Colonial Pine Hills. Someone had to pay for all that, along with the shopping trips to Minneapolis and Denver and the ridiculous spoilage of the growing number of grandkids. Would he ever get the nerve to tell her that to her face? *Hell no.*

It was pushing four-thirty when he made a right onto Catron. If the traffic and the roads cooperated, he would be there around five-fifteen. That would be good, since he promised he'd be there no later than half past the hour. Milo liked to be on time. He enjoyed being reliable. And he enjoyed his Mercedes. And his fancy clothes. He was also really fond of those expensive medications which, according to his doctor, should keep him alive to a ripe old age. There was no doubt a man with his multitudinous infirmities should rightly be retired by now, not driving through the dark and the cold at this ungodly hour. But then what? More visits to his overbearing, seemingly immortal mother-in-law?

The thought of mortality prompted him to pull over into the parking lot of the Holiday Inn on Sixteen. Before getting out of the car, he took in a deep breath to steel himself against the bitter cold. He held that breath until he was able to open the trunk and discover that he had, in fact, remembered to load the rifle.

"HE'S A LITTLE OVERWEIGHT. When was the last time you had his teeth cleaned?"

Parsifal shook nervously as the vet put the otoscope up to his ear. His watery, fearful eyes fixed imploringly on his human.

"I give him those dental chews," replied Sebastien, intentionally avoiding the question head on.

"I'll have Maureen set up an appointment for a cleaning. I'm afraid we'll have to put him under. He has a lot of plaque built up. See here." Barnadette Jacobs pulled back the dog's left cheek with her gloved thumb.

Sebastien nodded.

"So you say he hasn't been himself lately?"

"I don't know if he's sick or just tired. Or maybe it's hypoxia. We recently moved here from the West Coast. He's not used to the elevation."

"Oh? How long has it been?"

"A few months."

"Hmm." Dr. Jacobs made some notes on Parsifal's medical chart as she spoke. "That may be true—although he should have adapted by now. And his weight is certainly not helping the situation. I'd like him to lose three or four pounds. What are you feeding him?"

"Acclimatized, you mean?"

"I'm sorry?"

"He should have *acclimatized* to hypoxia, rather than adapted, I think you meant to say."

"Did I? Are you a doctor, Mr. Grey?"

Sebastien quickly looked down at Parsifal.

"No. I mean, yes. A PhD. I'm sorry about that. I didn't mean to be rude."

"Oh, you're fine, *Doctor* Grey. You may be right anyway. Well, Parsifal seems to be in pretty good shape for an eight-year-old. We will need to wait for the lab tests to come back, but I'm optimistic that if you can get some weight off of him it will make a big difference. How much exercise is he getting?"

"He hates the cold." Again, Sebastien avoided the question. "You think that might be it? Maybe the cold has got him down?"

"West Coast, you said? I would say so. Everyone moves a bit more slowly in the cold. He needs exercise and fresh air though, whether he likes it or not."

"What about you? Are you from around here? Originally?"

"Yes. Yes, I am."

Barnadette stood erect and clutched the clipboard tightly against her chest. *Was this a defensive posture?* he asked himself.

"But you lived in California," Sebastien offered as a part-question, part-declaration as he pointed to a certificate on the examination room wall.

"Ah, Davis. Yes. A very good veterinary school."

"Probably the best in the country," he replied with no hint of guile.

"You know it?"

"I'm from the East Bay."

"Small world, Dr. Grey. What brought you here?"

Damn. Sebastien stupidly failed to game plan for this.

"Please, call me Sebastien. I . . . I have family here. I recently retired."

The veterinarian smiled for the first time during their brief time together. Parsifal was still shaking.

"I don't know what surprises me more," she replied. "That you retired so young or that you came here to do it. You can't be any older than I am. And you must really like your family."

Sebastien strained to smile in return, grateful to have dodged the specifics of his new life or the truth of his semi-retirement, but his relief would be temporary, he knew. These occasions called for charm, or some sort of charisma, neither of which he felt he had. This was going to be awkward, but it was too late now.

"They're okay. What I really like about this place is how safe it is. My apartment in California must have gotten broken into half a dozen times. And I had a car stolen once. I bet not much happens around here."

Sebastien was never a good liar and was therefore unfit for undercover work, though he often used the art as an avoidance mechanism. Maybe he should have taken Tiffany's advice.

"We have our share of crime, Sebastien. Granted, I've never had a car stolen—although I don't drive expensive vehicles." Barnadette winked then smiled at him for the second time. "I saw you drive up."

Sebastien offered a nod as he scanned her for a motive as to why she would be watching him pull into the parking lot. Barnadette's face was un-made-up, plain, and somewhat wide. Her short nose was likewise broader than he would have thought, though the average person wouldn't have noticed one way or the other. But they would have noticed the diamond in her left nostril. Her mental eminence—chin—was less eminent than its anatomical label would lead one to expect. The epicanthus of her eyes folded just slightly where they met the bridge of her nose. Had he been pressed, Sebastien would have put her ancestry at three or four generations removed from Eastern European. She stood about five-ten, which may have been a little on the tall side for that part of the world, but then, the range of human variability was wide in all parts of the world.

"But if I were you, knowing what I know, I wouldn't get too complacent. Things do happen in the hills. Why, just a few months ago a couple of bikers were murdered up here. You may have heard about that."

What to say?

"I might have, now that you mention it. Doesn't that make you nervous? You don't live alone, do you?" Sebastien tried to feign concern rather than appearing transactional, which was how he felt in most interactions.

"I'm attached, Dr. Grey, if that's what you're getting at." Barnadette betrayed no humor in her statement.

Sebastien realized how bad that must have sounded. He tried to suppress his cringe. It was back to formalities. *Damn you, Sebastien. Such an ass.*

"Oh, no. I didn't mean that at all. I'm attached too. No, I just meant . . . do you feel safe here?"

"It's a wonderful place to live, especially up here in the hills. Folks look out for each other. They have more than their fair share of crime in Rapid City: vehicle thefts, burglaries, robberies. And things are a bit like the Wild West down along the highway. It's a great location for drug trafficking and human trafficking, for that matter. If you're apt to take rides from strangers, you may want to reconsider. Not that you fit the risk group for that sort of thing."

Barnadette gave Parsifal a rub on his head. "We'll want him back soon for that cleaning. I'm also going to have Maureen give you some printouts with information about helping him get to a healthier weight."

Sebastien drove away from the clinic wondering what in the world he was thinking. What was that supposed to accomplish? Aside from learning that he possessed poor dog-care skills, he left no wiser than he arrived when it came to the inner feelings of Barnadette Jacobs. But what did he expect? This was an impulsive move and netted the investigation nothing. He was lucky to get out without tipping off the last remaining suspect in the murder of Amber Harrison.

IF SEBASTIEN WAS of the opinion that the whole visit was a wash —and it was safe to say that he was—it was only because he had no way of knowing that at about the same time he pulled the Range Rover onto the highway, Barnadette Jacobs's ungloved fingers were pecking at the keyboard on her office laptop. The phrase "Custer County Cold Case," did not return many results, but she was able to bring up, most critically, that one article from the *Custer Signal*—the selfsame article that led to her expectation of a visit from the police about Amber Harrison's disappearance. Barnadette found what she was looking for in the second paragraph.

To assist in the cold case work, the sheriff's office has employed the services of Dr. Sebastien Grey, a forensic anthropologist from Califor-nia. It was this same Dr. Grey who helped to solve the grisly West Side

Silverback Motorcycle Club murders last month. *The* Signal's *own Derek Manly was able to leverage his hard-won connections in the law enforcement community to secure an exclusive interview with Dr. Grey, which will be posted to the* Signal's *website later this week.*

No, it was not a wash. Not by any means.

11

Peggy Harrison lived in a small single-story house with dark-gray wood siding and bright-white trim. The lower third of the house's facade was covered in ashlar veneer, and ashlar-wrapped pillars held up the covered porch, under which sat a swing chair. The low-gabled roof was covered in dark asphalt shingles. Tiffany took it all in from the front passenger seat of the rental car. The house looked newish, and the yard was obviously well cared for. It all seemed so idyllic, despite the rain. She wondered if this happy-looking house in Happy Valley, Oregon would seem less cheerful when they left it.

"Let's go. What are you waiting for?" Hank said as he ducked his head back into the rental car with his left hand on the driver's side door, poised to close it.

"I just hate this. It sucks."

"I know. Come on. I'm getting soaked out here."

Peggy Harrison answered the door almost before the bell stopped ringing. *Was she expecting them?* Tiffany asked herself.

"Mrs. Harrison, I'm Sergeant LeGris, and this is Detective

Reese. We're with the Custer County South Dakota Sheriff's Office. May we have a word with you?"

"You came a long way," replied the woman, stepping back to allow the pair into the house. "I take it this is about my daughter. Did you find her?"

Tiffany braced herself.

"Can we have a seat, Mrs. Harrison? We have some questions."

Peggy Harrison looked to be in her mid-fifties—Tiffany couldn't remember her exact age from the reports she had read. She was wearing jeans and a brown shawl sweater over a paisley-patterned tunic. There were no obvious signs of abiding stress or weariness on the woman's face, which appeared quite firm from Tiffany's seat across the living room. Nor were there indications of concealer to mask the years without her daughter.

"Mrs. Harrison, is there anyone else here? Do you live alone?"

"I live by myself, Sergeant. So please just tell me my daughter is dead. I've been expecting this."

A glimmer of moisture emerged from the corner of Peggy's otherwise stoic and fixed eyes.

"I'm sorry, Mrs. Harrison, but, yes, we have found your daughter. And I'm afraid she is dead."

A burst of compassion sent Tiffany to Peggy's side, where she kneeled next to her chair and placed a consoling arm on her back. The less-than-hardened detective blinked rapidly, hoping to disperse the tears pooling in her own eyes.

Neither Hank nor Tiffany said anything for several minutes as Peggy's tears turned to weeping. The crust she had built up over the years to protect her emotional and mental well-being was now fully shucked. It was a pitiful and wrenching moment.

Hank disappeared into the house somewhere, and Tiffany could hear a tap running. He came back a few minutes later with a glass of water and a wad of toilet paper, both of which he offered to Peggy.

"I couldn't find any tissues. Sorry."

Peggy looked up and grabbed the toilet paper. Hank set the water glass on the small side table, next to a book of crossword puzzles.

Peggy wiped her eyes and nose, then began crying again.

Tiffany returned to the couch and sat next to Hank.

"We're in no hurry," he whispered, looking at her.

Peggy Harrison continued to cry as the pair of detectives sat in silence. Tiffany looked away from the woman. She could at least give her grief some sort of privacy. Shifting her gaze to the wall behind Peggy, Tiffany noticed several framed pictures. Many of them featured Amber at various ages—from early childhood up through her high school years. She catalogued these in her mind, thinking they could be useful a little later. A couple of photos showed Peggy, Amber, and a boy a little younger than Amber, along with a man who was presumably Peggy's ex, Amber's father. The boy was quite obviously Amber's brother, whose existence was unknown to Tiffany until now. He would be a man now. Tiffany wondered where he was and how he would take this news.

On the fireplace mantle, to the right of the couch where Hank and Tiffany sat, stood a small brass clock. A thin beam of sunlight from the window behind her reflected off the bell-shaped dome that covered the clock, making it difficult to see the second hand. But the hour hand on the clock looked to be below the double-I. A surreptitious glance at the Chopard around her left wrist told her it was indeed well after three o'clock Custer time. The watch was a gift from Sebastien and looked to be absurdly expensive—she had never heard of that brand before, and a subsequent internet search in the privacy of her own home confirmed it probably cost more than her first car. She covered the silver and rose gold face with her sleeve and turned her attention to Peggy, who began to speak softly.

"Please. Can you tell me what happened to her?"

Tiffany shifted toward Hank, who cleared his throat.

"I'm going to be transparent with you, Mrs. Harrison. We wouldn't normally make this kind of visit in person. We would have the local police do it for us. But this one—your daughter, I mean—this one . . ."

Hank looked to Tiffany for help, which caught her off guard. Tiffany shook her head just enough to signal her lack of insight on the best way to put things.

"What I mean is that the investigation didn't go the way it should have. Mind you, I think everyone did the best they could with what we knew at the time."

"I don't understand, Sergeant. What are you trying to tell me?" Peggy was now tearing at the wad of soggy toilet paper in her lap.

"Amber is dead, like we said. But the fact is, she was dead long before she was even reported missing."

"I'm sorry. What?" Peggy moved forward in her chair and gripped the right armrest tightly, as if she were about to spring herself forward. "That's not right, Sergeant LeGris. That's not right at all. My Amber was alive and well until I reported her missing. I know that for a fact."

"And we need to talk to you about that, Mrs. Harrison," said Hank, "about what makes you think that. But before we do, you need to know that in September of 2012, human remains were found in eastern Custer County. Those remains went unidentified until a few days ago. Our lab matched the DNA from those remains with the . . . um . . . with the hair from your daughter's hairbrush, the one we took from her room."

Tiffany winced mentally every time Hank said the word "remains," but she was pleased he'd caught himself before mentioning the blood in the car. That was a bullet dodged.

"Oh my God. I don't know what to say. Are you sure? There must be a mistake. Are you sure?"

Hank opened the wine-colored leather portfolio, which had been sitting at his side. Peggy took the offered page, squinted at the cryptic technical details for a moment, then shook her head in confusion.

"What does this mean? I don't understand."

Tiffany approached Peggy and once again kneeled at her side.

"Mrs. Harrison," she began, pointing at the sheet, "this top line here . . . see these paired numbers? This is the genetic profile of the remains that were found. And see here. All of these numbers are the same. It's a perfect match. We're really sorry, Mrs. Harrison."

"Where has my daughter been, then?"

"That's what we're saying, ma'am. Your daughter is dead."

"No! I mean, if you found her body in 2012, where has it been? Where has my daughter's body been?"

Tiffany braced herself, resisting the urge to flee back to the couch. She recalled how Sebastien had once responded to her question about preparing himself for the worst decomp cases. His answer was blunt: *You can't prepare. You just have to do it.*

"Mrs. Harrison, your daughter's body has been in our coroner's office since it was discovered. It was found, as I mentioned, several months before your daughter was reported missing. Because of that, it didn't occur to anyone that it could be her. One of our forensic experts suggested we check it, just to be sure. That's how the match was made."

Peggy looked up from the lab report and directly into Tiffany's eyes. Moisture once again began to obscure both women's vision.

"I want to be clear, Mrs. Harrison," continued Hank, "I'm not making excuses for anything. We should have figured this out much sooner. We are incredibly sorry."

"We really are so sorry for the extra pain this has caused you," added Tiffany.

"How did she die? Can you tell me that?"

"We're not one hundred percent sure," replied Hank. "We know she was shot in the shoulder, but we can't determine if that wound was fatal or if there was more trauma that we haven't discovered yet."

Tiffany tried not to react to Hank's choice of words, but Peggy must have seen something in her face.

"What do you mean, 'haven't discovered'?"

After relating the circumstances in which her daughter's body was found, and the incomplete condition of Amber's remains, it was Tiffany's turn to make a water run to the kitchen. The poor woman must be nearing dehydration by now. Still, she was taking things a lot better than Tiffany feared. There were no railing accusations of incompetence on the part of the sheriff's office or threats to sue. At least not yet. Not that any of that should matter. The woman's daughter was dead. Murdered! In pieces, after all! She was due her anger. A tinge of gratitude emerged as she drained the glass at the kitchen sink, then filled it again for Peggy.

"Here. Have some water."

Peggy stared past Hank and out the front window while sipping from the glass.

"Mrs. Harrison, Detective Reese and I are going to do everything we can to find out what happened to Amber. I promise you we will get to the bottom of it. I know we can never bring her back, but we won't let this go. I promise."

Tiffany hoped Hank wasn't overselling things here, but then she remembered that Sebastien felt pretty certain this case shouldn't be too difficult to solve. Despite being the most optimistic of the trio, generally she was personally not so sure. There was a reason this case was cold for so long—and, based on what Sebastien said about the search, it seemed unlikely that the rest of Amber's remains would be found. Would that hamper things? It usually did, didn't it?

"Mrs. Harrison, who is this in the picture next to Amber?"

Hank looked at Tiffany, as if surprised by the non-sequitur.

"That's my son, Matthew."

"I didn't realize Amber had a brother."

Peggy didn't answer. Tiffany continued.

"He looks to be a few years older than Amber. Is that right?"

"Three years. Yes."

"Were they close?"

"Very close. They were pretty much inseparable until Matthew and I moved out here." Peggy almost smiled as she recollected.

"Must have been hard on him when his kid sister went missing," remarked Hank.

"When she was killed, you mean? Yes. He was devastated. Oh God! He'll be crushed when he hears!"

Touché, thought Tiffany.

"After you and Matthew moved here, did they stay close? Did they keep in contact?"

"Of course. I told you they were inseparable."

"Mrs. Harrison, did your son ever mention anything about Amber's disappearance? Did he have any theories? Or did Amber ever say anything to him that was out of character or cause for concern?"

"I thought she was angry with me."

"I'm sorry?"

Peggy wiped her nose with the toilet paper and her eyes with the back of her sweater sleeve.

"I was sure she hated me. Wouldn't return my phone calls. Her texts made it seem like she'd had enough of me. I don't know what I did. Oh God!"

"You didn't do anything wrong, Mrs. Harrison. That's the point. That's what we need to talk to you about. Whomever you were texting with, it was not Amber. Your daughter wasn't mad at you. She was . . ."

Hank didn't finish the statement, but his point hit home just the same. Peggy's eye grew wide, and her cheeks and shoulders lifted.

"You're right. I thought it was me. I thought . . . I've always tried to be a good mother. I didn't mean to push her away."

"And you didn't. You didn't, Mrs. Harrison. I'm sure you're a wonderful mother." Tiffany coupled her words with a soft hand on Peggy's shoulder. "Now, can you tell us more about those texts? What made you think she was unhappy with you?"

"I thought it was because I pressed her about her spending. But we had an agreement. There was to be no major purchases without clearing with me first. It's not like we were swimming in money."

Tiffany, once again sitting next to Hank, said, "You're referring to the computer?"

"That's right. But there was more than just that. A computer I could understand. At least she could use that for school. But the restaurants, the weekend trips, the clothes . . . we didn't have the money for all that."

"Mrs. Harrison, we now know, without any doubt, that the person with whom you were texting was not your daughter. She was not making those purchases. Somebody was impersonating her. That's why you could never get her on the phone."

Peggy nodded in agreement. "That does make sense. You know, she almost threatened me when I told her I wasn't going to pay the balance on the credit card? My Amber would never do that. And she would never have spent that money in the first place. She knew how difficult things had been since the divorce. Amber was a very responsible young woman."

Tiffany thought she detected an aura of relief envelope Peggy. This was an outcome she had not predicted for some reason. How monumental this must be for the poor woman to have the oppressively disjointed narrative about her daughter broken to pieces and replaced by something that made more sense. The truth will set you free, the Good Book said. This was as much a mission of mercy as it was a death notification. The weight coming off of Tiffany's own shoulders was almost palpable.

"Is there anything else about your interactions with Amber's phone—let's call it what it was—that stand out? In retrospect, that is. Knowing what we know now."

"It all stands out now, doesn't it? Her short answers to my questions about how things were with school, the arguing about the credit card, her never returning my calls or even answering them."

"What about the trips that were charged to your card? These were trips to where?"

Tiffany wondered if Sebastien would have lacked enough situational awareness to correct Hank's grammar in the middle of an interview. Probably not.

"That's another thing. Las Vegas? Tucson? Without asking me? And how do you do that in the middle of school like that?"

"I take it Amber didn't have any connections to either of those places." Tiffany had her notebook open on her lap, ready to note anything significant.

"No. Not at all. At least, not that I know of."

"I don't suppose, Mrs. Harrison, that you still have those credit card statements?" Hank asked.

"In fact, I do."

"You're kidding?"

Tiffany looked over at Hank, surprised by his response and wondering how Peggy would react.

"Sergeant, I'm an accountant. I have a habit of keeping financial records. And, unfortunately, those statements are the last tangible representation I have of my daughter. I thought so, anyway."

Peggy raised herself slowly from her chair and excused herself to retrieve the records.

"What about your phone records from back then? I don't suppose you have those?"

Peggy stopped halfway down the hallway that led to the bedrooms, turned, and shook her head. "No, I'm afraid I don't. My hoarding has its limits."

"I think we have enough for now, Hank. We need to leave her be," whispered Tiffany once Peggy was out of earshot.

"Not like this, Tiff. Not alone."

THE BAGGAGE HANDLERS on the tarmac looked like orange apparitions through the sheets of rain. *What an awful job that must be*, thought Hank.

"You want the window, boss?" Tiffany asked before snapping her seat belt in place.

"Nah, man. That looks miserable though. Glad I didn't check anything," Hank pointed out the jet's window. "It'll all be water-logged before it gets on the plane."

"You know, I was thinking . . ."

"Oh, yeah?"

"Credit card fraud is not exactly a solid motive for all the hassle involved in making Harrison appear to be alive. How much money could be involved in a laptop and some clothes?"

"The trips too. Now those are really interesting. What did Harrison say about those? One was Las Vegas and the other Phoenix? No wonder Peggy was pissed."

"Tucson, I believe is what she said."

"Same diff. In any case, we need to run those down. Do you have any idea what a miracle it was that Harrison kept those statements? But you're right. The motive is thin."

"What if the fraud was just an afterthought? What if Amber

was killed for a different reason and whoever killed her decided to take advantage financially by stringing her mother along?"

"You're starting to sound like my brother, Reese."

"Not such a bad thing, is it?"

"You're getting soft on me, Tiff. Don't go all loony like the doc. Is that a new watch?"

Hank picked up Tiffany's wrist and shook it gently, making her gracile hand flop back and forth.

"Yes, it is. And thanks for noticing."

"Looks damn expensive. A gift from the nerd, I suppose? We don't pay you enough for that kind of bling."

"Tease me all you want, Hank, but I know how much you like having me and your brother together. It warms your cold, black heart, doesn't it?"

"Yeah, yeah. Just do me a solid, will ya? Warn me before you graduate from fancy watches to engagement rings."

Hank folded his jacket and stuffed it behind his head, hoping to get some sleep. The sound of the jet engines gaining thrust and the murmur of the passengers settling in for the flight lulled him like a baby. He was almost asleep when he felt a jab to his right side.

"Huh? Wassat?"

"I asked you what you thought of Matthew Harrison."

"Oh. Seems like an okay guy. He gave all the right answers, anyway. Glad he lives nearby. I don't think Peggy should have to be alone. Wake me when they bring by the coffee, will ya?"

12

The conference room at Fortunatas Development's headquarters was long and spare. Most of the space was taken up by a wide glass conference table, which left barely sufficient room between it and the glass walls for proper handshakes and greetings.

A tall, gaunt man with a full head of silver hair stood from his chair and extended a cadaverously thin hand from the other side of the table.

"Dr. Grey, Peter Stern, senior partner here at Fortunatas. We are very grateful for your help. This is a damn mess."

Sebastien began to answer but was interrupted by an elegant woman in her late sixties who walked around the table and took his right hand between both of her own and forced eye contact.

"Abigail Fortune, Dr. Grey. I'm the managing partner and founder of this little operation. Thank you for coming down from the hills to see us."

Sebastien must have looked confused without realizing it.

"Yes, that is my name. 'Fortunatas' is merely a play on words, so to speak."

"Oh, well, that seems a bit . . ."

"Fortunate is the word you're looking for, Dr. Grey. And yes, it does work out nicely, doesn't it? Have a seat, Doctor. Here."

Sebastien lowered himself into the chair and pretended to adjust himself to a comfortable position while he looked around the room.

"Mr. Crane is unable to join us, Doctor. He has other obligations."

Abigail Fortune was a perceptive woman and was clearly in charge, as her title suggested. Peter Stern gave a more submissive impression.

"Well, Dr. Grey," Abigail began, her green eyes fixed directly at him, "Milo has briefed you on the main points of our dilemma, I think."

Peter reached down and retrieved a small box from the floor next to his chair, then set it on the table.

"This is it," he declared, pulling the lid off of the container. "It's not much, I have to say, but apparently there was enough."

"Hang on a minute."

Sebastien reached into his messenger bag and pulled out a six-inch-by-six-inch square beanbag, placing it on the table.

"There. Put it on that."

The bone was small and fragmentary, barely making a depression in the surface of the beanbag. Even still, the characteristics were unmistakable. It was part of a skull—the inner surfaces of the left and right eye orbits and about a half inch of forehead. Connecting them was the upper part of the nasal opening. Also present, protruding from the back of the fragment, was a structure that roughly resembled a pair of bat wings. Sebastien drew his head in for a closer look, coming within an inch or two of the bone.

"Looks like an orbital bone to me, Doctor," offered Peter.

"There's no such thing," Sebastien answered him without breaking from his examination.

"Re-ally?"

"Really. Not technically, anyway. The eye orbit is just a junction for several other bones. The sphenoid bone, for one. That's this wing-shaped structure here. And this little space between the wings, that's called the sella turcica, or Turkish saddle. That's where the pituitary gland sits."

"Re-ally?"

"Yes. And the rest of the orbit, which you see here, is made up of the frontal, ethmoid, lacrimal, maxilla, and zygomatic bones—although, the zygomatic, the bone of the outer wall, is missing in this individual."

"There's a lot more than that missing, Doctor." Abigail almost giggled as she said this. "It is native though, yes?"

"Yes."

"How in the world can you tell?" asked Peter.

"I'm supposing, to be completely honest. I don't know for sure. But take a look here, on the upper surface of the frontal bone."

Sebastien retrieved a pencil from his bag and used it to point to the surface of the eye socket, just behind and above where the eyes would be.

"See how this part of the bone looks spongy? There are all these little pinhole looking defects. That's not supposed to be like that. It should be smooth like the rest of the orbit. But what you see here is the orbital marrow, the blood cell producing area. When an individual does not have enough iron, either because of poor nutrition or some congenital condition like sickle cell trait, the marrow expands to allow for increased hematopoiesis—red blood cell formation. That's one theory, anyway. Others include infection or even scurvy. The condition is called cribra orbitalia."

Peter leaned over the table.

"You mean, that's where the blood is made?"

"It's one place, yes. Marrow is found in two of the leg bones, the upper arm bones, vertebrae, sternum, ribs, pelvis."

"And it's a native thing, this crib—?"

"Cribra orbitalia. Not exclusively. But, by some estimations, up to twenty-one percent of pre-modern skeletons in North America exhibit this type of pathology. It's far less likely for this kind of disease mechanism to go untreated in a modern person, native or otherwise."

"Thank you, Doctor Grey. This is helpful," said Abigail, though not convincingly.

Sebastien was still looking at the bone when he said, "I don't see how helpful it could be. This means your site likely contains more remains and even artifacts which, by law and by right, should be repatriated. I would recommend a second assessment and even excavation."

"Or, it could mean the bone was brought in with the fill, which is what we believe. Remember, Doctor, that is the purpose of our consulting you. Whether the bone is native is less relevant to our purpose. Either way, it is not from our site."

Sebastien sat back in his chair and knocked the eraser end of the pencil against his chin. Abigail looked at him with an obviously forced smile.

"Please, Dr. Grey. Do tell us what's on your mind."

"For the sake of transparency, I should inform you that . . ."

"You think this is a waste of time and a bunch of bull. We are well aware. Milo shared with us your hesitations. Please, Doctor, your concerns."

Abigail's stern and abrupt interruption, which was paired with a saccharine smile, dismayed Sebastien. There were no items he could raise without revealing his secret trip to the site, although Milo didn't expressly tell him not to go to the site alone. He thought for a moment, weighing the consequences of a handful of options. He decided the best response to her directness was to be blunt. Tit for tat.

"There was no dirt brought into that site, was there?"

"I beg your pardon."

Abigail's tone was still artificially pleasant, rather than confrontational.

"I visited the construction site. I looked at the soil profile from the water main trench. The dirt is uniform in that area and looks to be very consistent throughout the site. If there was no fill brought in, then the bone must have originated at the location, which means you have a problem."

The senior partner, Peter Stern, pointed a finger across the table.

"Now, look, young man. I—we—resent the implication that we have been deceptive. Furthermore, we do not appreciate you trespassing on our property. We have very strict insurance requirements, and you have exposed us to serious repercussions."

"At no point was I asked to stay out of the site. In fact, it could be argued that the opposite was implied. And you're already exposed. Are you not?"

Abigail rested her left hand on Peter's right bicep.

"Now, Peter. We should applaud young Dr. Grey for doing his due diligence. He's a professional, after all. What else should we have expected?"

Abigail's face remained unchanged, her stare steadfast.

"Out of curiosity, Dr. Grey, what are your credentials as a geologist? You must have formal training given your assessment of our soil."

"I have very little geological training, but your CRM consultants do. Their report mentioned nothing about fill dirt."

Stern smiled menacingly and said, "Dr. Grey, as you are aware, the fill was brought in after the consultants surveyed the site. That's the whole point. That's what we're saying. Milo, it seems, has misled us with his endorsement of his young anthropologist."

Abigail abruptly got up from her chair and collected her portfolio from the table.

"Come show us, Dr. Grey. Show us what you have seen on our site that makes you so sure. Peter, you'll drive."

A wave of anxiety and guilt rose through Sebastien. He felt like a kid who'd been caught stealing from the drugstore. But why? He did nothing wrong. And, in fact, he felt very sure about his conclusions.

"Fine," replied Peter. "I'll pull the car to the front."

"I can drive myself," declared Sebastien, trying to sound confident.

"I'm afraid that's not practical. We can't have private vehicles on the property. Again, it's a liability issue."

Sebastien turned briefly and watched the Fortunatas office building recede into the distance through the reflection of dark-gray clouds in the BMW's rear window. He felt cold, almost chilly, but he didn't know if it was due to the ambient temperature in the car or the feeling of vulnerability that crept over him from the backseat. Here he was, being driven away to who knew where by a couple of total strangers. Should he text Tiffany and tell her what he was doing and where he was going? No. She was very clear. This job was not in her purview. *You'll be fine, Sebastien. You're a big boy.*

Abigail rotated in the front passenger seat and smiled, showing her unnaturally bright teeth.

"Are you comfortable back there, Doctor? How's the temperature?"

"It's great. I'm fine. Is this . . . is this the right way?"

"We're avoiding downtown, Dr. Grey," replied Peter from behind the wheel. "You're new to the area, as I understand. You wouldn't know that, at this time of day, getting to the freeway can be a challenge."

Despite Peter's calm and rational reply, the anxiety continued to build as the busy streets with busy buildings and busy pedestrians turned into light industrial parks, then rural ranches, and finally open land.

As if reading his mind, Abigail turned to face him again and said, "You see all this land, Dr. Grey? There is terrific competition to buy it up. The landowners are making a mint off of firms like ours. And us, of course. Just about everything that is not Indian reservation is changing hands."

"What are you building?" Sebastien asked, trying to be polite.

"Up ahead we're going to make a left, which will take us over the freeway and to the site for the medical complex."

Sebastien sighed in relief. He swore he detected a tiny wink from Abigail.

"So, yes, we're definitely building our commercial portfolio. And the area up ahead was recently rezoned for industrial. We just purchased thirty acres, which we will turn into warehouses. We hope to flip some of them to one or two major retailers. This area is primed for distribution and fulfillment centers, being so close to the interstate."

Sebastien started to feel better. Abigail, Peter, and Milo weren't members of a crime syndicate. These were business people. This wasn't the drug trade, for goodness' sake. This was real estate development, geology, archaeology. Be rational, he told himself. This was fine.

Peter raised his eyes to the BMW's rearview mirror and said, "I'll tell you what though. Residential is the big thing around here. The population is growing and the housing inventory is far below projected needs. We've been holding on to a few thousand acres down south, and we recently—finally—got approval to put in four hundred single-family homes. It's a massive project."

"Yes, that is a very important project. Ours isn't the only development going in down there, but Custer County is primed for growth, and we're leading the way."

Peter made a left at an empty intersection and headed over

I-90. Sebastien now recognized the area from his earlier visit, but instead of feeling relieved, he belatedly registered something Peter said a few moments previously. *You're new to the area, as I understand.* Sebastien took his cell phone out.

"I'm afraid you'll get no cell service out here," Abigail said with the largest smile she had yet to throw at him.

Peter parked the car and got out to unlock the gate.

"Whose Mercedes is that?" Sebastien asked Abigail, referring to the maroon sedan parked off the road to the left.

"Why, I don't know."

Peter returned to the car and poked his head into the open driver's side door.

"Come on. Let's walk in. I'm afraid my car will get stuck if I drive onto the site."

Abigail alighted from the front seat and opened the rear passenger door for Sebastien. As he looked to place his feet on the ground, he noticed for the first time that Abigail's shoes were brown low-ankle hiking shoes that contradicted her stuffy gray tweed business suit.

"So, Doctor, there is the ditch the bone came from. Now, I must tell you I am very hands-on with these projects. I do specifically recall ordering fill dirt, which was needed to level the site. It came in from Stanley County, if I remember correctly."

"You do," affirmed Peter.

Sebastien looked around the site, for the second time, and once again failed to see any signs of leveling. He considered playing dumb, or at least dumber than he'd already played things—but, as was often the case with Sebastien Grey, he was unable to hold his tongue.

"How much leveling needed to be done? Look at the adjacent lots. All of them are just as level as this one. And your security guard told me the site was level before the improvements began. He also didn't remember any dirt being brought in."

Abigail made no response. She merely stood there, at the edge of the trench with her hands shoved into the pockets of her long wool coat, looking down into the hole.

Peter produced a cell phone and dialed a number. Once he put the phone up to his ear, he looked directly at Sebastien and said, "Dr. Grey, it gives me great pleasure to inform you that you are one giant pain in the ass. Hello? Milo? I believe we are ready on our end."

13

Milo lay prone on the ground behind a line of low bushes on the south side of the construction site. He did his best to remain still, but a patch of ice positioned just below his crotch was distracting him. Nearly resolved to finding a new hiding spot, his phone's earpiece began to ring. It was Peter.

"Roger that," he replied.

The view through the rifle's scope created a coin-shaped frame containing the back of Sebastien Grey's head and shoulders, as well as Peter tucking his phone back into his pocket. Milo shifted his aim to the right to avoid accidentally shooting his boss. He gave the trigger a long squeeze until the sound, smoke, and recoil punctured his senses.

Milo blew the smoke clear and peered through the scope again. The target was gone. Sebastien Grey had disappeared.

"Peter? What's going on?"

"He fell in the damn hole. You hit him and he fell in the hole."

A head-jerking laugh involuntarily leaped out of Milo's throat. He knew he was a good shot, but never had he gotten such a miraculous twofer: a hit and disposal all in one.

"See, Peter? You underestimate me. I am that good."

"Stop gloating and get over here. He's in the hole, but he's still alive," came the response from the phone.

"Well, take care of him."

"How? I don't have a gun."

This was fine, thought Milo. I have to do everything myself. He zipped up his rifle bag and threw the weapon into the trunk of his maroon Mercedes. The car fishtailed as he punched the gas on the dirt road. *Maybe he just needed new tires.*

Abigail and Peter were still in their same spots and still looking into the trench when he got there.

"Stand back," he said as he pointed the barrel into the hole.

There he was, that smart-ass punk, Sebastien Grey, squeezed between the walls of the trench, looking upward with wide, terrified eyes.

"Where did I get ya, you son of a bitch? Oh, your arm? Forgive me, Doctor, I was aiming for your enormous brain."

The anthropologist looked up at him, silent but shivering. He was obviously in shock and, hopefully, in a great deal of pain.

"You were right, Abby. You did bring in fill. We got us some Custer County dirt right here."

"You are charming, Peter. Milo, finish him off."

Milo kneeled down on the dirt and pushed the rifle under Sebastien's chin.

"Don't you worry, Dr. Grey," he chuckled. "My grandson will take great care of Detective Reese. Hell, if I were a few years younger, I would take care of her myself."

"Detective who?"

Milo turned to look at Abigail. "His partner. Some bitch cop up in Custer."

"Wait, you idiot!" Abigail rushed toward Milo, pushing the barrel of the rifle away from Sebastien. "You never told me the police were involved in this."

"Don't worry, she signed an NDA."

"An NDA? How stupid are you, Milo? You lawyers think a contract is the answer to everything. What did you tell her?"

Milo heard the blood thumping in his ears and felt his face warming. For a split second, he considered using the gun on Abigail. Peter's presence saved her life.

"She doesn't know anything! She's not involved."

"How do we know that? How do we know she's not on her way right now?"

"I . . . I texted her. She knows I'm here. She's coming. And others too," Sebastien said, his voice echoing from below.

Milo looked into the hole and saw Sebastien had shifted his body slightly. His right hand held up as if to stop a bullet. A dark red river was running out of the left cuff of his jacket and onto his left thigh.

"He's lying."

"How do you know that, Milo?" asked Peter.

"Damn it, Milo," spat Abigail.

Milo stood up and stuck a finger at Abigail.

"Damn it, yourself! Either way, we're going to kill him. That's the whole point, remember? He's probably dying anyway. It's too late now."

"What does she know, Milo?" Peter asked.

"Excellent question, Peter. What did you tell her, Milo? Did you give her the name Fortunatas? Does she know where the site is? Has she seen the map?"

Milo refused to answer. They obviously didn't trust him. There was no point.

"As long as they know where this place is . . ."

The sound of a diesel engine coming up the road interrupted Peter.

"It's the security guard. Get rid of that thing and get away from the trench."

Milo looked around. The only vegetation thick enough to

conceal the rifle was along the entry road. He calculated his chances and figured he could make it back to the gate and his car before the security guard reached the gate. He had no other options. And, if he could keep the guard from cutting his engine, he might be able to mask whatever noise that nuisance Sebastien Grey might try to make.

The two others followed along as Milo hobbled to the gate. They made it just as the guard's truck emerged from the last bend in the road. Milo didn't have a chance to open his trunk, so he tossed the rifle under the rear of the Mercedes.

"Hey, ya'll. Everything okay out here?"

"Yes, young man. We're fine. Say, you aren't the regular security for this site. Where is . . . uh . . . where is Bert?"

"Ol' Bert's AWOL."

"AWOL, you say? What happened?"

"Don't know. Who are ya'll, by the by? You got permission to be up here?"

Abigail stepped up to the idling truck.

"I am Mrs. Abigail Fortune, your employer and the owner of this site. You work for me."

"That right? What about you two?"

The man took out a small notebook and scribbled in it— ostensibly for recording the names of these sexagenarian interlopers.

"I'm Milo Crane, legal counsel for Fortunatas Development, and this is senior partner, Peter Stern."

The man in the truck appeared to be in his late twenties and was far less gullible than Milo had hoped. If only he hadn't shot Bert the day before while the poor jerk sat in his truck eating his breakfast behind an abandoned gas station east of the Air Force base.

"Look here, young man. We own this property and will not be treated as trespassers," added Peter.

"Uh huh. Counsel. Is that the one with the 'c' or the 's'?"

· · ·

"THAT'S IT. WE'RE CAUGHT," said Peter as the security guard drove away. "We need to implement the emergency protocol."

"Hold your horses," replied Milo. "He believed us. Do we look like criminals?"

"Milo, we have a half-dead man in a hole not a hundred yards from here."

Abigail motioned to the trench. "It's too late now, boys. We can't have Dr. Grey's corpse here. We have to move him."

Milo bent over with a loud grunt and pulled the rifle out from under his car. His knees made a painful cracking sound as he stood erect.

"It'll be easier if he's dead. Come on."

Anyone looking up from the trench—the trench that was dug to make a path for the water main—would have undoubtedly seen the visages of Milo Crane, Abigail Fortune, and Peter Stern pointed downward, each with a look that combined the telltale physiological signs of both panic and shock. But Doctor Grey was no longer lying in the trench in place to take the promised kill shot. No, this particular "giant pain in the ass" was several hundred yards to the north, on his belly, hiding behind an accumulation of wind-blown snow and using his good hand to fish for his cell phone.

THE NORTH WALL of the investigations conference room was almost completely covered by maps, diagrams, and charts. A dozen or so single sheets of paper rested atop the table, laid next to each other in an order that could only be obvious to Erin Morgan.

"You've been busy, haven't you?" offered Hank.

"Yes, I have. But you know I love this stuff. Will Dr. Grey be joining us?"

"He said he would try to," replied Tiffany. "What's this map?"

"Have a seat, and I'll take you through everything."

Erin pushed her round glasses up the bridge of her nose with one hand while leaning on her metallic red offset cane with the other. Her cerebral palsy made it difficult to balance.

"I analyzed all of the records for Amber Harrison's phone—it's a shame we only have records for the thirty days before she was reported missing and three days after. But I was able find some interesting things. It's a good thing you were able to get the cell tower listing, Tiffany. I'm a little surprised you pulled it off."

"It actually wasn't difficult at all. I think just about every version of a tower listing is handed over to law enforcement as a result of a search warrant at some point. Preserving them is fairly routine."

"So you're saying we know the location of Amber's phone when she—I mean, it—sent the texts to her mom?"

"Actually, no. Text messages are handled differently than phone calls. Texts are handled at the switch, not the tower."

Hank looked from the wall of information to Erin.

"Switch?"

"A switch is essentially a main hub for a group of towers. The towers receive information from the switch and push it to the phones. Likewise, the handset, aka phone, connects to the tower, which then communicates with the switch. For some reason—and I'm not a cell tower engineer, so take this with a grain of salt—the call detail record, or CDR, only records the switch number for a text, not the tower and sector. Also, back in 2012, there was no indicator on the CDR for texts. You could only tell it was a text if there was no tower number and no call duration on the records. It was the same way with voicemails."

"What about the calls? Can we tell where the phone was when it made a call?"

"We can, and that's what this map shows."

Erin motioned toward the large satellite map on the wall.

"These days, many cell companies can tell you approximately how many feet away from the tower a phone was when a handset connects to a tower. Back then that wasn't the case for these records. All we know is the number of the tower and the sector. If you draw a circle around a cell tower, then cut the circle up like a pie, the pieces would be your sectors. Most towers have three sectors, but some have more or less."

Hank stood up and walked over to the map, examining it closely.

"So we don't know how far the phone was when a call was made, but we know which side of the tower it was on," he said.

"That's right. And I know what you're going to ask next. How far does a tower go? There's no simple answer to that. Generally, a tower covers one-and-a-half to two miles. But I've worked cases where phones have connected to the tower from even farther away. It really depends on how busy a tower is and the terrain. If there is too much phone traffic near a tower, then a call might get diverted to the next nearest tower if it has a clear shot to get there. Of course, there are distance limits. But I once worked a missing persons case in Colorado where the phone of a missing person was hitting off a tower almost ten miles away. Search and rescue pinged his phone and found him way up on a mountain with a self-inflicted gunshot wound to the head."

"Not so helpful, then." Hank shook his head.

"Oh, on the contrary. Like I said, barring extreme circumstances, there is a limit. If a phone is hitting off a tower, by far the most logical explanation is that it is within a few miles of the tower. The sector becomes the next most important bit of information and very often people who analyze cell phone records make a major mistake when they get into sector data. Most people assume all sectors are the same. So, if a tower has three sectors, sector one points north, sector two points southeast, and sector three points southwest. That is not the case at all, yet most cell phone mapping programs plot them that way."

Erin walked over to the whiteboard, behind where Tiffany sat, and drew a circle.

"I'm probably going to bore you guys with this, but I think it's important."

"No, this is great," replied Hank. "Too bad my propeller-headed brother isn't here for this."

Tiffany looked down at her watch and grimaced.

"Maybe I should call him."

"Nah. It wouldn't hurt to be smarter than him in at least one thing. Proceed please, Erin."

"The key is knowing where the azimuth is, which is indicated on the tower listing."

"Oh, geez."

"Stay with me, Sergeant. The azimuth is the exact center of the sector, indicated in degrees. If a circle is three-hundred-and-sixty degrees—"

"And it is. I at least know that," laughed Hank.

"Color me shocked," added Tiffany.

Erin gave Tiffany a high-five before continuing.

"Let's say a tower has three sectors and the azimuth for sector one is at ten degrees. Three-hundred-and-sixty divided by three sectors means each sector is one-hundred-and-twenty degrees wide at the circumference. Sector one, then, would begin at three-hundred-and-ten degrees and end at seventy degrees."

"You didn't say there'd be math, Erin. Can we get to the good bits please?"

Tiffany got up and approached the map, her mouth open and eyes wide. She placed her index finger against the map and said, "Erin, this tower just west of Fairburn . . . what's the sector and azimuth?"

Erin scanned the CDR, which had been separated into single sheets and lined up on the table.

"There are two sectors that phone connected to on that tower. Sector one, with an azimuth of fifteen degrees, and sector two, which has an azimuth that is at one-hundred-and-thirty-five degrees."

Tiffany rotated her head slightly to the right, as if following the circumference of the tower.

"That means the phone was east of the tower, probably in or around Fairburn. So it's not like the phone was pinging off the west of that tower from a hilltop near Custer or something."

Erin nodded in agreement.

"And that's why I said that understanding sectors is very important."

"Okay," said Hank, approaching the map. "But we know Harrison was out there. That's where her body was found."

Tiffany shook her head. Her eyes were still wide.

"No, boss. This is based on Amber's phone records from thirty days before she was reported missing. In other words, about six months or so after she was dead. Whoever had her phone was in Fairburn, the same general area where her shoulder girdle was found."

Hank turned from the map and wagged a finger in Erin's direction. His mouth opened and closed like fish.

"Oh my goodness, Erin, you've actually made Hank speechless."

Erin walked back to the wall and pointed to another of the visuals she had made. It was a poster with icons that looked like cell phones connected by lines—some dashed, some solid, some thick, some thin, all terminating in arrows.

"Well, I'm not done. See here? This represents Amber Harrison's phone and the others phone numbers it connected with.

The thicker the line connecting the phones, the more times they connected. I ran each number out to see who it was assigned to. These phones here and here," Erin swept her hand across the chart as she explained, "belong to Peggy Harrison and Barnadette Jacobs, respectively. They're all texts. Most of the remaining numbers belong to retailers, customer service desks."

"So, buying stuff?"

"That's what I think, Sarge. There were also a couple of calls to a Las Vegas number that was registered to an Alex Stoyan back then. But now it's connected to a dry cleaner in Henderson."

"What about texts or calls to Shelly Shields's phone number?" asked Tiffany.

"Negative."

"Interesting." Tiffany bit her lower lip in concentration. "For the texts, can we get the content? What was said?"

"Nope. The cell companies stopped keeping those for more than a few weeks. They took up too much storage space, I think."

Hank turned to the map again.

"And were all of these calls made from the Fairburn towers?"

"Yes. They all hit one of those two sectors."

Still with his body toward the map, Hank rotated his head over his shoulder and almost got out an entire question.

"I don't suppose you ran out this Stoyan guy."

"Sure did. He's in federal prison for kidnapping."

14

Sebastien rolled onto his back to better reach his cell phone, which he had shoved in the front pocket of his trousers when he got out of Peter's car. He thought back to when Abigail told him there was no cell coverage out here. That had been a lie and probably should have tipped him off to the setup. But why were they setting him up? Why were they trying to kill him?

The voices in the distance seemed to be closing in. He needed to move farther away. He replaced his phone and rolled onto his right side, which resulted in an acute feeling of dizziness, like he might faint. Using two fingers, he carved a peephole into the snow pile. He could see the three of them standing there by the trench. They were gesticulating erratically. One of the two larger of the three figures—he could not tell who it was from this distance—shoved the other. They were arguing, panicking. Most importantly, they showed no signs of following him. And how could they? Even with a bullet-grazed arm, Sebastien was much fitter than any of them. Still, he needed more distance.

Blood was still draining down the side of his left arm. The

left leg of his khakis was now stained dull crimson over the top of the brown streaks of dirt resulting from his low crawl across the muddy earth. He removed his belt and tried to repurpose it into a tourniquet. It wouldn't quite stay tight around his bicep, but it did slow the bleeding a little. For some stupid reason, that line from Housman about "ensanguining the skies" came to his mind. He tried to remember the full poem, hoping it would keep him from fainting.

Sebastien got to his feet and looked back across the terrain over which he had crawled. It was a hundred yards at most from the construction site where he had found refuge to where the trench ended on the Fortunatas site. In the opposite direction, farther from danger, he could see several potential hiding spots —a portable toilet, an earthmover, a stack of concrete pipes—all of which were too obvious to provide cover. He would need to go farther north to where the land was covered with vegetation and, beyond that, to the line of trees that sprang up on the slope of a low hill.

The yelling behind him got suddenly louder. He turned. They had seen him. They were pointing now and waving for him to come back. *How stupid*, he thought.

Sebastien took a step toward safety, but his right leg gave out and pain shot up from the side of his right knee and into his lower thigh. He must have twisted his leg when he fell into the trench. He forced himself back up with a grunt and tried again, this time dragging his right foot rather than extending his leg fully. This was going to be slow. He looked back once more. One of them was walking toward him—not running but deliberately picking their way through the field. He was pretty sure it was Milo. The long, thin silhouette of the rifle confirmed this.

Setting his sights on the earthmover, he leaned forward for momentum and stumbled northward. A loud cracking sound echoed from behind him. It was the rifle. Milo was shooting at him. Was he hit? He didn't think so. But the pain in his arm and leg made it difficult to discern. He continued toward the earth-mover, trying to bend down and lower his profile, which made it more difficult to balance and slowed him down. He heard another shot from the rifle, but this one was followed instantly by a whizzing near his right ear. He threw himself on the ground and crawled the final ten feet for cover behind the trac-tor's giant tire.

"Come, now, Dr. Grey. Don't injure yourself further. You are only prolonging your pain."

Sebastien put his cheek on the ground and looked through the underside of the earthmover. He could see a pair of legs coming toward him, nearly at the line between the Fortunatas site and the one he was on now. He reached for his phone once more. Even if he didn't have time to call for help, having the phone in his hand might scare off the old psychopath. But it wasn't there. His cell phone must have fallen out when he stumbled. He looked again under the tractor. He saw that Milo was a few yards closer, but he didn't see his phone. Even if he did, he wouldn't be able to get to it before being shot. Running was his only chance. He needed to reach the tree-covered slope, which was now about fifty feet north beyond a patch of undeveloped land. There would be no cover between here and there. Milo would have a slow-moving target, unless Sebastien did something to distract him.

Looking on the ground around him, Sebastien saw there were several chunks of rock, each about the size of his fist. He took two up and crawled eastward, taking cover behind the back tire of the tractor. From there he could see Milo closing the distance with the rifle against his shoulder, sweeping the area in front of him with the barrel. Despite being older and obviously not in the best shape even for his age, Milo clearly knew what he was doing. The look on his face was terrifyingly confident and focused.

Sebastien wrapped his right fist around one of the rocks and took aim at the portable toilet, which was several yards to his left and Milo's right. Opting to forego sports in his youth, or ever, was now catching up to him. He couldn't remember the last time he threw anything—but it was too late now.

The *thud* of the rock hitting the plastic wall of the portable toilet caused Milo to stop sharply and turn toward the sound.

"Ah, there you are. Come on, now. You can't get away, Doctor."

The second rock was heavier than the first, though the side of Milo's head would make for a smaller target. Sebastien heaved again.

Milo let out a scream and fell to the ground, dropping the rifle. Blood ran down and over his ear and cheek from the top of his head. *Nice shot to the left parietal. That should leave a radiating fracture.*

With Milo screaming, cussing, and writhing on the frozen earth, Sebastien now faced a choice. He could head for the trees, as he had planned, or he could further the offensive and try to reach the rifle before Milo regained himself. Maybe he could put a bullet in Milo's head instead of the other way round. It would be risky. The old man was much closer to the rifle than he was, and it could all be over in a flash.

Sebastien took another look toward the trees, calculating in his mind the comparative risks of both options. When he turned back, he saw Milo reaching for the rifle with his free hand while blood from his head poured through the fingers of his other. It was too late. He willed his injured leg to bear weight and dashed for the slope.

THE BAG of groceries slipped from Tiffany's grasp while she tried to simultaneously answer her phone and unlock her front door. An orange rolled into the entry hall and toward Mist, who jumped at it playfully.

"Hey, Hank. What's up?"

"Have you seen my brother?"

"No, I tried to call him after I left the office, but he didn't answer."

"Any idea where he might be? I already checked his place."

"He's probably just out with friends or something. I'm sure he'll be back soon."

"Are you day drinking, Reese? My brother has no friends. And where the hell would he be if not with you?"

"I don't think you're giving your brother credit, Hank. He's really come out of his shell recently."

"Name one."

"What?"

"Name just one friend he's made, besides you, obviously."

"Why are you being mean?"

"One."

Tiffany blew a few strands of hair from her eyes and looked to the ceiling.

"Fine. Gerry Good Crow."

"Gerry from the coroner's office? What? Do they go bowling or something?"

"With all due respect, Sarge, what's your point here?"

"My point is, Sebastien missed an important case meeting, which he would never do. He lives for this crap. What's going on, Detective?"

Tiffany felt a numbness fill her chest and radiate down her legs. Sebastien's little side job should never have been an issue. She had no plans to bring it up either. It was nobody's business, for one. And for two, she didn't want Hank or anyone else at the sheriff's office to think Sebastien wasn't fully dedicated to the cold case work. He was just a contractor anyway. It shouldn't matter. But Hank's concern was making her worry. She was now contemplating all of the ways in which the Fortunatas case could go wrong. Logically, she couldn't think of that many, but her imagination was providing all kinds of wild scenarios. It was time to come clean.

"I don't know. Last I heard from him, he told me he was going to an appointment with a client."

"A client? What do you mean, a client?"

"Your brother agreed to handle a forensic case. Actually, it's not really forensic at all. It was some archaeology thing."

"Where?"

"Rapid City, I think. Oh, geez, do you think he got robbed or something?"

"Sebastien got robbed on an archaeological site in Rapid City? What's really going on, Tiffany?"

"It's not a big deal. A real estate development company asked him to look at some remains that were found on a construction site. They're Native American, apparently. But there's a disagreement about whether the bones are actually from the site. They've asked Sebastien to take a look at them and the location they were found in."

"Oh. Well, that doesn't sound like such a big deal. But why would he still be there? It's been dark for over an hour."

Tiffany gazed out her dining room window at the blackness. Hank was right. There was no reason for him to be gone this long. She tried to think of any other business that could have kept Sebastien in town.

"Maybe his clients invited him to dinner or something. Or maybe he had to do some shopping in town."

"But why not return a text or even answer his phone?"

Hank was right, she realized. Something was off here.

"Do you think we should go into town and see if we can find him?"

"You mean just randomly drive around? That doesn't sound very effective. Do you know where this development site is?"

"No, but the address is in Sebastien's apartment."

"Okay, I'm on my way to pick you up," replied Hank.

Mist was still mewing and swatting at the fruit on the entry floor, but Tiffany was too busy biting her fingernails at the kitchen table to think of her spilled groceries.

15

———

"**B**rian, it's for you." The man held his palm over the portable phone and yelled into the depths of the machine shop.

"What's that?"

"Phone. For you."

Brian Crawford flipped the switch on the side of the massive rectangular press causing the sound of grinding metal to whirr to a stop.

"Yo."

"Brian."

"Yeah, what's up?"

"We need you out here right now. We have an issue that needs to be handled."

"I can't. I'm working late to finish a job."

"That's exactly what I need you for."

"Where are you? What happened?"

"I'm sitting in the emergency room of Pennington General. But I need you to get out to the north side development and help Peter."

"Help him do what?"

"Get your ass out there now, sonny boy."

"You're going to get me fired."

"Fired? My lad, you will be in jail by morning if you don't get out there and help your uncle. And quickly. Bring a gun and some rope."

Brian's boss waved to him from the other side of the shop and tapped his bare left wrist with the index and middle fingers of his right hand.

"I told you, didn't I? I ain't getting mixed up in that anymore. I thought we were done anyway. 'No more,' you said."

"Circumstances warranted that we take some measures of self-preservation. Now, I would love to go into the details for you, but I'm a bit indisposed at the moment."

Brian wasn't sure what "indisposed" meant, but he thought it had something to do with Milo not being able to talk. It didn't much matter though. He couldn't afford to lose this job, nor could he quite see the urgency. After all, it had been nearly ten years since they left the business, and anyone who knew anything was either dead or too guilty to give themselves up.

Brian hung up the phone and retrieved his protective goggles from the work counter. After double-checking his tolerances and blowing away the accumulated swarf, he hit the switch on the press and got back to work. Sure, he would help out his Uncle Peter, just as soon as he was no longer "indisposed."

SEBASTIEN'S CONCERN about being followed up the hill proved needless. Milo was badly hurt by that rock, and appeared to have lost his enthusiasm. What a miraculous throw and, he now realized, a fortuitous choice of projectile. Thinking back to the feel of that rock in his hand, he recalled its one sharp edge. Surely that very edge had connected with Milo's cranium. It reminded him of the Oldowan choppers used by the earliest hominins to scrape meat from the bone. Did he have anthropology on the brain even with the loss of blood and shooting leg pain, or was this just his mind's way of distracting himself from the inevitability of freezing to death?

They were gone now. He saw them from his perch on the hill, hiding behind the fattest tree he could find. Abigail and Peter picked their way through the construction site and helped Milo to his feet. Abigail even took off her scarf and tied it around Milo's head. The old man looked like he was wearing a 1950s head wrap. He was still pissed though. That much was clear. A few times Milo raised the rifle in the direction of the hill, only to have it tugged away from him by Peter.

Sebastien only saw one pair of headlights recede from the road next to the construction site. So maybe not all three of them were gone. That ruled out going back down the hill to the main road. He would be walking back into their hands. He could barely even walk! So, no phone and no way to walk out— at least not quickly. But he had to move, even if his leg slowed him down. They all saw him escape up the hill. They knew which direction he ran. So which direction now? Sebastien looked around, seeing only darkness and the small red and white lights of the cars passing on the distant highway beyond the road to the gate.

His best option was to move farther up and over the hill, but first he checked his arm. The belt did a good job of staunching the bleeding. The blood trail down his arm and hand was now thick and sticky. He winced in pain as he worked a finger under the belt and directly into his wound, trying to assess the depth. The tip of his finger went in about an eighth of an inch. He rubbed the tip of his finger against his thumb. The bleeding had stopped. The pressure from the belt and the cold had no doubt worked to his advantage.

A couple of times while dragging his bad leg up the hill, he found himself reaching again for his phone, thinking to use its flashlight function to help him find his way in the dark. Stupid how dependent on technology modern humans had become. Overspecialized, really. Too far in one direction of evolution, like the Zinjanthropus from a million and a half years ago. Also known as "Nutcracker Man" because of his massive jaws and teeth, that particular species of human ancestor was way too dependent on a vegetable diet. Then the Ice Age came. Poof! In a geological heartbeat, Nutcracker Man went extinct. Sebastien was experiencing his own personal Ice Age now. Was his dependence on his cell phone going to lead to his own extinction?

The hill flattened out. He had reached the top. Behind him, the trees formed a wall of utter blackness. To the left he could see clouds touching the horizon. Light from the moon traced their billowing edges. To the right was more of the same, but there were fewer clouds, and the night sky in this direction was freckled with stars. Directly ahead the horizon was broken up into dark geometric shapes—a few rectangles and a square. These must be buildings. Maybe they were occupied.

The frigid air was stinging his lungs, yet sweat was beading on his forehead. This was an ominous combination, he realized. In order to distract himself, he employed his usual technique— an internal dialogue of fretting and wondering. The Socratic method turned inward. He thought about Tiffany. Was she thinking of him? Did she realize he was gone? Would she be worried or indifferent? Would he survive long enough to propose—properly propose? And, oh yes, he would do that. And soon too. *If* he survived. Could this be a sign? *Better get your act together, Sebastien. Don't waste time. If you get back—no!—when you get back you need to seal this deal. But will she say yes? Is it too soon? Oh Lord.*

He shifted his thoughts to the events that led him here, to this wind-chilled plateau on the west side of the northern plains. He knew this was all wrong—or, at least, he *should* have known. Sitting in the back of Peter's BMW, he had that feeling of dread, but he couldn't reconcile it at the time. Now, looking back, it was clearly all bad. First of all, there was no chance in hell that any native tribe would allow a bunch of business people to walk off with a sacred piece of one of their ancestors —and certainly not for the purpose of scientific examination. He should have put that together long before being shot, crippled, and turned to ice. What would he look like when he was dead and the animals had gotten to him? Would somebody be poking at his corpse as it lay inside a thicket? *Oh Lord.*

The entire premise was stupid . . . yet he fell for it. What an idiot! Who in their right mind would undertake such a project? A native bone is a native bone, and no act of God or the devil will stop a proper archaeological assessment when remains or artifacts have been found. In hindsight it was all obvious. The bone didn't come out of any site, at least not recently. It was probably stolen to begin with. And what about the CRM company's assessment of the site? Sebastien was fairly confident these were fake or doctored. Same with the coroner's report from Pennington County. But how? More importantly, why? Why would Milo get him involved? Did they really need validation of their backfill story, or were they just using it as a ruse to get his attention? What was the motive?

Ah. Motive. *You're a fool, Sebastien. Motive is far more critical than you realized. In the absence of hard data, motive may be all you have.* Why lure him out to a pre-made hole in the ground and try to pick him off from long range? He didn't know anybody in South Dakota except for a few people at the sheriff's office and the coroner's office. Besides his family and Tiffany, that was really it. Sure, he had a few acquaintances. Could this be related to the earlier cases? Was this the West Side Silverbacks taking revenge? No, that couldn't be. Milo and his cohorts were not an outlaw motorcycle gang. What about the Boxwood Torso case? Now, that seemed a little more likely. But that homicide was thirty years old. Who would be left to exact revenge for the handful of villains he helped to put in jail? The only other truly culpable person in that case was dead.

Speaking of those earlier cases, he had gotten a fair amount of press since moving up here. It dawned on him that, while he may not know a lot of people, a lot of people knew him. At least, they knew *of* him. And didn't Milo mention something about his reputation? Yes, he did. Tiffany's, too. Didn't Milo *also* bring up the Amber Harrison case? Yes . . . it was the first thing he mentioned. He even offered to help. This must be the connection. But how would Milo and Fortunatas be connected?

16

"Sharon, it's Tiffany Reese. I have an exigent circumstance. I need to track a cell phone."

Hank and Tiffany were headed east in Hank's Tahoe after retrieving all of the Fortunatas documents from Sebastien's apartment, including the site map with the address. There was still no word from Sebastien. He hadn't answered their texts or calls, which was unusual for him. Tiffany tried to quell her panic and keep herself in law-enforcement-officer mode, but it was growing more difficult by the minute. Tracking Sebastien's cell phone might be premature—he was an adult, after all, and had only been "missing" for half a day—but waiting any longer was not on the table.

Tiffany gave the dispatcher the number and repeated it two more times, each followed by an impassioned "hurry!"

"Nine-two-five area code?" asked Sharon. "Is that your boyfriend, Doctor Grey?"

Tiffany ended the call and turned to Hank, who stared out over the steering wheel.

"Dispatch is on it. They're going to text me right back."

"Good."

"And how does everyone know that Sebastien and I are dating?"

"It's a small pond, Tiff. And my brother has made a pretty big splash."

Tiffany pushed a loud sigh through her lips.

"You going to be okay?"

She answered with a nod.

"I'm sure the little rat is fine. How much trouble could he be in? I'll tell ya this much, when we do get ahold of him, I'm going to tear him a new one," declared Hank.

How much trouble could he be in? Tiffany thought about that question and tried to answer it for herself. Knowing what she knew about Hank's brother, she couldn't imagine him subjecting himself to danger. Sebastien was no risk taker. She had picked up that much in the less than six months she'd known him. He wasn't all timidity and meekness though. She'd seen Sebastien stand up for himself—and for her!—enough times to know he could have a hair-trigger temper. But that was only in the face of some perceived wrong, and it was never with any hint of violence.

The cold window felt good on her skin as she rested her forehead against it, following the white line on the edge of the road as it passed by. Should she tell Hank about Sebastien's reservations about his little side job? Clearly he saw some ominous signs. He was suspicious. But she talked him out of those suspicions, didn't she? She tempted him with talk about her expensive taste in rings. No, that was not true. *Don't even go there*, she scolded herself. Sebastien knew full well she was joking.

Tiffany's phone dinged from between her knees on the passenger seat. It was dispatch.

"They say his phone is hitting off a tower at five-thousand-one Redtail Road in Rapid City. They're alerting RCPD."

"Is that near the construction site Sebastien was working?"

Tiffany pulled up the map on her phone and unfolded the site survey over her knees. Hank switched on the cab's interior light.

"You know it is. That tower looks to be southeast by a few miles, just off the highway."

"Remember what Erin told us. The tower could actually be quite a few miles from his phone. Can they be any more specific?"

Tiffany scrolled through the text from dispatch.

"Here it is. It says approximately twelve thousand feet northwest of sector one." Tiffany punched some numbers into her phone. "That's just over two miles."

"Okay, good," replied Hank. "And sector one. Which direction did Erin say that one pointed in?"

Tiffany lifted her head, thinking for a moment. "Remember, we don't know for sure. It all depends on the azi-something. But generally I think that's the one that faces north."

"Call dispatch back and have them make sure RCPD knows that. And let them know we'll be there in about twenty."

In the distance, beyond the entry gate, beams from half a dozen flashlights were cutting through the dark like lightsabers. Tiffany unbelted herself and jumped down from the Tahoe. Hank quickly followed.

"What the hell are they doing all the way up there?" she asked.

The pair made their way through the entry gate, which was wide open with the padlock obviously cut. Hank's own flashlight illuminated the ground as they headed north toward the searchers.

"Hey, you shouldn't be here. I'm going to have to ask you to leave the premises."

Hank trained his flashlight onto his badge, which was clipped to his belt.

"Sergeant Hank LeGris of the Custer County SO. This is

Detective Tiffany Reese."

"Geez, Sarge. Not in the eyes." Tiffany raised her forearm to block the two-thousand lumens that seared her corneas.

"Sorry."

"Oh, right," replied the uniformed woman who had approached them. "This is one of your guys we're looking for."

"Uh . . . sort of."

Tiffany quickly offered a correction to Hank's response. "Yes, it is. The missing person is our forensic scientist."

Tiffany heard a dog bark from up by the others, followed by some elevated voices.

"Any sign of him?" she inquired, tilting her head in the direction of the commotion.

"No, but we got his phone. It was lying in the mud in the next lot up. We also found some blood nearby—in two different places actually. The dog just got here. We're tracking it now. Come on up."

The area was completely flat and unencumbered, save for a stack of concrete pipes, a portable toilet, and a large earth-moving machine of some type. A little farther ahead, between the pipes and the portable toilet, two officers were examining the ground. A third was holding his flashlight under his arm while rolling out crime-scene tape between stakes. The officer who led them to the scene pointed northward and said, "The dog's got a scent."

Tiffany made to follow the officer, but Hank pulled at her elbow.

"Hang on. Look at that."

Hank's flashlight illuminated the ground a few feet to the right of them. It was a pile of snow, depressed in the middle and spotted with a dark liquid.

"He was here. He must have come onto the property from the gate. I don't see another way on."

Hank pointed the flashlight back in the direction from

which they came.

"According to the diagram, if I remember right, the bone was found in a trench to the east of the gate. What made him come back up this way? If it was him."

Hank waved his flashlight as an invitation for Tiffany to follow him back to the gate. Once there, Tiffany pointed eastward.

"Shine it this way," she said.

Sparse patches of snow sparkled under the beam as they proceeded carefully, trying to avoid falling into the trench. They needn't have worried. The darkness of the pit stood out in sharp contrast to the rest of the earth.

"Oh, man."

Tiffany looked down and saw what Hank had seen in the flashlight's brilliance. It was more dark liquid puddling at the bottom and smeared along the wall of the trench.

"And look there. Drag marks away from the hole."

"Dragging or crawling?"

"All right, I've seen enough, Reese. Now tell me everything you know about Sebastien's innocent little side job."

Tiffany insisted there wasn't much to tell, but still she unfolded everything to her sergeant. She told him about Milo, Fortunatas, the mysterious bone, and the envelope of money. She also confessed her part in coaxing Sebastien out of his initial reservations. Getting it all out helped her realize it was really not that sinister after all. It didn't sound high-risk or dangerous, anyway. If anything, it all seemed pretty silly. Thankfully, Hank seemed to concur.

"Is that it?" he asked. "And they were paying him a few thou?"

"I swear, Sarge. Unless Sebastien found out more, that's all there is to it."

"Obviously your boyfriend got himself into some sort of trouble."

"You keep saying that, but Sebastien isn't just my boyfriend. He's your brother and an important part of the team."

Hank looked back toward the searchers, who were now farther north, beyond the construction site.

"Nope. When there's trouble, he's all yours. Pull up that map on your phone, will ya?"

THE LARGE BLACK shape on the horizon turned out to be a barn. He knocked on the large swing door in the hopes that someone would be inside. Judging from the number of cows he'd just passed by in the pasture, and the piles of manure he'd stepped in, it was a good bet that some *thing* was in there, at least. At this point, he wasn't prepared to be picky. Some shelter would be welcome, if nothing else.

There was no answer, but the door creaked considerably as he pulled it open. His presence was now heralded. Sebastien's heart took a shot of adrenaline when he heard a horse neighing from deeper in the darkness. This was a positive sign. He closed the door behind him and stood stock-still in a blackness so thick he could almost feel it pressing down on his shoulders, willing him to the ground. He obliged the feeling and sat with his back against the door, waiting for his eyes to adjust so he could better make out his surroundings. There was more neighing, followed by a cat meowing—then, silence again.

After sitting for a few minutes, he felt an overwhelming lassitude. He must have burned through his last endorphin molecule—endorphins, stored in the pituitary gland, which sat inside the sella turcica of the sphenoid bone. And so it came full circle. It always came back around, back to where it started, didn't it?

Sebastien's head fell forward with a jerk, which roused him from his near plunge into slumber. He needed to fight it. He had to be alert and aware or else he would wake in the morning with Milo smiling over him with that rifle. Or maybe he wouldn't wake at all.

A soft purring to his immediate right, between his hip and the side of the barn, signaled the presence of one of the barn's residents. He reached down and felt for the cat, receiving some rough licks to his fingers.

"Well, hi, there, little guy. Where's your family? Are they nearby? You must have a human who takes care of you. Or do you eat rats and mice? Probably both, I bet."

Sebastien felt around the fur of the cat's neck and found a thin collar with a tag attached. It was too dark to read the tag, but it didn't matter. He'd found safety. There must be people nearby. He thanked the cat and reached into the darkness for something to use as leverage so he could stand up.

THE TRUCK WITH "A&M FABRICATION" stenciled on the doors sat idling on the Highway 90 frontage road. From here, Brian could see the flurry of activity in the distance. There were numerous lights, some red and blue, most the color of daylight, flashing, bobbing and bouncing. He looked up through the windshield expecting to see a helicopter with a high-powered spotlight scanning the ground, but there wasn't one that he could see—not yet, anyway. Regardless, there was no way in the world he was going up there. Game over, man. He thumbed Peter's number into his cell phone.

"Dude, where are you? The cops are all over up here."

"You should have been a Rhodes Scholar, Brian. I took off at the first sign of law enforcement. What took you so long?"

"Like I told Milo, I had to finish a job."

"That might have been a poor choice. We needed you. Sebastien Grey is out there somewhere and he's the only thing standing between us and life in prison. God willing, he's dead. But if he's not, and the police get to him first, you won't need that little job."

"Sebastien Grey? Who's that?"

"He's the guy the sheriff up in Custer brought in to work those cold cases. You know, like the Amber Harrison homicide."

"Homicide? Nobody knows that for sure."

"I'm afraid they do. And if they don't yet, it's only a matter of time."

"So what now?" asked Brian.

"First off, stay far away from there."

"Yeah, no kidding, Uncle Pete."

"You got your gun?"

Brian reached behind the truck's bench seat and felt around.

"Yeah, I got it."

"Good. Now, remember this—and don't write it down— head east on 90, then take the County Road Four exit. Turn left and head north about four miles. When you get to the top of the hill, make another left. Just a second, let me zoom in. Ah, yes. That's Spur Ranch Road. Make a left on that. Head about three miles and you'll see a road to the right. It dead ends about a quarter mile up. There's some ranches back in there. That's where Grey was headed when he got away. Don't do anything stupid or suspicious, but try and find him. You might get lucky. If you see him, shoot him."

"Well, that wouldn't be suspicious at all."

"This is not a joke, Brian. Don't let us down."

Let us down, thought Brian. *This whole deal was done and over until you old idiots opened it up like a can of tuna.* He should never have let himself get lured into this, but he was young and thought he was tough. He wanted to be a big shot, a player, a kingpin. Now all he wanted was to keep a low profile and take care of his wife and kids. He should be a lot more disturbed by everything that went down, everything they did. A normal person would feel bad about it. But not Brian. He had something missing inside. It must run in the family.

"What if the cops already found him?"

"What does it look like out there? What are the police doing?"

"I don't know. I just see a bunch of lights."

"They're still looking."

"How do you know?"

"Look, Brian. It's doesn't really matter. Just go where I told you. If you see the police, turn around and call me when you get back to the highway."

Brian tapped his fingers against the top of the truck door. He eyes darted around the dim cab. There was a lot to consider here. Peter was making this sound too easy.

"And what y'all going to do? You and Milo and Grandma. You aren't bailing on me, are ya? Y'all gonna be gone, aren't ya?"

"Get a grip, Brian. We're family. You're not on drugs again, are you? Don't lose your nerve."

Brian hung up and put the truck in reverse, punching the accelerator to affect a one-eighty on the gravel road. Now pointing south, he pulled the shifter into drive and headed for Highway 90.

Spur Ranch Road appeared pretty desolate. There was just one house on the left side, right at the turn from County Road 4. There were no lights on in the home, but Brian killed the truck's headlights as he drove past just in case. He pressed the reset button on the trip odometer and kept one eye on it. The road was sloping upward, climbing above what passed for civilization. Light pollution from Rapid City glowed faintly out his driver's side window. The distance and darkness made him feel a little more confident about not getting caught.

Brian lurched his head forward and slammed on the truck's brakes as dark shapes bounced from his right side periphery and into the road. He squinted. It was two deer heading down to lower ground. He waited, as there were always a few more—in his experience, anyway. Sure enough, more deer followed the first two and descended the dark slope. He took his foot off the brake pedal and continued his slow cruise up the hill.

Peter failed to figure out that the right turn was more like four miles up the road, not three. Nor did he disclose that there was a large house on the corner. Maybe it wasn't there on Peter's version of the map, Brian considered. No. It was clearly an old home. It could even be an estate, it was so big. Oh, damn! A square of yellow light came from one of the upstairs windows. Brian reversed for about thirty yards and left the truck on the shoulder of the road. Walking would be a lot safer.

He shoved the pistol into his belt at the small of his back and gently closed the truck door. Cutting across the sparsely wooded area to the east of the home, rather than following the road past the house, seemed a better plan. So he headed north-west in the darkness with only faint moonlight to reveal any obstacles on the ground, his breath forming a vapor. The earth was muddy and pocked. He nearly twisted his ankle more than once in holes that were a little too perfect to have been left by animals. Empty post holes, probably.

After walking for three or four minutes, Brian found himself at the end of the small road Peter had told him about. To his left he saw the rear of the house, only there were more lights visible on this side, all from the second level—and, unlike the side yard, the area to the back of the house looked to be manicured and maintained. He lowered himself and crept along through the grass behind the patio, on which were several chairs and a table. Up ahead, just beyond the house, he saw a large building, prob-ably a barn, by the shape of it. It was dark and could make a good hiding spot.

A shrill squeaking sound punctured the quiet as he took his next step forward. It came from a dog's toy, which he smashed under one of his steel-toe work boots. He froze and watched the back of the house. Sure enough, a light came on inside the home on the lower level. This was followed by an exterior light over the patio. Brian ran forward and dove behind the bushes that bordered the north side of the grass.

The back door opened and a woman came out. She was dressed in a robe and carrying a shotgun. She scanned the backyard, squinting, then walked onto the patio and raised the shotgun. Brian held his breath. The woman continued walking onto the grass directly toward his hiding place. He nearly wet himself. She was a mere thirty feet away and looked eager to blow something to pieces. The woman swept the shotgun to the right, away from him, then slowly brought it back in his direction. He couldn't tell if she saw him, but she was now pointing the barrel of the shotgun directly at him. He reached behind him and put his hand on the grip of his pistol. If he could avoid using it on this crazed housewife, he might still use it on his Uncle Pete.

Psycho lady lowered the shotgun and turned. Brian exhaled silently and watched as she walked back toward the house. She muttered something unintelligible and swung her right leg forward. The dog toy went flying onto the patio and bounced off of one of the chairs.

Once the coast was clear, Brian got up out the bushes and made for the barn. With that lady in the house, and who knew who else, his pistol would not be an option. He'd have to kill that guy as quietly as possible, if he could find him. This was a bad position to be in. He should have asked Pete if the guy was armed. Not that it would change anything. Uncle Pete would simply say: *We don't have a choice.* Fortunately, Brian always carried his custom-made hunting knife. He was proud of it and liked to show it off. It was one of the perks of working in the shop too. He had a pretty good side business making custom knives. He patted his thigh, confirming the antler handle still stuck up from the leather sheath.

17

There was nothing in his immediate proximity to grab ahold of, so Sebastien crawled forward, feeling the floor with his hand. A thin layer of straw covered the floor, some of which was moist. He tried not to think of what the cause for that could be as he groped his way deeper into the barn, like a blind beggar.

His hand struck something metal just above the floor. It was the spade end of a shovel, which had to be leaning against something. The horse stall, maybe? A few inches closer brought confirmation. Sebastien tried to find the top of the stable wall with his left hand, but his arm had stiffened in pain. He sat on his backside and used his feet to push his body back against the stable. From this position he could pull himself up with the handle of the shovel.

A flicker of light strobed across the far end of the barn. It was coming from outside at the rear of the building, seeping in between the gaps in the siding. As tempting as it was to think he was saved, Sebastien held himself still. He had no way of knowing who was out there, coming toward the barn with a flashlight. It could be the property owner, but it didn't mean he wouldn't get shot as an intruder. Maybe it was Milo. It didn't seem like he had made it too far from the construction site. It might be a better idea to stay low, he told himself. Stay low and stay still.

He felt the cat again, rubbing against his leg with the crown of its head.

"Shh," he whispered.

The light was closer, coming in from the side of the barn now. Dead vegetation snapped under the feet of whoever was out there. Sebastien began to doubt it was the property owner, only because they were walking very slowly, stopping at intervals to shine the light through the spaces in the siding boards. The cat was no longer moving, obviously alarmed at the approaching visitor. Sebastien took this to be a bad sign too.

Suddenly the cat pressed its paws into Sebastien's leg and sprang upward to the top of the stable wall, knocking the shovel off balance in the process. The resulting cacophony of metal against wood startled the horse, causing it to stomp and neigh. As if the cat hadn't done enough, it too began to vocalize the alarm.

"Who's in there?" came a voice from outside.

Sebastien froze.

"Come on out. I've got a gun."

A beam of light came in directly through the cracks, a little to Sebastien's left. The man had a flashlight or maybe a cell phone. Maybe it was the rancher. Sebastien was about to respond when the voice came again.

"That you, Grey?"

Sebastien reached out and found the handle of the shovel. He lifted it into his lap with his good arm and held it like a lance.

"Come on, man. I'm a cop. Let me give you a ride down. You okay? Are you hurt or anything? Dude, you must be freezing."

That was the answer Sebastien needed. There were way too

many things amiss to think the police were here to rescue him. Firstly, the police wouldn't be whispering. Secondly, *"Come on, man"*? *"I'm a cop"*? *"Dude"*? No way. Sure, police do talk like that, like everyone else—hell, his brother Hank was a great example —but not when they're trying to affect a commanding presence in an uncertain circumstance. Sebastien had been around cops for years, too long to not be tuned into such a nuance. He wrapped his fingers more tightly around the shovel and breathed through his nose.

The man was on the move again. The radiance from the flashlight flickered toward the front of the barn.

"Who the hell is out here?"

It was the voice of a woman coming from the same direction that the man with the flashlight had come.

"I've got a shotgun, and I'll take your head off. You hear me?"

The unmistakable sound of a pump-action shotgun being racked emphasized the woman's seriousness. The situation just got a lot worse.

One of the barn doors opened just enough for a man-sized shadow to enter. This resulted in a metallic skirl from the door hinges.

"Oh, that's it. I'm going to shoot right through the damn barn. I'll take your head off, you damn tweaker copper thief. Frank, get those dogs out here!"

A momentary blast of light hit Sebastien right in the face, followed by a shuffling sound. Whoever had entered the barn was now sitting right next to Sebastien.

"You better keep your mouth shut, man," the shadow barked. "That bitch is crazy."

Sebastien pointed the shovel at the man.

"Don't come near me. I'll scream."

"You'll scream? Oh, for . . ."

"Who are . . .?"

A blade of cold metal pressed against Sebastien's throat before he could finish his question.

"Shut up."

What sounded like a pack of wild dogs barking and yelping emerged from some distance behind the barn. They were headed this way, prodded on by another voice, not the woman's.

"Get 'em, girls. Sic! Sic!"

"He's in here," yelled the woman, who was now just outside the barn door.

"You say one word and I'll put a bullet in you and them people," muttered the shadow man, as he pressed the knife a little deeper into Sebastien's skin before jumping up and disappearing into the back of the barn.

Both barn doors flew open with a bang, and two huge dogs were on top of Sebastien in an instant. One pulled at his bloodied pant leg, the other pinned him to the ground while gaping and growling. Great strings of dog slobber fell into Sebastien's eyes and mouth.

Someone lifted a switch and the space became bathed in light.

"Come on, Penny, Molly. Get off the boy." The man pulled at the leash of the Rottweiler that was on top of Sebastien.

"What happened to you, boy?"

The woman with the shotgun looked down at Sebastien, surveying his various injuries and bloodstains. Despite her evident concern, she still had the barrel trained directly at him.

"That's what he gets when he messes with the girls."

"That weren't the girls, Frank. Look at him. What happened, son? You look like you need help."

Sebastien lay there on his back. He dared not point or motion to the rear of the barn, nor did he even mouth a warning to the ranchers. He didn't want to get them killed.

"Geez, Theresa. The man's busted all to hell. Can you get up, boy? Penny! Stay off of him."

The man snapped at the dog and approached Sebastien, kneeling over him. He looked like he was about to pat Sebastien down, but something gave him pause—probably the sight of all the blood and dirt.

"You need to answer me. What's your name? How did you get here? Can't you talk?"

Sebastien shifted his eyes to the lady again. She still had the shotgun at the ready. There was a good chance she could pick off the shadow man, but he had to get out of the way.

"He's got a gun," yelled out Sebastien, just before rolling over and putting his good arm over his head. Sound waves from the gun battle smashed into his eardrums and the smell of hay and gunpowder filled his nose. A crushing weight against his back pinned him against the floor. He opened his eyes and saw the massive black head of a dog drooped over his shoulder. The dog's eyes rolled upward and its tongue painted his cheek with spit as Sebastien turned his head to the right. Still, he dared not try to extricate himself for fear of being struck by the gunfire that continued to fly over his head.

The chaos of the volley ceased, and Sebastien heard the woman scream "Frank!" He looked up just in time to see his attacker emerge from behind the back wall of the stable, pistol in hand. He lowered and covered his head once again, expecting to be shot. Instead he felt the man push the dog's body off of his back.

"Come on, prick!" the man shouted.

The man pulled Sebastien by the back of his shirt along the floor toward the rear of the barn. In less than a few seconds, Sebastien found himself outside. He tasted the rough grass and dirt and felt the dewy moisture. Once completely out of the barn, the man flipped him onto his back.

"Get up," he ordered.

"Who are you? What are you doing?"

Without replying, the man threaded his arms under Sebastien's shoulders and lifted him onto his feet.

"I can't walk. Get your hands off me!" cried Sebastien, before his head exploded in pain, before the stars filled his eyes, before his muscles went limp and his consciousness left him.

"DID YOU HEAR THAT?" asked Tiffany.

Hank nodded and gunned the Tahoe to the top of the hill. He parked it in front of a large old house and they both jumped out, drawing their weapons and readying their flashlights.

"Call it in," ordered Hank.

Hank went to the front door and did a knock and announce. Tiffany peered into the front room window. There were lights on at the back of the house but no movement within.

"It's coming from behind the house."

Hank stabbed his finger in the direction of the frantic barking, and Tiffany nodded.

The pair hurried up the side of the house until they reached the back corner. Hank poked his head forward just enough to see into the backyard.

"Follow me."

Before Hank could move, Tiffany grabbed his shoulder.

"Are you okay?"

"What are you talking about, Reese?"

"Well. You know. You've been through . . . I mean, you just got . . ."

"Detective Reese, shut your friggin' pie hole and follow me. There's a light on over the patio. Stay out of it."

Hank ran forward beyond the end of the patio, and Tiffany followed him. Once on the grass, they went low and surveyed the area. With the last of the booming echoes faded into the night, they were able to make out the sound of someone yelling.

"It's coming from that building," Tiffany said.

"Wait? Do you hear that? Someone's calling for help."

They approached carefully at first, unable to discern much, but got a better look within fifty yards.

Somebody was jumping and waving at them.

"Cover me," Hank said to Tiffany.

Tiffany advanced another dozen yards and took a position behind a tree. She watched as Hank ran toward the animated figure. His weapon was still drawn. She heard him shout.

"Keep your hands up. Keep 'em up."

She lost Hank in the shadows to the side of the building, so she moved closer and took a position behind a shed on the far side of the house. Her radio crackled with life. It was Hank. He was calling for medical.

Tiffany rushed ahead, past the woman who had been flagging them over. She was holding a large dark dog by the collar. The animal was agitated, snapping and barking at Tiffany.

"Get that thing locked away," Tiffany instructed.

She turned the corner to the front of the barn, spotting Hank's kneeling figure silhouetted against the light from the barn.

"Oh my God, is that Sebastien?" she asked.

"No. It's the guy who lives here. He's been shot in the leg. The medical bag is in the back of the Tahoe. Go get it—the Tahoe, I mean. Drive right up here."

Tiffany turned to run back to the Tahoe, getting a look inside the barn as she did so.

"Is he okay?"

"He'd be better with that medical bag!" shouted Hank.

WITHIN A QUARTER OF AN HOUR, the place was a veritable hive. Law enforcement from Rapid City and Pennington County were setting up lights, taping off the scene, and taking statements.

"Is he going to live?"

The Pennington County sheriff deputy tried to sound reassuring.

"Yes, ma'am. We think so. The paramedics said your husband was lucky."

"What about Penny?"

"Penny, ma'am?"

"My dog."

The deputy glanced into the barn.

"I'm afraid not."

"Did you check? Did someone check?

"She's dead, ma'am. I'm sorry. She might have saved your life though. Tell me again what happened once more. I'll need an official statement."

Theresa recounted how she heard noises in her backyard and went out to check on what it could be. They've had problems with thefts recently.

"And did you have the shotgun when you went out to check?"

"Yes, I did. But I didn't see anything. It was only when I went back in and upstairs that I saw a light by the barn. The bedroom window faces that way."

"I see. And you went back out? Pretty brave of you, ma'am."

"I know how to use a shotgun, Deputy."

The deputy once again looked toward the barn door.

"Yes, you certainly do. So, you came down the second time. What next?"

"I heard a sound in the barn. Someone was in there. I told Frank to bring the dogs out. Sure enough, they went ballistic. We opened the barn door and flipped on the light. He was just lying there."

"Who was just lying there? The man with the gun?"

"No, the other man. He looked injured. Frank went to see if he needed help and the man yelled something like, 'He has a gun!' That's when it started."

"That's when the shooting started?"

"Right. I saw the guy—the guy with the gun—pop up from behind the horse stall. He shot at Frank. Penny jumped at him. That's when she got shot."

"Uh huh. And what happened next? What did you do?"

"Well, Deputy, I took a shot at him, but I must have missed. Blew a hole through the barn though. He fired back, and I tried to take another shot at 'em. The gun jammed. That's when I saw the man on the ground—the injured man—get dragged through the back of the barn. The guy who was shooting at me just dragged him and took off."

"Did you see where they went?"

"No. I checked on Frank."

"And what about him?" The deputy pointed with his pen at the agitated Rottweiler. "Did he chase after the guy?"

"You mean her? No. Molly stayed by Frank the whole time."

MILO WAS WALKED out of the hospital at three that morning. The doctors wanted to keep him overnight, but he declined, Edith's badgering notwithstanding. It was a nasty contusion accompanied by a low-grade concussion, but his skull was not broken. Head injuries bled like the dickens though. That was what the doctor told him. Not that he needed any further education in that department. He was glad he wasn't wearing his good coat when that prick Grey hit him with the rock.

No one other than Abigail and Peter knew what had actually happened. And Grey himself, of course. No, he'd told the emergency room doctor he had a bad fall coming out of his office on a patch of ice. Whoever was responsible for clearing the snow and laying the salt was gonna get sued. They could bet their lives on it, or so he said.

Without knowing what was going on with Grey, he simply could not afford to be reposing in the hospital. Milo was not prone to anxiety or excessive worry, but in this case he was very much on edge. Grey needed to be dead. Every cat was, or would be, out of the proverbial bag now. In hindsight, proactively going after the Custer County forensic anthropologist was a bad idea of the highest magnitude. But what was done was done. And, in the absence of news about Grey's demise, Milo's first priority was to collect his passport from his safe at home and his emergency stash from his safe deposit box at the bank. There was another regret. It was hard to flee when he had to wait for the bank to open.

Edith steered the Cadillac into their neighborhood and approached the left turn that would bring them home.

"Are you sure you're all right, dear?" she asked. "You seem out of sorts."

"I just cracked my skull open, Edith. That's doesn't make for a good mood. And I'm tired. I have a lot to do tomorrow, and I need to get up early."

"You shouldn't be working tomorrow. You need to rest, and I don't think you broke your skull. The doctor said you got a bad cut and a bruise."

Milo didn't reply. Arguing was pointless.

"Wait. Stop here."

"What is it?"

Edith pulled to the curb and leaned toward her husband, craning to see what he was seeing.

"You know what, sweetheart. You're right. I'm in no shape to work. What do you say we spend a couple of days at the lake house?"

"That would be lovely! What a wonderful idea. You should

sleep in a little before we go. I'll call Peter in the morning and tell him to leave you be."

Before Edith could pull the shifter into drive, Milo put his hand on hers.

"No. Let's go now. I'll be able to sleep longer if we go out there as soon as we can."

Edith sat back in the driver's seat and pursed her lips at him.

"What about packing?" she asked.

"Bah! We have everything we need out there already. And you know Peter. He'll just send someone after me if I don't come in. And I don't need that. The doc said my blood pressure was up too."

"Did he say that? I don't remem—"

"Edith, just turn around. We'll be there before the sun comes up."

18

"It was that truck, that truck we passed. Whoever was in that truck had Sebastien."

"We don't know that for sure. But it makes sense."

They were standing on the large front porch of Milo's two-story home in Colonial Pine Hills. The neighborhood was quiet at this time of night, but it was probably always quiet. There was no answer and no response to Hank's demands to open the door, so he motioned to the Pennington County sheriff deputies to force it open. The sound of the door being bashed was quickly followed by lights being switched on in homes along the street.

"Milo Crane! Pennington County sheriff! Come on out! Make yourself known!"

Once the residence was cleared by Pennington County, Tiffany and Hank walked into the entry hall. The house was dark, except for a small table lamp illuminating the front room.

"I'll take upstairs," said Tiffany.

Hank nodded and proceeded to search the living room. The local deputies likewise spread out for the search.

There were four bedrooms upstairs. Tiffany searched each

of them carefully. She went through dresser drawers, looked under mattresses and beds, pulled pictures and mirrors off walls, and even felt for hollow spots under the carpet. She wasn't sure exactly what she was looking for, but Milo had to be involved somehow and, that being the case, there must be some clue pointing toward where Sebastien had been taken.

She crossed the landing at the top of the stairs and entered the master bedroom. Tiffany ran her hands over the duvet that covered the large bed. She lifted the mattress but found nothing. There were dressers on two of the walls and nightstands on either side of the bed. Tiffany looked through all of these, finding only what one would expect: clothes, underwear, socks, as well as a revolver in the top drawer of one of the nightstands, which she unloaded and bagged. A sense of urgency and disappointment started to take hold, but what did she expect to find —a file folder labeled, "This is where I take my victims"?

Tiffany let out a whistle as she entered the walk-in closet. It was massive and featured two built-in wardrobes, one of which was in the center of the closet. She patted down the clothing items that hung around the perimeter of the space, discovering several folded bills in large denominations—mostly fifties and hundreds, a few twenties. She replaced these and pushed aside the hanging clothes to see what, if anything, was behind them. The closet was lined with cedar panels—of course it was!—but nothing was stashed in the darkness.

The floor of the closet was neat and orderly, covered by possibly hundreds of shoes that were paired up and ready to go. There was something about their arrangement that seemed off, or maybe it was the opposite—as she stepped back for a broader look, she noticed the shoes were arranged underneath the hanging items they would most likely be worn with. At least, it seemed that way to Tiffany. She got on her knees and searched through every pair, once again finding nothing.

Shifting her attention upward, she saw that a shelf lined the walls of the closet near the ceiling. On this shelf were dozens of shoeboxes, double stacked—and shoeboxes, she knew from the many searches she had participated in, often contained the most important things. She excitedly pulled these down and went through them, but with a sense of humorous irony, she found only women's shoes in the boxes—the most predictable find was the least expected.

Tiffany now stood in the middle of the closet, surrounded by spilled shoeboxes and just about every type of footwear a person could want. She was under no obligation to restore the order she had so enthusiastically destroyed, she knew. But she wasn't that kind of cop. And besides, now that the search was beginning to look futile, she wasn't even certain about Milo's culpability in Sebastien's disappearance. There was no point in leaving his place in shambles.

After reboxing the shoes, she began to stack them on the shelf once more. Getting them replaced in their original order would be impossible, so she opted for speed over accuracy. Tiffany was anxious to find out what, if anything, the others had uncovered. However, her haste didn't prevent her from noticing the square aperture in the ceiling above the shelf—an attic door.

"Where are you going, Reese?" Hank asked as she passed him in the family room.

"The garage," she responded. "I'm looking for a ladder. I wanna get into the attic."

"Sounds dangerous. Let me help."

Hank paused his search through the bookshelf in the family room and followed Tiffany into the garage.

"Very funny, Hank. I can handle myself."

"I know you can, Detective. But I like your company better than these locals."

The attic was unfinished and filled with blown-in insulation and exposed studs, joists, and beams. Tiffany reached down into the side pocket of her cargo pants and pulled out a pair of leather gloves while Hank held the ladder. With her hands protected, she ascended to the penultimate rung and patted around the insulation near the attic opening.

"Watch out for raccoons. Those suckers are mean."

Tiffany lowered her head through the opening and gave Hank a look.

"I don't understand how you can joke, boss. Sebastien is in real trouble."

"I know he is. Why do you think I'm joking? I'm trying not to think of the worst-case scenario."

After a few minutes of searching, Tiffany's hand found something buried in the insulation, just below a section of duct. It was about the size of her hand.

"Got something. There's something here."

"Nice! What is it?"

"Gross. It's a dead bird. Hang on, I'll throw it down."

"Wait! No, don't do tha—. Oh, I see. You're as worried as I am."

Tiffany turned on the ladder with her head still in the attic and resumed fingering through the insulation. Doing so reminded her of when she had searched the slope of the creek in the hills last summer with Hank and Sebastien, though she was ungloved for most of that effort. Her mind wandered a bit. She tried to recall if she felt anything for Sebastien on that sunny day. Did she have any idea what that fateful collaboration would ultimately produce, both professionally and personally?

She made another ninety-degree turn on the ladder. On the third pat into the cloud-like material, her hand struck something hard and flat. Excitedly, she cleared off the insulation to reveal a small lockbox.

"A safe! I found a safe!"

"Bingo!" called up Hank. "It's always the attic with these bozos."

The box was relatively light. She handed it down to Hank, then went back into the attic and poked around some more.

"Is there a key up there?" Hank was trying the lid of the lock-box, which was a little smaller than a briefcase.

"I'm not seeing one. Let's just bust it open."

Tiffany and Hank went into the garage again and searched through the various cabinets and drawers built into the garage wall. Tiffany found a hammer and a large flathead screwdriver.

"I don't know if that's gonna open it."

"It's worth a shot, boss."

Tiffany wedged a screwdriver in the seam between the lock-box's lid and the base, wiggling the tool and testing the strength of the lock. It wouldn't budge. She handed the hammer to Hank and motioned for him to use it against the heel of the screw-driver, which she held in place under the keyhole.

"Hold that sucker down," he told her.

Hank drove the hammer against the screwdriver with loud reverberating blows.

"I don't think it's going to give, Sarge."

"It'll give. Here, let's do this." Hank took the lockbox and put it on its back edge. "Hold it there," he said.

Hank position the screwdriver with the tip wedged in the gap of the lockbox's door, and drove the screwdriver downward with a series of grunts that matched the tempo of the hammer. Cracking and popping sounds echoed throughout the garage and probably throughout the entire neighborhood. Finally, after several strikes, the box opened like a clam.

The contents of the lockbox consisted of typical items that one might want to keep secure. There were passports in the names of Milo and Edith Crane, car titles for a Mercedes and a Cadillac, birth certificates, and various pieces of jewelry. At the bottom of the safe was a file folder. Tiffany pulled it out and opened it on the garage's workbench.

"Ah, look at this," she said.

"It's like paperwork for the house—mortgage and title-type stuff."

"Yeah," agreed Tiffany, holding up one of the stapled stacks. "But not just this house. Look at this address. Dumont."

"That's up in Lawrence County. Maybe it's a vacation home? Lots of city people have lake houses up there."

"Yes, and maybe that's where Sebastien is."

The fluorescent bars on the garage ceiling reflected off of Tiffany's widened brown eyes. Hank seemed uncertain.

"Maybe," he said. "I guess we can get someone out there. But I don't know. I mean, look at the pictures around this place. I haven't met this guy—I know you have—but he looks like an old dude. He doesn't look like he would kidnap or hurt anybody."

"I know that, Hank. But he's connected. He's involved somehow."

"Okay, but we need to hit this guy's office too. What did you say the company was called?"

"Fortunatas Development. The address is on the paperwork for the construction site. I left it in the Tahoe."

"Hang tight a sec."

Tiffany watched Hank disappear into the house, then went back to rifling through the lockbox. Examining the jewelry in the yellow fluorescent light of the garage did not tell her anything about where she might find her boyfriend, who was almost certainly in peril, but she needed to do *something*. She couldn't just stand there while her mind imagined horrible images of Sebastien on an autopsy table because they couldn't get to him fast enough. How would that be for irony! The examiner becomes the examined! It was unthinkable. They just got started, she and Sebastien. And they were too good of a team to let it all end because of some stupid CRM job. This was supposed to be easy, laughably mundane. Her eyes began to moisten as she looked around the garage, searching for some clue.

"All right, here's the deal. You and I are going to hit this lake house, pronto. Rapid City is getting a search warrant for the office. These fellas are going to go there next. Oh, and get this. The crime scene techs found fingerprints all over that barn. And yes, they're processing them as we speak. This is everyone's priority, Tiff."

"Are we going to have the locals go to the lake house and see if he's there? It would be a lot quicker that way."

Hank looked dubious.

"I just don't know. You never can tell with those small departments in the middle of nowhere. You know how it is. They drive by, everything looks quiet, and they don't even stop."

"I think you're being a little unfair, Hank. I'm sure they know what they're doing. I'm worried. Sebastien could be dead. They could've killed him by now."

"I know you are, Tiffany, and I am too. That's why I want to handle this. And think about it, the guy at the ranch had a gun. He could easily have killed Sebastien in the barn then took off. He could've killed that lady too. He took Sebastien alive. I think that's a good sign. Don't get me wrong . . . I have no idea what's going on here. But again, Sebastien could be getting loaded into the coroner's van up at that ranch right now, but he isn't."

Tiffany tried to think through Hank's logic. She had to admit, it did make sense—not that she felt any better about it. Sebastien was obviously in danger, and who knew what was happening to him at that very moment? They had to find him quickly. She didn't necessarily agree with Hank's opinion about the locals up at the lake, but she understood where he was coming from.

"How long do you think it will take us to get there?" asked Tiffany.

"An hour and fifteen if we haul ass."

"Okay, then. Let's haul ass."

They headed north in silence, each lost in their own

thoughts, imagining their own scenarios. Soon, they broke free of any semblance of civilization. The plains with their grassy coverings yielded to coniferous forests, blanketed in deep snow. Thirty minutes into the trip the sun was just barely breaching the horizon behind them, casting an amber glow into the Tahoe.

Tiffany watched the trees go by to avoid closing her eyes. She was wrapped in fatigue and the rhythm of the tires on the plowed road was threatening to lull her into a deep sleep. But she couldn't afford to get a nap in, fearing she would be too drowsy to be of use when they reached their destination. Fortunately, an unrelenting anxiety rescued her from being overtaken by sleep.

Hank couldn't find the road listed on the paperwork for Milo's lake house, so they stopped at a diner for coffee and insight. It was one of those stereotypical mom-and-pop stores that happened to feature a small restaurant with checkered cloths on small rectangular tables, and farm implements nailed to the wall. The coffee was thick and the customers sparse.

"There's one other thing you might be able to help us with," said Hank to the middle-aged woman who stood behind the counter.

"What's that, honey?" the woman replied, tipping a coffee pot over Hank's newly emptied cup.

"We're looking for this address. I can't seem to find the road. I guess you could say we're a bit lost. Any idea where this is?"

Hank pulled a folded piece of paper from his jacket and flattened it onto the counter. The waitress put on a pair of large glasses, which had been hanging from a chain around her neck, then simultaneously looked down and rotated her head over the page.

"Oh, sure," she said. "You're from Rapid City, are ya?"

Hank and Tiffany replied affirmatively in unison.

"Then you would have passed that road about three miles

back. There isn't really a sign for it, at least not like an official one. It's just a piece of wood nailed to a tree."

"That must be why we missed it," offered Tiffany.

"A lot of people miss that road. Not that many people try to find it. That's them fancy lake houses. Those kinds of folks generally discourage traffic or visitors."

Hank tapped the counter.

"So, this address is up that road? Any idea about how far?"

The woman picked up the sheet of paper and brought it closer to her face.

"Sixty-Three-Seventy-Three. Oh, sure, that's the Crane place. It's just a few miles up."

Tiffany was impressed.

"Excuse me, ma'am, but how do you know that? You don't know everyone's address up here, do you?"

The woman peered at Tiffany from over the top of her reading glasses.

"Yes, I do, young lady. I deliver the mail in this zip code. What are you doing up here, may I ask? It's pretty early. And, like I said, those lake house folks don't like visitors much—especially ol' Milo and Edith."

Hank showed the woman his badge. Tiffany did the same.

"Oh no, is there some sort of trouble?" The waitress appeared genuinely concerned.

"No. No, ma'am. We just need to pay the Cranes a visit. There's nothing to worry about."

Tiffany quickly interjected, "You haven't seen them, have you? Recently? Today, I mean."

"Why, yes. Are you sure they're not in trouble?"

It occurred to Tiffany that the woman was likely the hub of Dumont gossip. Working at the diner and serving as postmistress in such a small town would definitely give her the inside scoop on just about everything that happens within a five-mile radius.

"No, ma'am," Hank replied with a disarming tone. "Like I said, no trouble. We're just trying to track them down because we recovered some property that we think came out of a burglary at their place in town. We were hoping they could take a look at the items and verify if they do belong to them."

The woman wiped her hands on her apron and smiled in relief.

"Oh, well that makes sense. Too bad about the burglary. That's why folks come up this way. Everybody knows everybody up here and people who don't belong tend to stick out like piss in the snow. Just last summer, the Hendricksons had a stereo stolen right out of their boat. And it was on their own dock too! It turned out to be the Carpenter's drug-addled nephew and his pregnant girlfriend. Only sixteen! Can you imagine? Now, the Carpenters don't exactly agree with the politics around here either. But law and order is important, isn't it? You two understand that, I'm sure. But the Carpenters—well, they'll figure it out."

Hank was still laughing at the yellow snow simile. Tiffany found it less amusing, feeling they were wasting their time with small talk in the diner.

"But you did see them?" Tiffany demanded.

"Yes. I saw Mrs. Crane earlier—about an hour ago, in fact. I guess you could say you just missed her."

"Really? They're here now?"

"She is. I'm not sure about Mr. Crane. But she was in here earlier, picking up some supplies."

Hank and Tiffany pushed their way through the door of the store-slash-diner, which slammed behind them with a bang.

Tiffany snapped on her seatbelt and said, "They're here. Could be just a coincidence, though."

Hank gave only a doubtful grunt in response.

"Should we call for backup?"

"For a couple of fogeys? No, I think we can handle it, Reese."

19

With the aid of the waitress's instructions, finding the road wasn't too problematic. The plank of wood that marked the turn was painted roughly the same shade of brown as the tree trunk to which it was affixed, and the lettering on the sign was white. In the middle of the snowy woods, the sign was near perfectly camouflaged.

From the highway, the road was unplowed, but the Tahoe easily crawled through, deepening the slush-filled tracks left by other vehicles. Through the trees on their left side, they saw the early morning sun shimmer off the still lake. Across the lake, homes with large decks and steep stairwells straddled the steep slope that led from the road to the water's edge and down to the water. It was only logical to conclude that the homes on this side of the lake would be similar—appearing as one story from the road, but really two levels, with the lower being concealed behind the decline.

Tiffany and Hank both squinted into the tree-broken sunrise, trying to make out the house numbers as the Tahoe finally reached the first of the homes on the west side of the lake. All the structures were similar in design—cedar and river stone exteriors and pale-red metal roofs. The main concession to originality seemed to be the various small statues that bordered driveways and front porches: moose, bear, deer, bison, and even Bigfoot.

"There. That's it." Tiffany pointed over the steering wheel.

Hank pulled as far as he could to the opposite side of the road, and the pair surveyed the front of Milo's house. The front porch was covered and to the left of it was a large picture window, through which could be seen another window on the lake side of the home. The interior of the house, at least what they could see of it, was filled with the early morning's radiance. But neither detected any movement within the home or signs of anyone having tramped up the snow-covered walk and through the front door. There were, however, tire tracks in the driveway that terminated at the garage door.

"Interesting."

"What, Hank? What do you see?"

"Look at the driveway. See the tire tracks in the snow? They're way wider than the tracks from four tires rolling through once"

Tiffany wasn't following. She shook her head and replied, "Okay. What are you getting at? You think more than one car drove into the garage?"

Hank looked at her, signaling disappointment with his half-rolled eyes.

"I won't tell your smarty-pants boyfriend you said that. No, if there were two cars in that garage, there would be four distinct tracks on the driveway, a pair on each side. Probably, anyway. What I mean is that someone drove the car in, then backed out and drove it in again."

"They've entered twice. Okay. I see that. What does it mean?" Tiffany chose to ignore her sergeant's condescending reprimand.

"The lady at the store said Crane's wife was in there earlier.

She was alone. Now, it could be that she went here first, then left later for groceries. But if you needed supplies for your stay, wouldn't you just go to the store first, then back to the house? Why make an extra trip in the cold?"

"No offense, boss, but I think you're overanalyzing. Are you trying to channel Sebastien? What if she needed to check to see what she already had in the house before going to the store? And why would it matter anyway?"

"Am I? If your Crane guy wanted to keep a low profile, he wouldn't show up in the town's version of Grand Central, would he? Not with that busybody working in the place. He'd get dropped off first."

"What's the plan? Just walk up to the front door?"

"Unless you have a better idea."

Hank didn't wait for a response before sliding out of the Tahoe. Tiffany followed him across the snowy road toward the house.

"Mrs. Crane? Mrs. Crane? This is the Custer County sheriff. I would like to have a word with you."

Tiffany was shivering next to Hank on the porch. It must have been a good twenty degrees colder up here than it was down in town.

"Mrs. Crane, we know you're here. Please come to the door. We're here on official business."

Tiffany brought her face up to the leaded sidelight window, next to the front door. There was a shadow playing off the wall in the hallway to the left. She looked at Hank and pointed in the direction of the movement.

"Someone's definitely in there," she said.

The pair waited several more minutes, but still no one came to the door.

"That's it. I'm going around to the back."

"Wait. I'll go with you."

"No, you stay here in case someone tries to leave out the front."

The sound of snow crunching broke the eerie stillness as Hank crossed the driveway to the side gate. Once she could no longer hear it, Tiffany tried another few knocks on the door, then waited. Still nothing.

Tiffany turned on the doorstep and blew hot breath into her palms as she looked up and down the road in front of the house. It was beautiful here. Just the kind of place she would like to have one day. It was probably a little too rural for Sebastien, but the houses were set fifty yards or so from each other and featured pine trees serving as privacy fences. The doctor would appreciate the solitude. Oh, Sebastien. Where the hell was he?

On the opposite side of the road, the sun illuminated the outer edge of a thick forest. Some of the trees were circumscribed by pink ribbons. Tiffany hoped inwardly they weren't tagged for removal. That would be a shame. Maybe they were going to clear the land for more lots. Such a move would make her livid if she lived up here. Way to spoil a view.

As she turned toward the door, Tiffany thought she caught sight of snow falling from a tree limb. She traced the trees upward, expecting to find a squirrel or bird, but it was too dark to see. That's why they call it the Black Hills.

A shadow fell across one of the columns that held up the porch roof. Light from inside the home was momentarily obscured. Someone was moving about in the hallway. She spun around just in time for the front door to open. It was an older woman dressed in jeans and a heavy wool sweater. Her hair was short and gray, and her eyes were bright blue. Her wide, pleasant smile was obviously forced.

"Can I help you?" she asked.

"I hope so. I'm Det. Reese with the Custer County Sheriff's Office."

Edith Crane took Tiffany's offered hand as she stuck her head past the threshold, looking left and right.

"Where is the man who was with you?"

"Oh, he'll be right back. He just went to the car."

"What can I do for you? Is there some sort of problem?"

"Ma'am is your husband home? It's him we're looking for."

"My husband is asleep. He's had a very traumatic evening."

"May I ask what happened?

"I'm afraid he took a fall. His head is horribly injured. He really needs to sleep. The doctor insisted. I'll have to ask you to come back later."

Tiffany tried to look concerned, but it was not Milo she was most concerned about.

"I'm so sorry to hear that. When did this happen?"

Edith's face lit up. Her eyes widened.

"Is that why you're here? Milo's accident?"

Several options manifested themselves in Tiffany's mind as she searched for a response. Whatever happened to Milo, an accident—real or not—could be a good cover story for her visit. Maybe Edith was helping Milo set up an alibi and this would be good opportunity to dismantle it. That wouldn't help her find Sebastien though. No. She would have to be direct.

"No, Mrs. Crane. I'm here on a separate matter. I'm loo—"

"Detective, I'm going to have to ask you to come back later."

Tiffany stuck her toe in the door before Edith had it fully closed.

"I'm sorry, ma'am, but that's not at all possible. You see, I'm looking for a missing person and I believe your husband knows where he is."

"I'm sorry, Miss. But I don't think Milo knows anything about that."

Edith responded with a certainness that troubled Tiffany. *She must know*, she thought. She's covering for him.

"With all respect, ma'am, I need to ask him that myself."

"You'll have to come back, Detective. My husband has got a concussion and he's in no state to speak with anyone. Doctor's orders. I told you that."

"Fine, Mrs. Crane. In that case, I'll just wait in my car until the warrant arrives."

"Warrant? Whatever do you need a warrant for?"

"And I've already told you that. I'll be in my car. Let me know if your husband becomes available before that warrant gets here and we take apart your pretty house."

Tiffany was firm yet smiling. She turned to walk down from the porch.

"Uh . . . Detective."

Tiffany pivoted to face Edith, concealing her smirk.

"Yes, ma'am."

"You really shouldn't be out there in the cold. Why don't you come in. I'll make some coffee."

"Thank you, Mrs. Crane. Coffee would be wonderful."

The Crane's lake house was as immaculate as their Rapid City home. The interior walls of the living room were covered in redwood planks set diagonally. On the table in the entry stood two framed pictures, one of a large family beaming wide smiles with the lake in the background. The other was a picture of Edith wearing a summer hat and holding a rose near her cheek.

"That's a lovely picture, Mrs. Crane. Was that professionally done?"

"No, Milo took that. He is a whiz with a camera. Thank goodness, too, because I'm not."

Tiffany followed her through the living room and into a small breakfast nook behind the kitchen. A large picture window framed the lake behind the house.

"Sit here. Make yourself comfortable."

Edith pulled a chair out for Tiffany who sat, taking a furtive look through the window and into the backyard. She didn't see any sign of Hank.

Edith walked to the kitchen and lifted the pot from the coffee maker. The act reminded Tiffany of Mickey McCallister's slit throat and Sebastien's eye for detail. It seemed like so long ago that Sebastien helped out on that first case.

"What do you take in yours, Detective Reese?"

"Black is fine for me, thank you. So, can you tell me more about what happened to your husband last night?"

"I told you. He slipped on the ice outside of his office. He says he wants to sue them, but I don't think he will. He was just angry and probably embarrassed. Milo has had a lot of health issues in the last few years, and I think it's hurting his pride, if I may be honest. But I told him, it's not a big deal. These things happen, don't they?"

"Yes, ma'am, I suppose they do. Were you with Mr. Crane when he fell?"

"I was at home. He called me when he was on the way to the hospital."

"So, you didn't actually see him fall?"

Edith handed the mug to Tiffany and sat opposite her at the breakfast table.

"I didn't. What are you trying to say? Are you saying you don't think he fell? Believe me, Detective. I've seen his head. It looks awful. Milo is on blood thinners, you know. And I can show you his clothes, if you really want to see them. They're ruined, of course."

"No, I believe you, ma'am. I mean, I believe that your husband got injured. I'm just trying to figure out what really happened."

"I told you what happened. And who is this missing person?"

"He's a colleague of mine. A Doctor Sebastien Grey. He is a forensic scientist with the Custer County Sheriff's Office. Have you ever heard of him?"

Edith held the cup up to her lips and blew gently on the hot liquid.

"No, I don't believe I have. Should I have?"

"I just was wondering, ma'am, if your husband had mentioned him before."

The woman shook her head and said, "You know, my Milo doesn't work criminal cases. He's a corporate lawyer—real estate, to be more specific. He tells me he doesn't like it very much. He's getting ready to retire soon anyway."

"You weren't aware that your husband engaged Dr. Grey to help him in a real estate matter? It involves a site that Fortunatas Development is improving on the northeast side of Rapid City. Apparently, there were some bones found on the site. Your husband asked Dr. Grey for his opinion on how they may have gotten there."

"He didn't say anything about that to me. Sounds very boring. Milo doesn't talk much about his work with me, thank heavens. I have better things to think about."

"Such as?"

"Grandchildren, for one. And I take care of my mother. She's in a home, you know. I think Milo resents the time I spend with her. But what am I to do? So, you think my husband's work has something to do with your missing scientist?"

"Yes. I'm sure of it. You see, your husband and my—I mean, Dr. Grey—were scheduled to meet yesterday afternoon. We have evidence that Dr. Grey was at the site in question, and we have further evidence that he was injured while there. We know he was forcibly taken from the area last night. I don't think it's a coincidence all of that happened on the day your husband sustained an injury. So that's two people working on the same real estate matter getting hurt on the same day—really at the same time."

Edith put her coffee down and turned in her chair to face Tiffany.

"Are you saying you think Milo is responsible for the disappearance of this man, Dr. Grey? Why ever would he do that?"

"I'm not saying he's responsible, ma'am, but I do think it's all connected. That's why I need to talk to him—and I'd like to do so as soon as possible. Are you sure he's too incapacitated to have a quick word with me?"

Edith let out a breath.

"It does sound rather important, doesn't it?"

"Life and death, Mrs. Crane."

"In that case, I suppose I'll see what I can do."

Tiffany took another look out the back window once Edith left the kitchen. There was still no sign of Hank. She walked through the single French door and onto the balcony that sat outside the breakfast area to get a better view behind the house. She didn't see her sergeant, but she did see two sets of tracks in the snow leading from the back of the house to the right, southward. She lifted her hand to shield her eyes from the glare of the sun and followed the tracks with her eyes. They reached all the way to, and beyond, the closest neighbor's house. What in the world was going on?

20

Sebastien was tossed into the darkness, landing on cold concrete. The door slammed behind him, extinguishing a thin wedge of light before he could make out his surroundings.

At no point during the last hour did Sebastien get a decent view of the man who held a knife to his throat, threatened him, yanked him out of the barn, pushed a gun into the small of his back, and forced him into a truck. Aside from the muted threats uttered in the barn, and the one time the man growled at him to "shut up and sit still" during the drive, he never clearly heard his abductor's voice either. Maybe that was due to the gun battle back in the barn, which continued to ring in his ears. All he could discern was that the man was much younger than the trio of near geriatrics who lured him into this mess.

Sebastien waited in the blackness for a few minutes, listening for a clue indicating what his abductor might be doing on the opposite side of the door. He heard nothing. For the second time that day, he found himself sitting in pitch blackness.

"Hello?" he whispered, wondering if he was alone. There was no reply other than the soft echo of his own voice.

The space was small and must be empty, he concluded. The echo and coolness of the air reminded Sebastien of that time Tiffany took him to Wind Cave. Tiffany. Surely by now she and Hank were missing him. Tiffany was a great detective. It wouldn't take her long to find the Fortunatas site and come looking for him. Maybe she already had. But where was he now? Why was he brought here? Would they be able to find him? Clearly Milo was trying to kill him. But it wasn't Milo who brought him here. Who was it? And why was he alive?

He extended his right arm in front of him at ninety degrees, then moved it to his right, rotating on his backside to complete a full circle sweep of his immediate surroundings. He felt nothing. Then, using his feet and his good arm, he pushed himself backward a few feet and conducted the same sweep. Still nothing. He gave himself another scoot backward, this time hitting a wall.

Based on this little experiment, Sebastien estimated the room to be no more than ten feet from the door to the back wall. He turned to his left and did the same reverse push along the wall, this time hitting something within just a few feet. Reaching behind himself, he felt a cardboard box.

The door to the room abruptly swung open, allowing light to fill the space. The shape of a man rushed at him and pulled him to his feet by the shoulders of his recently purchased Moncler Grenoble ski jacket, which was, of course, destroyed at this point—torn, bloodied, shot through. Sixteen hundred dollars. How stupid.

Based on shape and size, the man was most likely the same person who had brought him here. Only now he was wearing a ski mask as he violently removed Sebastien's jacket, sweater, and shirt, exposing his naked torso. Who was this guy? What the hell was going on?

"What are you doing?" Sebastien demanded, fearful his trousers would be next.

Sebastien got no verbal response, but the man's purpose became very clear when he produced a role of gauze and rolled it over his wounded arm with a technique that was indelicate at best.

"I guess you're not going to kill me, then."

His abductor pulled a large knife from his hip and held it in front of Sebastien's eyes. Sebastien gulped and opened his mouth to say something but was interrupted when, in one deft motion, the guy slashed the knife through the gauze and pushed him to the ground. Sebastien landed on his left side. His injury slammed against the concrete, sending a wave of pain up his arm and into his neck and chest. The man, and the light, evaporated through the door.

Sebastien reeled in pain on the floor, which felt like a sheet of ice against his bare skin. Fortunately, during the few moments the door was open, he was able to get a good look at the room. He dragged himself toward where the man had tossed his jacket and reached outward.

After putting on his jacket, Sebastien sat still, trying to recall what he had observed of the space. The floor was concrete—he knew that already—and the walls were constructed of concrete block. The ceiling was sheetrock. He did not see any vents in the ceiling, but then he didn't get a look at the ceiling behind him. One of the walls was lined with boxes. The other was bare. A metal drum sat in the far-left corner, a few feet from the door, which looked to be metal.

Sebastien ignored the painful protests from his leg and shoulder as he forced himself to his feet and stumbled toward the door. The doorknob would not turn at all, and jerking it back and forth produced no movement either. Next, he pointed himself in the direction of the cardboard boxes stacked along the wall. If he couldn't get out through the door, and the room was otherwise solid, his best hope for escape would be to find something he could use as a weapon. He might be able to over-power his captor the next time he came in the room. There didn't seem to be any other way.

The boxes were light. He could easily lift them and even shake them. The first box he tried was folded shut. He reached in and found clothing. Feeling through, he could make out soft items, some clearly silk or satin. Lingerie, probably. There were bras too. There must be females living here, he figured. Or maybe this guy was a cross dresser?

The next two boxes produced the same kind of clothing. The fourth box was taped shut, but he was able to peel through the seal rather easily. He found several pump and spray bottles in the box, which reminded him of shampoo or lotion. There were also several pieces of loose jewelry—earrings, necklaces, rings—and three wallets, the kind women carry in their purses.

Sebastien's mind shifted. He was no longer looking for something to use as a weapon. The Amber Harrison murder investigation just took a tremendous leap forward in his estima-tion. And what was more, although the boxes didn't reveal the location of his concrete jail, he would bet all the cash in Milo's envelope that train tracks would be within walking—or running—distance.

HANK ROUNDED the corner at the side of the house and peered down the slope toward the backyard and the lake beyond. On this side of the house there were a few windows on the upper level and two windows on the level below. He saw no move-ment or people inside, although the windows on the upper level at the back were too high for him to investigate. There was no way for him to know if anyone was up there looking down on him as he slinked down the hill.

At the very back of the house there was a balcony on the south side of the upper level and a large deck off the lower that looked out over the lake. He noticed a trail of footprints in the snow heading from a sliding glass door to stairs on the east side of the deck. Hank continued along the edge of the deck, keeping an eye on the back of the house. He saw that the footprints continued southward in the snow.

Hank stood behind the far corner of the deck and pondered his next move. The footprints appeared to be relatively fresh, and they probably were, considering the Cranes—at least one of them—had only just made it to town. Add to that the fact no one answered the front door, and it was looking like the occupants had chosen to run off rather than talk. There was just the one set of footprints though.

Hank approached the sliding glass door. The sunlight behind him shone into the interior of the home, revealing a large bedroom, with a bathroom on the opposite side and a dresser against the left wall. The bed was unmade. He finger-tapped on the glass and waited. There was no answer. He knocked again, this time with four knuckles, and followed that up with a vocal demand. Still nothing.

On the other side of the window at the south of the home, there was a family room with couches, a large TV, a built-in wet bar, and a wood stove. Along the right wall of the room was a staircase connecting the lower and upper levels. Hank could see to the top of the stairs. There were no signs of life, no homicidal geriatrics. Behind the staircase was the beginning of a hallway. This obviously connected the family room with the bedroom. He knocked on the window, getting the same result as before.

Hank turned and followed the footprints down the deck stairs. Ahead of him lay a blanket of white stillness that terminated in the edge of the lake and a dock. Hank whistled to himself, admiring both the dock and the extra-long pontoon suspended in the slip a few feet over the frozen water. The snowy earth between himself and the dock was undisturbed. He turned to follow the footprints southward.

The tracks ran parallel to the house and extended past a patio with snow-covered furniture and a ring of stone with a fire pit in the center. About sixty feet beyond that, a line of thick pine trees separated the Crane's property from their neighbor's. The tracks went right through the trees at a ninety-degree angle. They were not left by someone meandering through the snow to enjoy the cool morning air, Hank realized. No, these tracks were left by someone with a fixed determination and purpose. They formed a straight line from the bottom of the deck stairs to the trees. Hank put his palm on the grip of his pistol and approached.

"Mr. Crane," he called, "sheriff's office here. Come on out."

All was stillness. The snow seemed to absorb his voice as it left his throat. Silence was the only reply.

Hank squeezed through the branches with his pistol leading the way. It was all clear. He looked down for evidence that whoever left the tracks paused to hide behind the trees. But no, the footprints continued straight through the neighbor's yard and beyond for several yards. Whoever had made these tracks had a long head start. Yep, it was probably Milo, Hank decided. He probably heard them at the door and took off.

The tracks disappeared behind a woodpile, a perfect ambush spot. Hank turned toward the lake and crouched on the neighbor's dock, all the while keeping an eye over his shoulder. From this new vantage point, he could see behind the woodpile. There was no one there. Hank was beginning to feel a little silly, trekking all the way out here, so far from his partner, his backup. Maybe it was Tiffany who needed the backup. Maybe he should go back and check on her. He resolved to do so once he followed the tracks a little farther.

The snow behind the woodpile bore the signs he'd been looking for, the marks he'd expected to find behind the trees.

The track-maker had indeed taken cover behind the stacks of wood, stamping an oblong depression in the snow and mixing it with the dark earth. From this spot, the path of prints took a sharp turn westward, toward the road.

Hank paused at the edge of the road, seeing that the tracks continued to the opposite side, which was heavily forested. He realized he would have a distinct disadvantage if someone— Milo, for example—was in there hiding behind a tree in the darkness, waiting to strike. He reached for his radio, thinking to call Tiffany for backup, but decided that remaining quiet was his best option.

The trail was remarkably easy to follow, the blackness notwithstanding. Aside from some rabbit prints and divots made by falling pine cones, the deep snow was undisturbed. The prints made another right turn fifteen yards into the trees. The tracks were forming a great circle and heading right back to where they started, toward Tiffany.

Hank double-timed it northward, taking special care to step inside the already existing tracks to minimize the sound of crunching snow that could reveal his presence. After traveling for approximately two minutes, he found a naked spot in the trees and could get a good view back toward the house. He had made it past the south-side neighbor and was roughly twenty-five yards from being parallel to Milo's front door.

There was movement up ahead and to his right, in the direction of the track line. Hank went to his knees behind a thick curtain of branches and waited to see what or, more likely, who it could be. He strained his eyes but saw no further motion. He needed to get closer. Up ahead but to the left of the tracks, he saw a direct path to a hiding spot that would put him within fifteen feet of the activity. He would need to take extra care to avoid making too much noise.

He raised himself halfway up and into a bent over position. It seemed to take several minutes for Hank to creep ahead; he was moving so slowly, so cautiously, all the while keeping his pistol trained in the direction of the movement. Once in place, he lowered himself and parted the branches just enough to get a look.

As he expected, it was a person. They were lying prone in the snow, dressed in a thick green coat, green pants, and a brown cap. What was he doing?

As if to answer the unspoken question, Hank saw the man lift something up in front of his face. After squinting and shifting his position by a few inches, he now saw it was a rifle, its scope raised to the man's eye, its barrel pointed directly at the Crane's front door. Hank raised his own pistol and took aim.

21

Edith returned to the breakfast room, spotted Tiffany on the balcony, and went out to join her.

"What are you doing out here?" she asked.

"It's a lovely view, isn't it? I would love to live at a place like this. Is that your boat too?" Tiffany pointed over the rail of the balcony.

"Yes, it is, although we don't use it much."

Tiffany turned to look at the woman and noticed a pall of concern over her face.

"What's wrong?" she asked. "Is your husband coming out?"

"I . . . I can't find him. He's not in bed. He's not in the bathroom."

"What do you mean, you can't find him? Where could he be?"

Edith lifted her hands in a sign of resignation. "I don't know. I truly have no idea."

Tiffany rushed past Edith, pulling her pistol from its holster as she reached the living room.

"Mr. Crane. Milo. Where are you? I need to talk to you."

She continued into the hall, stopping at the first bedroom on the left. She observed only a desk and couch and a small closet on one wall. She pulled open the closet door and stepped back, pointing her weapon.

"Milo, come out of there."

Using the end of her pistol, she pushed aside the clothes that hung in the closet, exposing only a vacuum cleaner.

She then searched the next bedroom, sweeping her pistol under the bed and looking through the closet. Nothing.

She exited into the hall with her weapon sweeping left and right.

Edith screamed, "Don't shoot! What are you doing? Are you going to shoot my Milo?"

Tiffany ignored her and continued into a bathroom at the end of the hallway. The shower curtain stood open. There was nowhere for Milo to hide here.

There was one final room on this level. Tiffany turned left out of the bathroom and searched it.

"What's downstairs?"

"The master bedroom. That's where Milo is. I mean, that's where he *was*."

Tiffany went back toward the entry, stopping at the interior garage door. There was one car in the garage.

"How many cars are here?"

"One car. My car. Will you please put down that gun? Milo wouldn't hurt anybody!"

Tiffany scrambled down the stairs to the lower level, keeping her back to the wall and her pistol pointed over the banister. She emerged into a large family room with couches, a bar, a wood stove, and a huge flat-screen television—all of which, excepting the wood stove, she searched behind. On the far side of the family room was another hall that led to the master bedroom.

"Milo, come out! Come out here now!"

There was no response, no movement, and no sound.

Tiffany cautiously got down on her knees and lifted the bed skirt, finding only some rolls of wrapping paper and a pair of slippers. The master bathroom, which was to the left of the bed, was also empty. Tiffany proceeded to the sliding glass door, which led from the master bedroom to the backyard, and saw the footprints heading out of the bedroom along with another pair of prints that came from the side of the house. The last prints stopped in front of the bedroom slider and continued toward the living room window. Those were Hank's footprints, she realized. They, like the prints that led from the master bedroom, ultimately headed down the back of the deck and to the right.

Tiffany dashed upstairs, into the family room.

"You stay here," she said.

"What's going on?" Edith replied.

"Just stay right there. Don't move until I get back."

Tiffany made for the front door and pulled it open. Just then, the entry sidelight exploded, sending thousands of tiny glass fragments into the entryway. Tiffany threw her hands in front of her face and dove to the ground.

HANK STOOD over Milo with both hands gripping his weapon, which was pointed downward over the man's lifeless body. However, Hank's eyes were focused on the front door of the house across the street.

"Come on, Tiff. Come on," he begged into the cold air.

He gave Milo a few shoves with the toe of his boot. The man was dead. The bullet went into his head behind his right ear and exited through the left side of his forehead—which, strangely enough, was already covered by a large bandage that was now hanging by one edge, gently flapping through the smoke coming out Milo's skull.

This was the guy, the old guy who caused all this trouble?

Hank looked back toward the house and saw movement—feet moving in the doorway. He holstered his weapon and stomped out of the forest and across the road.

"Geez, are you okay, Reese?"

Tiffany walked out onto the porch, patting her legs and chest for signs of injury.

"I think I'm fine. I didn't get hit. Wait. Where's . . . oh no!"

"What is it, Reese?"

Hank ran onto the porch and followed Tiffany into the house.

In the living room lay Edith Crane. A bullet, Milo's bullet, had pierced the sidelight and struck her right in the sternum. The expanding pool of blood in the entry pushed broken glass toward the baseboards.

WITHIN TEN MINUTES, every cop in Lawrence County was on the scene—though there weren't that many of them.

"Crazy bastard."

"Let's hope the same thing didn't happen to Sebastien," replied Tiffany. "That poor woman had no idea."

"You really think so, Reese? I find that hard to believe."

"Somehow, I believe it."

"Are you sure you looked everywhere? No sign of Sebastien here or anybody else?"

Tiffany shook her head.

"He's not in there. But now we know that Milo is behind whatever happened. He's involved."

"I agree, but that guy doesn't fit the description of the man who took Sebastien from the barn." Hank pointed across the street to the trees. "Did you check the garage for the truck we passed last night?"

"There's only a Cadillac in there. Registered to Edith Crane, according to the locals."

Once Hank and Tiffany finished giving their statements to the Lawrence County deputies, they got back in the Tahoe and headed south.

"Where do we go from here?" asked Tiffany.

"We need to figure out who else is connected to this thing. This ain't a one-man deal. Hopefully Rapid City came up with something at Fortunatas Development."

Hank's phone rang, and he pulled it out of his pocket and put it on speaker.

"Good morning, sir."

"Sergeant, what the hell's going on up there?"

Hank looked over at Tiffany in the passenger seat and pulled back his lips in a feigned look of alarm.

"Oh, you know, Lieutenant. Same old thing, different day."

"Stop with the crap, Sergeant. There's nothing remotely amusing about our people trespassing on Lawrence County's patch and picking off the citizenry."

"We were there on business, sir. I can assure you of that."

"The Dr. Grey thing?"

"That's correct. We had information suggesting he could be held captive up here. Turns out he wasn't, but the guy we suspected tried to shoot Deputy Reese."

"She's okay, I assume. I would've heard if that wasn't the case. Right, Sergeant?"

"I'm fine, sir," replied Tiffany. "He missed me. Unfortunately, he did hit an innocent woman. His wife."

"That's tragic."

"You should have been there, sir. I hit him just as he was shooting."

Tiffany slapped Hank on the knee and mouthed a profanity.

"Well, well done, Sergeant. A little odd to be bragging about such a thing, but we'll let the department psychologist untangle that one."

"Yes, sir. We still don't know where Dr. Grey is though."

"Hopefully this helps. Rapid City crime scene techs processed the fingerprints from last night's scene. They recovered several sets of fingerprints from the barn. Some of them aren't in our database."

"Probably Dr. Grey's, sir."

"Right. That's what I was thinking. But others came back to the residents and a third person. A man named Brian Crawford. He's a Custer County guy according to the DMV, but he has no record."

Tiffany looked over at Hank, then down at the phone and back up at Hank. Her mouth had fallen open.

"What?" whispered Hank.

"I've heard that name," she said

"You mean you've dealt with him?" asked Lieutenant Breed.

"No, no. But I've heard that name before. Let me think."

"While you're thinking about that, Reese, I want you two to get with Erin in crime analysis and run out your dead guy. We need to know who he's connected to, who his relatives and business associates are, and everyone else he's connected to for that matter. Somebody on that list is going to know where Dr. Grey is."

"Yes, sir. That's a great idea," answered Tiffany.

"Didn't you already call her?" mouthed Hank.

Tiffany smiled and nodded.

Despite a valiant effort to stay alert, Tiffany nodded off. She should never have rested her head against the passenger door, which surrendered her to overwhelming fatigue. Interestingly, though, she began to dream—one of those lucid dreams where the dreamer controls the scene, like changing the channel on a television.

The dream started with Tiffany kneeling over Edith Crane's

body. A flower was resting against the dead woman's pale cheek —the same flower from the picture of Edith that stood in the lake house entry. She turned her head at the weight of a hand placed on her shoulder. Turning her head, she saw Milo Crane smiling at her. His teeth were yellow, and his breath smelled of coffee. Tucked in his left armpit was a rifle, a thin wisp of smoke lacing up from the barrel.

"My girl, come with me. We are free."

Tiffany changed the channel in her mind. She was now in front of Sebastien's building, honking her car horn impatiently. Sebastien emerged and got in the car. She noticed he was bleeding through a bandage on his neck, and she leaned over to give him a kiss. The next thing she knew, they were driving on the road toward Lead behind a huge semi-truck. Tiffany pulled off the road at the spot where Shelly Shields had been hit. She looked in her rearview mirror and saw flashing lights from a patrol car. An officer knocked against her window and asked, "Did you see what happened?"

Hank must have been lost in his thoughts, as Tiffany's voice startled him.

"What the . . . I thought you were asleep. You trying to get us killed, Reese?"

"I remember. I remember it now."

"What are you talking about?"

I remember where I heard the name the lieutenant gave us. I mean, I read it. It was in the report about Shelly Shields's accident up in Lead. Brian Crawford was the name of the witness who called it in. He was on the road behind the truck when it hit Shields and knocked her over the guardrail.

22

Sebastien was beginning to doubt his plan. It was shortly after searching through the boxes that he determined he would need to try a different tactic. He was in no condition to fight his way out. True, his current plan counted heavily on the kidnapper's gullibility. But it was worth a shot.

The moisture from his breath settled on his forehead and cheeks as it ricocheted off the metal. It was difficult to keep track of time, but he estimated he'd been hiding under the overturned barrel for at least a half hour. His knees were fully flexed, and a sharp pain shot out from his right patella upward and laterally. He swallowed the agony and distracted himself by pondering the Amber Harrison case.

The pieces of the puzzle, at least the pieces he had in his possession, were fitting together nicely. To be sure, many pieces were still missing, but a picture was starting to form. Amber Harrison was either a victim of human trafficking or, less likely, a participant in the general scheme. Sebastien was certain it was one or the other. And he would bet Milo's stack of money that not too far from this place he could find the train tracks he'd walked along just a few days ago. Amber had been here in this very room.

Sebastien realized all these present troubles began when it came to light that the remains of the shoulder girdle in the coroner's freezer could possibly belong to Amber Harrison. Somebody must have talked—despite the sheriff's directions to keep things quiet. Not that Sebastien thought there was some conspiracy or that someone tipped off Milo to warn him. No, it was probably just as simple as someone relaying the fantastical news that the sheriff's office was about to crack the Harrison case. Didn't Milo himself say he was well connected when he visited Sebastien's apartment? He had friends in the sheriff's office, he said. And wasn't it the Amber Harrison case that Milo first mentioned during that portentous visit, before anything about native bones, or real estate, or fill dirt, or NAGPRA ever came up? No wonder Sebastien felt uncomfortable and suspicious. This entire ordeal was an effort to lure Sebastien to the site, kill him, and perhaps bury him right there. But was Tiffany part of that too? Didn't Milo say that day when he came to visit that he had been watching him? He knew Tiffany was there. Did Milo originally hope to draw Tiffany to the site as well and kill them both? It seemed likely.

But why? Why did Milo feel compelled to get the upper hand on the investigation? There must be some reason the discovery that the remains belonged to Harrison would lead the sheriff back to Milo and Fortunatas Development. Maybe it was just paranoia. Maybe the old man was losing his nerve.

Questions sprang up in Sebastien's mind like a whack-a-mole game. Who was impersonating Harrison during the fall of 2012? Was it Barnadette Jacobs? Maybe, but Sebastien doubted that. More likely it was that other roommate. What was her name? Shelly Shields—that was it. No, it was too suspicious that Shelly left school and the house not long after the remains were found.

He looked forward to getting some of these answers from Milo himself, but first he needed to get out of here. He was being spared for the moment, even given a bandage for his arm, but they ultimately wanted him dead. That was the entire plan to begin with. So why was it that this crazy guy—the psychopath who brought him here, threw him in this dark room, stripped off his jacket, and rendered first aid—was keeping Sebastien alive?

Whatever the answer, he had limited time to act, and there was no way he was going to sit around and wait to be killed. He would not allow himself to be ripped from the happiness that had so recently found him. Sebastien did not know anything about the next life or whether there even was one. He was not prone to speculating about matters of religion or spirituality. But even if there was a heaven, he was doubtful it could provide the happiness that Tiffany had already given him. It was too early to lose that. And to lose his brother with whom he had so recently reconciled. He wanted to see his niece, Kirby, grow up to be an adult smart-ass instead of a child one. He wanted to hold his new baby nephew, who was due any day now. No, he would not go gently. There was a puzzle to be solved and a future to embrace.

Sebastien's musings were interrupted by the sound of the door being unlocked. He held his breath and tried not to shake. The door opened and he heard a man say, "Okay, you, it's time to ... what the hell?"

The man ran off somewhere, back into the house. Did Sebastien's plan work? *Could* it have worked? Was this guy that stupid? But what to do now? Should he wait or make a run for it?

This window of opportunity would not stay open, he realized. He stood up and pulled the barrel from over his head, setting it down carefully to avoid making any noise. Sticking his head out of the door just enough to take in his surroundings, he saw a hallway leading to his left and another leading to his right. On the left, the hallway took a sharp turn about eight feet from the door. To the right, it led into a larger room, where he could see some furniture, a fireplace, and children's toys strewn about. The room continued to the right, but that side of the space was obscured by the hallway wall. On the left side of the room was a door leading outside. Through the glass in the door, he saw concrete stairs leading upward to the backyard. He was in a walkout basement, and that door, and those stairs, would lead him to freedom. He was less than ten feet away.

Sebastien made a break for the door, ignoring the pain in his, now swollen, knee. Reaching the knob, he found with great relief that it was unlocked. He had the door open a crack when something heavy hit him from behind, causing him to crash forward and into a coffee table. Someone was on his back, pinning him against the floor. He tried to turn and face the man, but the man's knees were crushing Sebastien's arms as he lay prone.

"Where are you going? You ain't getting out of here."

It was the same man from before.

Sebastien squirmed, trying to knock the man off his back and arms, but it was no use. He was overpowered, caught.

"Let's get you back in the hole and let you cool down before you hurt yourself."

The man began to pull him by his feet back toward the room. It was a familiar scenario, but this time Sebastien was prepared. He kicked his good leg free, flipped onto his back, and pointed a bottle of hairspray directly into the man's face, pressing down hard on the release. His captor screamed and fell backward into the hallway, covering his eyes. Sebastien got up and gave him a few more seconds' worth of *superior hold for an active lifestyle*, then scrambled out the door and up the stairs.

At the top of the stairs lay a grassy backyard separated from an open field by a short picket fence. Sebastien made a run for it, looking back before throwing himself over the fence and into the open field behind the property. The man was nowhere to be seen. Sebastien pressed forward, barely able to lift his right foot. Whether it was due to the cold or the shock, he was starting to feel numb, on autopilot, trapped in a bad dream.

The field ended at barbed-wire fence bordering a dirt road. He crawled under the fence, catching his already shredded jacket on the barbs and pulling it from his naked torso. Several hundred feet up the road to his right, he could see a small house. He considered heading toward it, but he didn't trust that decision. The house was too close to the place from which he'd escaped. It might be part of the same property, or maybe the residents were in tight with the man who took him. Sebastien crawled underneath the fence on the other side of the road, scraping his back against two barbs.

Naked from the waist up, pants dyed in blood, a bloody bandage around his left bicep—he'd be easy to spot, and one hell of a sight. For the next twenty minutes, he kept his head on a swivel, looking for signs of being followed.

He crossed a shallow creek and went up a short hill on the opposite side, which flattened onto a landscaped plateau with grass, a gravel U-shaped driveway in front of a colonial-style house, a large barn, and a corral. He knocked on the door of the house.

"I don't suppose I could use your phone?"

The boy who answered couldn't have been more than ten or eleven years old. He stared at the bloodied and broken visitor with a horrified gape. The plate of food he carried in his left hand quivered.

"Mom," the boy called out, still staring at Sebastien. "There's a guy at the door. And I don't think he's selling nothin."

23

"You're lucky, you know that?" declared Tiffany, smiling.

"This kind of thing never happened to me in California."

"How bored you must have been," replied Hank. "You can always go back if you can't handle it here, Mr. Big City."

Sebastien glanced up at Tiffany with questioning eyes. She smiled down at him and leaned over to deliver a kiss.

"Dr. Grey isn't going anywhere. We have an investigation to finish—and a body to exhume."

"A body to exhume?" replied Sebastien.

Hank rolled his eyes. "You really do know how to turn him on, don't you, Reese?"

Tiffany pushed Sebastien's wheelchair out of the hospital doors and up to the Tahoe. Hank hurried ahead to open the passenger door.

"Where are we going? And what's this about an exhumation?"

"We're going to Rapid City PD. They're interviewing Crawford as we speak. Once they're done, I want a turn with him."

"Good. Maybe he can lead us to Milo and the others."

Hank reached over to fasten Sebastien's seat belt. "Let me get that for ya. And, by the way, your buddy Milo is no longer a threat."

"What do you mean? Did you arrest him?"

Tiffany got in the back passenger seat and leaned forward to her left, reaching her head into the space between the front seats.

"Hank shot him. He's dead. Poor guy."

"'Poor guy'? What are you smoking, Reese? He tried to shoot you. I saved your butt."

"I know that. I just feel bad that it had to be done."

"Tried to shoot you? Are you okay, Tiffany?"

"I'm fine, Sebastien. One hundred percent."

Hank started the Tahoe and put it in gear.

"Hey, Tiffany, why don't you tell your boyfriend about Shelly Shields?"

"Oh, yeah, that's the exhumation I mentioned. I was so worried about you that I forgot to tell you last night."

"Isn't that cute?" laughed Hank.

"You hush, boss. Anyway, Lieutenant Breed told us some of the fingerprints on the barn came back to Brian Crawford. I remembered having read the accident report for Shelly Shields's hit and run. The witness who called it in was Brian Crawford."

Sebastien's mouth dropped.

"You're saying that Shelly Shields, Harrison's roommate, is dead?"

"I know. Very interesting, right? She was hitchhiking up on 14A near Lead when a semi-truck swerved onto the shoulder and hit her, sending her over the guardrail and down into a ditch. The witness who saw the accident and first reported it was the same guy who had you locked up in his basement. This was shortly after Harrison's mother reported her missing."

"Which explains why we don't have an interview from her," added Hank.

"I'm assuming Shields was autopsied."

"Of course," answered Tiffany. "Nothing was found that could rule out the accident. But, with a supposed eyewitness and no suspicion of foul play—aside from hit and run—they closed the case quickly. No one other than Crawford saw it happen, and law enforcement couldn't locate the truck."

"You're right, Tiffany," replied Sebastien. "We need to look at Shields's autopsy report, if not her body."

"I'm chasing that down now, waiting for Gerry at the coroner's office to call back. So, what is the prognosis, Sebastien? What did the doctors say?" asked Tiffany.

"Same thing you said, really. I was lucky. The wound on my arm isn't too deep and didn't hit any major vessels. They stitched it up."

"What about the leg?" Hank nodded toward Sebastien's brace.

"Grade two sprain of the lateral collateral ligament. Hopefully it won't require surgery. I won't know for a few weeks though. I just have to try to stay off of it and keep it iced."

"I'm really glad you're okay." Tiffany put her hands on his shoulders and gave him a squeeze.

"I am too," said Hank. "We'll drop you off at home on the way so you can rest up."

"No way," exclaimed Sebastien. "It would be stupid to drive all the way to Custer, then drive back to Rapid City. I can go with you . . . I'm fine."

"Suit yourself, bro. I wouldn't want to be stupid. Now, what are we thinking here? On the Amber Harrison deal."

Sebastien turned slightly in his seat to put both Hank and Tiffany in his field of vision.

"I believe it's clear now," began Sebastien, "that there never was an issue with native bones at the Fortunatas Development site. I don't know where they got the skull fragment, but I'm sure it was obtained illegally. It will have to go back to the tribal authorities, if we can recover it."

"The whole thing was a ruse?" asked Tiffany.

"I'm sure of it. Do you remember when Milo came to the apartment? The first thing he mentioned was the Harrison cold case."

Hank turned his head and growled, "You were there, Reese? You were there when this whole thing started?"

"I just happened to be there, Hank. I was an unwilling participant in that meeting. Neither of us expected that Milo, or anyone else, would visit the apartment."

"She's correct. Believe me, I discourage visitors."

Hank looked irritated but let Sebastien continue.

"Anyway, it was obvious to me from the beginning that the Amber Harrison case was on Milo's mind the whole time. I think Milo, Abigail Fortune, and Peter Stern fabricated this whole thing."

"And why would they do that, Sebastien?" asked Hank.

"Very simple. It was a distraction. Either that or they were trying to stay close to the Harrison investigation. They ultimately wanted me out of the way. Somebody at the sheriff's office, or somebody who is connected to someone there, told Milo that the Fairburn remains were being compared to Harrison's DNA. Milo knew we would be working the case—and he obviously knew I was helping."

"You're saying that this Milo guy was so afraid of your big brain that he tried to take you out before you got to the truth?" Hank scoffed.

"It makes perfect sense to me," Tiffany interjected. "Especially since they had access to a construction site in a remote area. It wouldn't have been that risky. You know, if they made Amber disappear so successfully, they probably thought they could do the same with Sebastien."

"Exactly," replied Sebastien. "I would only add that it wasn't so much about my so-called 'big brain' as it was about how crazy they were."

"And what's the motive?" asked Hank. "What does a real estate developer have to do with a murdered woman?"

As they drove toward the Rapid City Police Department, Sebastien laid out his theory of the crimes. He told them about finding the women's clothing, underwear, makeup, and wallets in Crawford's basement.

"There were several boxes of the stuff," he told them. "Unless there's a women's volleyball team living in that house, and they keep their personal belongings in storage, what I saw was clear evidence of burglary, robbery, theft, or more likely, human trafficking. And that could be the connection to Harrison."

"Did you happen to see her wallet in there with the others?" Tiffany asked.

"I didn't get a look inside the wallets. I could just tell they were wallets."

"Normally, I would accuse you of stretching to a conclusion on that one, Sebastien. But I think you're spot-on there."

"Wow! You're agreeing with me, Hank?" Sebastien smiled.

Tiffany acted out a histrionic gasp from the back seat.

"Yeah, yeah. Whatever. When RCPD searched Crawford's house, they found a lot more than that. There were also boxes of personal lubricant, condoms, and even Plan B pills. We're talking large quantities of all that. The guy could stock a drug store on Vegas Boulevard, although the stuff was all old and expired. Remind me to ask you how you know so much about the contraband related to sex trafficking, little brother. Do we need to run you in for an interview?"

Sebastien was getting better at ignoring his brother's jibes.

"Speaking of Vegas," said Tiffany, "remember what Erin said about one of the phone numbers from Harrison's cell phone

Where the Blood is Made

records? It belonged to a guy from Las Vegas. A guy who's now in federal prison for kidnapping."

Hank's phone beeped.

"Hey, Melissa. Yeah, Sebastien's good, just a bit beat up. What's that? You want to talk to him?"

Hank handed the phone over to Sebastien.

"Hello? No, I'm okay, really. You did? And what did you find out? Are you sure? Same spelling and age? Hmm. Thanks for doing that, I owe you. I . . . er . . . I love you too."

"You hittin' on my wife, Sebastien?" Hank grabbed him playfully behind the neck.

"What was that all about?" inquired Tiffany.

"I asked Melissa to look up Barnadette Jacobs' social media accounts. She seems to know how that stuff works—I do not. Specifically, I was hoping she might be connected to a 'Brian.'"

"And?" Hank lost patience with the pregnant pause.

"Jacobs doesn't have a direct connection to anyone by that name. However, she *is* connected to a 'Brian Crawford' through someone else."

"Ho-ly."

"Who is the connection?" demanded Tiffany.

"A man by the name of Adam Bell."

"That's the guy who threw the Christmas Eve party that Harrison missed."

"Yes. Do you suppose we could run out to Crawford's house before we go to the police department?"

"Why, Sebastien?" asked Tiffany. "I'm pretty sure that place is sealed up. We can't go in."

"I don't want to go in. I just want to verify something before we talk to Crawford."

Forty-five minutes later, the trio were headed north in silence, away from Fairburn. The drive to Crawford's place revealed enough information to speculate about what happened to Amber Harrison all those years ago. Especially relevant was the discovery that, to reach the scene of Sebastien's captivity, it was necessary to cross the very same train tracks near where Harrison's remains were found. The consensus ran along the following lines, with some minor details yet to be agreed upon.

In the late spring or early summer of 2012, Harrison found herself in the clutches of Brian Crawford, who abducted her for the purposes of trafficking her—probably to a network of like-minded villains in Las Vegas, or Tucson, or who knows where. Perhaps Harrison was voluntarily mixed-up in the scheme, but this seems unlikely given that she apparently escaped, or nearly did so until a bullet shot through her left scapula.

Whether Harrison made it to the train tracks on her own or collapsed short of the tracks and was conveyed there, it was impossible to say. But it was Sebastien's suggestion that her being intentionally placed on the tracks was more likely, given the blood transfer from her body to her car. How convenient it would be for Harrison to be run over by a train, making her death attributable to an accident.

Why make it seem as though Amber Harrison was still alive? Pure greed was as good a reason as any. The perpetrators must have been anxiously awaiting news in the media of Harrison's death, but failing to hear of any, they changed tactic. If they could make it seem as though she were still alive, still attending school, still working at the gym, they could not only use her credit card but string her poor mother along to keep the money coming. That part of the plan required a willing participant in the form of a female.

The cell phone data made it clear that Harrison's phone was in the vicinity of Brian Crawford's Fairburn home. Whoever played the role of Amber using her phone was doing so from Crawford's. The tower address, sector, and azimuth were going to corroborate that. And which of Amber's roommates was dating a mysterious "Brian"?

Tiffany as much as confirmed that theory when she reported

—with great satisfaction—what she discovered during her visit to the Black Hills Fitness and Climbing Club. Shelly Shields was Amber's supervisor at the gym. She would have ample opportunity to doctor the time cards, making it seem as though Amber were alive and well, at least from a work perspective. But was Shields the one impersonating Harrison at school? They agreed that such was likely the case, though the truth of that may be beyond reach.

∼

THE INVESTIGATIONS huddle room at Rapid City Police Department doubled as a viewing area for the half a dozen interview rooms. A wood table stood in the middle of the space, surrounded by chairs. A bank of monitors and recording equipment took up an entire wall.

Tiffany, Hank, and Sebastien were introduced to the Rapid City detectives by their supervisor, Sgt. Ramos. One of them, a large man with tattooed forearms and a bushy mustache, offered Sebastien his hand.

"So, you're the guy? Glad to see you're all right."

Sebastien leaned on his crutches and shook the man's hand.

"Thank you," he said. "I appreciate everything you've done, especially picking up Crawford." Sebastien motioned to one of the monitors, which showed a defiant-looking Brian Crawford sitting alone in an interview room.

"No sweat."

"He looks a lot different than I expected." Sebastien approached the monitor. "I never got a good look at him. I expected him to look . . . I don't know . . . crazier." Crawford looked to be in his mid-thirties. He was muscular and tall, his long legs reached all the way under the table. He wore a Colorado Rockies baseball cap, a blue flannel shirt bulging in the arms, blue jeans with stained thighs, and heavy boots.

"He's just a punk," returned the detective. "Looks like someone did a number on him. He looks like a raccoon. Was that you, Doctor?"

Sebastien nodded and said, "I hit him with some hairspray."

The detective gave Sebastien a fist bump and said, "Whatever works, my dude."

One of the RCPD detectives, who appeared to be the freshest of the bunch, was especially happy to meet Tiffany.

"Tiffany Reese, damn glad to meet you. I've heard a lot of good things. I'm Jason Kraft."

Kraft was clean-shaven and, unlike the others, dressed in a suit and tie.

"Really?" Tiffany smiled but her tone made her sound dubious. "How in the world have you heard of me?"

"You know, around the office. Say, the fellas and I are going for drinks later. Wanna join?"

"You're not on your way to church?" Tiffany quipped.

Kraft looked down at himself.

"Oh, no. No, I had court this morning."

Hank glanced at Sebastien, who had turned from the monitor, and stifled a chuckle. The anthropologist looked like he wanted to run Kraft through with one of his crutches.

"I'm only joking with you," replied Tiffany. "Thanks for the invitation, but we're kind of in the middle of things here."

"Yeah, sure. Here. Take my card in case you ever need anything. Just give me a buzz or whatever, you know."

"Is he talking?" Hank asked.

"He's denying everything," answered Sgt. Ramos. "We told him Dr. Grey described his basement perfectly, and that his broken coffee table substantiates the doctor's version of things. And his fingerprints too. He knows he's screwed. But he won't talk."

"Did he invoke?"

"No, Sergeant LeGris, he hasn't."

"Mind if we take a shot at him?"

"You can come in with me," offered Ramos.

"Brian, this is Sergeant Hank LeGris from Custer County."

Ramos took the chair immediately next to Crawford, while Hank sat on the other side of the table.

Crawford made no reply, except to fold his arms a little more tightly and pull his feet in.

Hank thought about asking Crawford whether he was curious about having Custer County involved, but decided against it. In his considerable experience, it was always best to let the home team take the lead.

"Are you still going with the story that you don't know what we're talking about?"

Ramos leaned in for effect.

"I don't." Crawford uncrossed his arms and raised his hands. Hank recognized the usual criminal tactic of acting dumbfounded.

"Really? I've left you alone in this room for a half an hour, and you still haven't come up with any decent explanations for why your fingerprints were on the barn or why your basement was all torn up. You're just going to deny it and pretend it will go away? It's not going away, Brian. You shot a man up at that ranch. You're lucky he's going to live, but still, aggravated assault with a firearm is a big deal. Animal cruelty too. Hell, half this town would hang you just for that. And that gun we got from your place, the one in the kitchen drawer, I bet it's going to much the slugs they took out of the barn."

"You're high. I don't know what you're talking about."

"Did it hurt, Brian, when Dr. Grey popped you in the face and gave you those shiners?"

"He didn't hit me! It was damn hairspray!"

"Forgive me, I misspoke. Hairspray is exactly what Dr. Grey said it was. Isn't that right, Sergeant LeGris?"

Hank ignored the question but took the opportunity to

change the angle of attack. He calmly asked, "Mr. Crawford, how do you know Milo Crane?"

Brian's lips parted slightly then closed, like a fish.

"I don't . . ."

"Ah-ah, Brian. I didn't ask you *if* you know Milo Crane. I asked you *how* you know him. Spare us the bull."

Brian's eyes went to the top of the table.

Hank and Ramos made eye contact just long enough to get on the same page. They both let the silence take over.

"He works for my uncle," Crawford finally muttered.

"Peter Stern, you mean?" The blow landed hard. Crawford's eyes got big and terrified. Hank decided to hit him again. "Does he work for Fortunatas Development along with Abigail Fortune?"

Hank watched Crawford's posture soften. Ramos saw it too. He raised his eyebrows at his Custer County counterpart.

"That's okay, Brian. We already know all that. So, what brought you out to the ranch the other night?"

"I told you. I don't know nothing about that."

"Hell of a coincidence though, isn't it?" continued Hank. "The ranch practically overlooks the construction site your Uncle Peter owns. Yes, I know he's your uncle. You don't think we're a bunch of idiots, do you? We know everything. And that site . . . that's the same place Milo and your uncle were at that afternoon. Will wonders never cease? Oh, and just out of curiosity, were you and Milo close?"

Brian inclined his head.

"What do you mean, 'were'?"

"You haven't heard? Your old buddy Milo took a shot at one of our detectives the other day. Unfortunately for him we were able to intervene. I'm sorry to say that Milo Crane is deceased."

Crawford's face changed dramatically. It was obvious that Hank's statement was going to change everything.

"Like I said, Brian, we know that Milo was at the site that

day, and we know that Peter was at the site that day. And we also know that Milo and your Uncle Peter asked Dr. Grey to meet them at the site that day. In fact, it was Peter and Abigail who drove the doctor out there. We also know it was Milo who took a shot at him. His aim is as bad as yours, apparently. That's two attempted murder charges, in case you're counting."

"I didn't do that. I didn't do anything." Crawford said the words, but the statement lacked conviction.

"Conspiracy, then." Ramos was getting in on the fun, following Hank's lead.

"This is quite the mess you've gotten yourself into."

"Look," Brian began, "I don't know anything about Dr. Grey. I had nothing to do with him. I didn't even know he was there. I didn't even know that my uncle was there or Milo or my grand—."

Crawford caught himself, but not quickly enough. Hank acted as if he'd already known.

"Now we're getting there. Tell us, Brian, if you didn't know that your uncle or grandmother would be out there, why the hell were you out there?"

"Look, I was at work. I was working. You can ask my boss. I didn't even want to leave. Milo called me and said they were in trouble. He said there was a problem. He told me where to go and told me to bring a gun. I didn't even know what was up there! I was walking around in the dark. I didn't even know what was going on, I swear! As far as I knew, someone had hurt them. For all I knew, they could've been kidnapped."

"That's well and good, Brian. If that's the case, why did you grab Dr. Grey and take him back to your place? And why did you shoot the rancher? It should've been obvious they were the only ones there."

Brian looked toward the wall. Hank and Ramos gave him a few minutes, but he still offered no answer.

"Okay," Hank said. "Let's change the subject. You don't

wanna talk about the other night? Fine. Let's talk about some-thing else. Let's talk about something that happened, oh, I don't know, about ten years ago. You ever heard of a girl named Amber Harrison?"

"Never heard of her."

"Maybe you just forgot. A lot of water goes under the bridge in ten years. Let me jog your memory. You shot Amber Harrison and left her on the train tracks out by your place."

"You're delusional."

"Am I? How about the girl you killed and dumped off the side of 14A up by Lead? Shelly Shields, I think her name was."

"I'm done. I want a lawyer."

"SUIT YOURSELF," replied Ramos. "You're pretty much toast anyway—here and in Custer County. Isn't that right, Sergeant LeGris?"

Hank stood up and said, "I would say so. Burned on both sides. They'll have to scrape you off with a knife."

24

"What's this?" asked Sebastien, taking the folder from Tiffany. He was sitting on his sofa with his injured leg up on his coffee table. Parsifal lay next to him with his head in Sebastien's lap.

"Gerry says the exhumation is a no-can-do. Even if we could get a court order, which would take an act of God, the ground is too frozen."

"Frozen? Already?"

"Yes, already. That folder contains plan B. It's the accident report from Lawrence County, including statements from Brian Crawford. Autopsy results are also in there. I figured this might be the next best thing."

Tiffany sat down next to Sebastien, on the opposite side from Parsifal, and put her arm over his shoulders.

"Ooh, careful. You're leaning on my bad arm."

Tiffany sat up straight to give his arm some space.

"Sorry. I didn't think about that. How's it going, anyway? Are you feeling any better?"

"A little. The arm is still sore, and the doctor thinks I'll have a scar, despite the stitches."

"Then let me warn you. I think scars are sexy."

Sebastien replied with wide eyes and an impish grin. Tiffany laughed.

"Actually, I didn't come out here to become rugged like my brother. I'm glad to hear you're into it though."

"What about the leg? How's that feeling?"

"Not too bad. I'll be wearing the brace for a few weeks."

Tiffany smiled mischievously and stroked his hair.

"What are you thinking, Tiffany?"

"You need a haircut, my love."

"A little preoccupied these days. But I'll take it under advisement."

"Good, you do that. I have a great idea. Are you ready for it?"

Sebastien thought about all of the ways to respond, about the way he *wanted* to respond. Maybe it was the pain, or his recent multiple brushes with death, prompting him to consider if he could scrape up the courage . . .

"I'm listening."

"You know my brother, Mitch, the rodeo clown?"

"You told me about him."

"He's got this RV. It's beautiful. Got everything you could ever want. Mitch said we could borrow it anytime we like. Let's get out of here—once you're on your feet again. I've always wanted to take a trip to the coast."

"Are you serious?"

"Yes. Why wouldn't I be? We need a vacation. I want to get to know you better. Away from all this, I mean." Tiffany tossed the folder onto the coffee table with contempt and folded her legs up to her chest.

"I think it's a great idea, Tiffany. I'm excited. But . . . an RV? I don't know. We could always fly. It'd be a lot quicker."

"Bor-ing, Dr. Grey. What about all the places in between here and there? What about adventure?"

"What about marrying me?"

Tiffany laughed, but he kept a straight face.

"I'm serious. I love you."

Tiffany sat up and turned to face him. Her face lost some color.

"Oh . . . Sebastien. I love you too. I do. It's just so . . . I didn't expect this."

"Look, I know this isn't the way these things are supposed to go, but I have no idea how to be romantic. I just know I want to be with you. You're everything to me."

Tiffany sat back, facing the large window again. She took his hand in hers.

"I've been engaged before. Have I told you that?"

"I had no idea. What happened?"

"He got cold feet. I think he's in Florida now, running a fishing charter."

"What an idiot!"

"Would you hate me, Sebastien, if I said I wanted to think about it a bit?"

"No, no. I'm sorry. I shouldn't have ambushed you like this. I think I'm just . . ."

"Stop it, Sebastien. You don't understand. Yes, I will marry you. But not yet. Let's get to know each other a little more. And in the meantime, you can think of something a little more dramatic for a proposal."

Sebastien knew he should feel disappointed, maybe even rejected. But he didn't. Maybe it was her sincere smile, her warmth, or the way she held his hand in hers. Her response only made him more certain she would be well worth the exercise in patience.

"I'm sure I can come up with something a lot better."

"I know you can. For now, though, I'm dying to know what you think of that." Tiffany motioned to the folder.

"Let's find out." Sebastien emptied the contents onto his lap. Parsifal jumped down from the sofa and moped his way to his basket in the kitchen.

First, Sebastien took up the accident report. He tried to clear his mind of any sort of bias, realizing it was possible for Brian Crawford's involvement to be a coincidence. They still did not have evidence that Brian Crawford was the Brian who Shelly Shields had been dating. And Brian was still not talking.

He skimmed over the time of day, weather conditions, and other incidental circumstances of the accident, then read through Crawford's statement:

I was doing about thirty-five in the northbound lane of 14A, just south of Lead. At the entrance to the quarry, a truck pulled out in front of me. It cut me off. I had to slam on my brakes, but the truck accelerated quickly. It probably got up to fifty. I noticed the driver was weaving a little bit, crossing the center line. I thought maybe he was drunk. Anyway, as he rounded the right-hand curve just south of town, I saw a lady standing on the shoulder. She had her thumb out and was waving it at the truck while walking backward. She was obviously hitchhiking, trying to get the driver to stop. That's when I saw the truck drift onto the shoulder and hit the girl. Her body went flying over the guardrail and into the ditch. I was in shock. I expected to see the truck's brake lights go on, but he didn't even stop. He didn't even slow down. I pulled off the road and jumped out of my car. When I looked into the ditch, I saw the lady lying down there.

Crawford was asked if he could tell whether the woman was dead. He responded that he felt she was dead. He did not see her moving and could not detect her breathing at all. However, he also stated he did not try to approach the woman or render first aid. The ditch was too steep, he said. There was no way he could get down there without injuring himself.

When asked if he could describe the truck, or if he had gotten a license plate, he said he did not get the plate, but he was pretty sure it was a belly dumper with two trailers.

"It doesn't look like the officer on the scene asked Crawford about why he was there or where he was going," announced Sebastien, without looking up from the report.

"Why would he? He was just a witness. At least, they thought he was. There was no reason to think otherwise or be suspicious of Crawford."

Sebastien flipped the pages of the accident report. "I don't see where they try to reconstruct the accident either."

Tiffany leaned over and flipped some of the pages in the report as it sat on his lap. "I don't see one either," she replied. "That would make sense though, wouldn't it? It's not like there were any cars on scene. There wasn't a collision. And look here. It says that Crawford's car showed no signs of having been in an accident."

"They took him at his word," said Sebastien.

The autopsy report provided essentially the same investigative narrative as the accident report—except it also included a diagram of Shields's position in the ravine. She was found lying parallel to the highway, on her back, with her arms splayed out above her head.

It was also noted in the autopsy report that Shields had fractures to the rear and left side of her skull. She also had a fractured right forearm. The cause of death was listed as impact trauma to the head. Manner of death was accidental. The toxicology report stated that Shields did not have any alcohol or other impairing substances in her system at the time of death.

Sebastien handed a stack of photos to Tiffany. "Take a look at these. They're the autopsy photos. Very interesting."

"What am I looking for?"

Sebastien pointed to one of the photos.

"Here, on her skull. They shaved her hair so you can see the damage to the left parietal and left portion of the occipital."

"You mean her head is crushed? Yeah, that looks pretty bad. Is that the kind of thing that could happen because of the car accident?"

Sebastien thought for a second. "Yes, it's possible. Certainly. Especially for someone outside of a vehicle. A person could get hit and thrown and knock their head against all manner of things. The velocity of a truck going fifty-odd miles per hour would absolutely be sufficient to cause major trauma."

"So maybe Crawford was telling the truth?"

"I don't think so. Where's all the other trauma? The broken legs? The broken vertebrae? Why no mention of rib fractures? I mean where are all the other injuries? And she should be bruised all over."

"The report said her right arm was broken." Tiffany thumbed through the photos and found one that showed Shields's right arm. "Although it doesn't look broken to me here."

Sebastien found the envelope of radiographs in the folder. He held up each in turn against the light from the front window.

"Here. See this x-ray? That's the right ulna—that would be in the forearm. And this dark line, that's the break mentioned in the autopsy report."

Tiffany took the sheet from him. "That doesn't look too significant."

"No, it would be very significant," Sebastien replied. "It would be very painful. And it's also not easy to get that kind of fracture right in the middle of the ulna. You see, that's a depression fracture. That wasn't made because the arm was twisted or caught in something and snapped. Something hit her forearm."

"Are you saying that's a defensive wound?"

"Yes, I am. That is a classic parry fracture. She lifted her hand to protect her head against an impact."

"Would you expect to see something like that in a car crash?"

"Lifting your arms to cover your head isn't exactly a typical reaction to having a truck plow into you. No, it's more a reaction to protecting your head from being hit by something like a fist, a bat, or a hammer."

"This fracture was done before the accident."

"But what accident? We don't have any evidence of an accident except an eyewitness statement from a person who we think was known to the victim and who we know is a violent criminal. And look at this. See how Shields's body is lying in the ditch? It's parallel to the road, and her arms are above her head. What does that look like to you?"

Tiffany examined the scene diagram, then went back to the photographs and found the one of the body lying in the ditch.

"Damn. It looks like two people—one at her feet and one at her arms—laid her there."

"Looks like it to me. A very low effort staging. I'm surprised law enforcement didn't pick up on that to begin with. I'd also be willing to bet that the two people who put her there were Brian Crawford and Milo Crane."

"Milo is kind of old to be dragging bodies into ditches. Don't you think?"

"Ten years ago?"

Tiffany frowned, flipping through the pictures. "But how do we prove it? How do we connect Crawford to the body?"

"Wait." Sebastien put his hand on Tiffany's. "Let me see that."

"What? What do you see?" Tiffany leaned in.

"Look here on the pinky and ring fingers of her right hand. What is that on there? Is that dirt?"

"I don't know. It's hard to tell. It could be, I guess."

"Do me a favor. Would you grab my magnifying glass? It's in my desk, top drawer in the center."

Tiffany came back with the magnifier and handed it to Sebastien.

"It almost looks like ink or lead. Take a look."

"I see it. But what is it and what does it mean?"

Sebastien closed his eyes and looked up for a moment. "Do me a favor."

"Another favor?"

"In my desk drawer there's a pencil and a pad of paper."

Tiffany handed him the paper and pencil.

Sebastien took the pencil and used it to scribble on the paper. He erased the marks, then scribbled some more. He did this a few more times.

"What are you writing, Sebastien? What are you doing?"

Just a little experiment. Sebastien held out his right hand and presented the backs of his fingers to Tiffany. "Look at my hand. See the smudges on my fingers? Looks a lot like the dirt on the Shields's right hand."

"I'm not following you, Sebastien."

"Watch carefully." Sebastien put the pad of paper on his lap and wrote "Amber Harrison" in large letters. Next, he flipped the pencil over and erased the page. "See that? When I erase the pencil marks, I have a habit of brushing off the eraser dust with the back of my writing hand. I think most people do. It's too late to prove it, but I believe this shows that on the day she was killed, Shields used a pencil to write and erase—a lot. Was she in class that day, taking a test or doing an assignment? We already know she dropped out of the university midway through that fall semester. If she wasn't in school officially, why was she going to school unofficially? Was she there impersonating Amber?"

25

Barnadette opened the door almost before the final knock. She did not look at all happy to see Tiffany and Sebastien standing on her porch.

"I knew you were with the police, Dr. Grey. You didn't have me fooled. Now, what do you want? I've told you everything I know. What happened to your leg?"

Sebastien's chest tightened as he waited for a sideways look from Tiffany. He should have known this would happen. He was too anxious to confront Barnadette. Tiffany never took her eyes off of the woman in the doorway. *Guess I'll have to deal with that later*, he thought.

"Just a sprained knee."

"Miss Jacobs, we're here to tell you something. It's Bell. Adam Bell is the person with whom you co-hosted the Christmas Eve party."

"Okay."

"You said you forgot."

"And I did. I did forget."

"What about Shelly Shields's boyfriend? You told me you didn't know his last name."

"I didn't. Still don't." Jacobs's answers were curt, with a tone of irritation. "What are you getting at?"

"May we come in, Miss Jacobs?"

Barnadette didn't answer, but she opened the door and made way for the pair to come through.

As Tiffany continued her inquiries, Sebastien watched Barnadette's face closely. He thought he could detect the woman softening. He wondered how long she would take to crack.

"Miss Jacobs, you told me and the original investigators that you were arguing with Amber over the rent. She wasn't paying her share, you said."

"That's true. With Amber out, we couldn't afford the rent."

"We?" Tiffany asked.

"Shelly and I. She was still paying her share, even though she wasn't staying there."

"And when did you sign the lease for the house? Do you remember?"

"I'm sorry. I really don't recall. You must understand, this was all a long time ago."

"We do understand, Miss Jacobs. Let me help you with that. It was a six-month lease, just like the semester prior. You signed it in August. *You* signed it. And Shelly Shields. But, unlike the spring semester, Amber Harrison didn't sign the lease. We spoke to the landlord. He still owns the property and still rents it out to students. Thank goodness."

"Ye-es. Thank . . . goodness," Barnadette muttered.

"You see where we're going with this." Tiffany spoke softly, almost sympathetically. "You never expected Amber to share the rent. You never expected her to live with you because she was dead. Murdered. So how did you cover her third of the rent?"

Barnadette shot up from the loveseat opposite the couch.

"Murdered! I had no idea! I don't know what you're talking about!"

"You may not have known, but you definitely had a hunch,"

interrupted Sebastien. "They were paying you to keep quiet, weren't they?"

"Wait . . . seriously, I don't—"

"You do, Barnadette. You do. Don't waste our time. Crawford is in custody in Rapid City. He's telling them everything. The guy can't shut up. So, what is he going to say about you? Bell, too. We paid him a visit. Interesting guy. He denied everything, of course. So now is a good time for you to jump the line and tell your story."

Barnadette sat down again, tucking her hands between her blue-jean-covered thighs.

"Let me take a crack at a scenario, Dr. Jacobs—I'm going to call you doctor . . . you deserve that much. I think you saw Adam Bell drop Amber's car off in your driveway. And I also believe he knew you saw him. He, Brian Crawford, and Shelly Shields paid you off. As long as you didn't say anything, they would pay Amber's share of the rent. Do you know where that money came from?"

Barnadette replied with a soft "no."

"It came from Amber Harrison," Tiffany broke in. "They killed her, siphoned off her credit card, and paid you a share of the proceeds. So, whether you like it or not, you're in this. Now, we're willing to discuss how deep."

"WHAT MAKES you think Bell dropped the car off?"

They were in Tiffany's cruiser, headed to the loft.

"She didn't deny it," Sebastien replied.

"I noticed that. But how did you guess?"

"Any idea what percentage of men are five-foot-five or under?"

Tiffany shot Sebastien a bewildered glance.

"Seven-point-two percent. That's pretty low. How tall do

you think Bell was?"

"He's a little guy, that's for sure. About five-four, I'd say. Poor fella."

"Remember what the forensics people said about Harrison's car? When they searched it, they found the driver's seat was pulled way forward."

"That's pretty clever, Sebastien."

"Not really. It's practically a trope."

Tiffany's phone called out through the car's speakers.

"Hey there, Erin. You're on speaker. It's me and Dr. Grey."

"Oh, Dr. Grey, I am so glad we got you back."

"Thank you, Erin. So am I."

"Whatcha got, Erin?"

"I just ran our players through the public databases and I thought it might be important that you hear what I found sooner rather than later."

"Shoot."

"It's a little complicated."

"No problem, Erin. I'll explain it to Dr. Grey later." Tiffany's alabaster teeth made her pale skin look almost dark.

"Haha. That's funny. Anyway, I found out that Brian Crawford's dad is in prison."

Sebastien looked over at Tiffany and mouthed, "Human trafficking."

"What's he in for?"

"Human trafficking. Turns out, he went down with that guy from Vegas, Alex Stoyan. They couldn't prove trafficking on Stoyan, so he got kidnapping. Or maybe he turned on Roger Stern."

Sebastien blurted out, "Stern! You're telling us Brian is a Stern! As in, Peter Stern?"

"Technically, no. Brian's mother went back to her maiden name after she and Roger divorced. And she did the same for

Brian. But, yes, Brian Crawford's father is Roger Stern, who is in prison. And there's something else."

"There's more? You are the best, Erin."

"I know. The house out in Fairburn, where Dr. Grey was taken, it doesn't belong to Brian Crawford. It's his legal address, but the home is owned by Peter Stern and Fortunatas Development. Which brings me to Abigail Fortune. She's Crawford's aunt."

Tiffany thanked Erin and ended the call.

"We already knew that Crawford's uncle was Stern. We just didn't know how. But the fact that Crawford's father is in prison for trafficking is huge."

"It proves I've been wrong, if nothing else," declared Sebastien.

"What do you mean?"

"I thought Harrison was taken in an attempt to traffic her. I no longer think that's the case. Crawford had nothing to do with the trafficking. Neither did Abigail or Milo."

"I'm not sure that makes sense, Sebastien. Or maybe I just don't follow you. Are you saying Crawford didn't kill Harrison? And if Fortunatas is not a front for trafficking, why were they trying to take you out?"

"No, I'm almost certain he did. But I don't believe that a girl like Harrison would be kidnapped for trafficking by people who knew her. That's not usually how that works. No, she was killed because she saw something at the Fairburn place. She was going to go to the police. Something forced her to flee and somebody —probably Brian—chased her down, shot her, and left her on the train tracks. We know there were two people involved in that, since there was blood transfer on the passenger's seat of Harrison's car. Makes sense that Adam Bell was number two."

"Brian was trying to protect his uncle, then?"

Sebastien rubbed his right knee as he contemplated Tiffany's question.

"You okay?"

"Yep. Still hurts like a bear though. Yes, I do think that was his motive, along with protecting his father. My guess is that the evidence I found in Stern's house would further incriminate his father and his uncle. Or perhaps he was recruited by Stern to take care of Harrison. He was an ancillary figure in Fortunatas' larger trafficking operation, at any rate. This also resolves something else that has been bothering me."

"Oh?"

"Why did Crawford take me alive? Why not shoot me in the barn or slit my throat? Putting me in his basement was a major risk."

"Why do you think he did it, then?"

"Leverage. He needed a card to play in case the others left him in the lurch."

"What about Milo and Abigail?"

"Milo was a lawyer who doubled as an old-school killer. Abigail was just trying to protect her nephew and brothers."

"Sebastien, I hate to channel your brother, but I think you're jumping to conclusions."

"Can we go talk to Crawford again?"

"I HAVE TO TELL YA, Pete. No offense meant, but that was a stupid plan."

"Do not respond to that, Mr. Stern. Sergeant, unless you have some evidence, beyond the word of a violent young man, I must insist that my client be released at once."

Stern's lawyer had her arms folded on the interview room table. She leaned in for optimal intimidation. Her face was less than a foot from Hank's.

"You must have forgotten about the victim. A Dr. Grey."

Hank broke eye contact with the lawyer and spoke directly to Stern. "You know the name, don't ya, Pete?"

"Do not answer that."

Hank moved his eyes back across the table. "Dr. Grey has given us a statement to the effect that you participated in the attack on him. In fact, you were the one who called Milo Crane and stated, 'We're ready on our side.' The phone records will help corroborate that. As will the fingerprints."

"Fingerprints?" Stern's voice cracked.

"Mr. Stern, I will handle this. Sergeant LeGris, to what are you referring?"

Hank tossed a tri-folded sheet across the table.

"A search warrant for your client. You see, Dr. Grey is a forensic scientist, which you knew. But being one of the evidence-minded kind of people, he made sure to put his fingers and hands all over your pretty leather back seat. Like I said, Pete, it was a dumbass plan."

The lawyer took up the page and began to skim. Hank suspected it was more for show than anything else.

"And, as long as we're talking about witnesses, let's not forget your nephew. He told us everything. He said you and your brother were running a trafficking ring. Only, it was Roger who got popped, along with some guy named Alex Stoyan. That's a good brother you got there, Pete, not throwing you under the bus and all. Too bad Amber Harrison showed up at your house with Shelly Shields for a private party with your nephew and his buddy. Although, it turns out, Harrison wasn't much of a partier. Brian wouldn't say how the poor girl ended up in the storage room, but I have my theories. Maybe she ran in there to hide from Brian, or his friend Adam. Maybe one or both were getting a bit too handsy, if you know what I mean. Hell, given the family penchant for abduction, they probably threw her in there to scare her into complying. However it went down, Harrison was a smart girl. She saw what you had in your basement for what it was. She was going to the cops to report what they did to her and what she found in the house. She urged Shields to go with her. But, no. Her loyalty to your nephew was bigger than her sense of right and wrong. I can only imagine what was going through Harrison's head — stuck out there with a couple of degenerate yahoos and a false friend. Anyway, here we are. Oh, and Brian says it was your idea to make it look like Harrison was still alive. I'm not a lawyer, but I bet we can squeeze a felony murder with your name on it out of that. What do you think, counselor?"

"Sergeant, my client maintains it is his sister, Abigail Fortune, who is behind this whole conspiracy. Mr. Stern had no idea what she was up to."

"You know, you have a point there. We'll have to ask her that when she gets here. My team picked her up at Rapid City Regional Airport a few minutes ago."

Hank capped this final statement off with a gratuitous wink.

EPILOGUE

D r. Grey, I am delighted to learn that you have decided to purchase "Winter Thunder." I do maintain it will set your home apart from all others. In fact, I propose we have an open house to celebrate. We could make it a welcome-to-town party for you, as well. What does your schedule look like for the middle of April? A month should be plenty of time to prepare and send out the invitations. And don't you feel bothered with the details. I will handle everything.

Yours,

Tabitha

Sebastien closed the email. He would respond later. How he became such a people-pleaser, he did not know, but buying the painting seemed like the neighborly thing to do—and Tabitha was his neighbor now. It was time to step out of his comfort zone a bit and become more of a part of his adopted home, although four grand was a pretty hefty price to pay for such personal progress. What happened to thirty-five? Oh well. Tiffany would be proud of him.

The cheap blinds that covered the RV window made a metallic sound as he lifted them to get a better look at Tiffany.

There she was, lying on a beach chair about twenty yards away, reading a book. Her white bikini almost matched her skin, but she was turning a bit pink in the Southern California sun. She would need more sunblock—and he would bring it to her as soon as he finished checking his email and messages.

Bro,

Melissa says if you come back married she will kill you both. Her words, not mine. So take that under advisement. She expects to be invited to the wedding, if you ever con that sweet lady into settling. Tell Tiff that Hank Junior is now big enough for the bouncy seat she got him. It's a big hit, except it makes the little bugger spit up. Of course, Tiffany will probably think that's funny.

Drive safe. And, remember, Detective Reese has limited PTO. We need her back as soon as possible. And you, too, maybe. Just a little.

Hank.

Even Hank and Melissa were on to the subject of marriage. Sebastien considered this a good sign. Maybe he wasn't so far off the mark with his plans. This thought prompted him to continue checking his new emails.

Monsieur Grey,

All possible arrangements have been made. The Opera de Paris billets are secured, as are the Tour du Gastronomie reservations. You must understand that Hotel Cinge Blanc will require payment in full at the time of arrival. Please do let me know if plans change.

Marcel Gugot, Concierge

Sebastien opened the door to the RV, shielding his eyes from the sun as it reflected off the sand. Tiffany was a shadow, a silhouette, from where he stood. She looked up from her book at him.

"Well? How are things back at home?" she called out.

Sebastien turned to look at Parsifal, who showed no signs of interest in the sea air. He closed the RV door and made his way to Tiffany.

"Hank says thanks for the seat you got Hank Junior. He loves it apparently."

"I'm glad to hear that. Lie here, next to me." Tiffany stretched her beach towel to accommodate Sebastien.

"They want to throw me a party back in Custer. Tabitha, my tenant who owns the gallery, offered to host it."

"And you said yes?"

"I haven't replied. But I will say yes."

"I'm proud of you. Oh, is that the lady who took you for four grand when you bought the ugly painting of the bison?"

"Yes. And there is another thing. I've been asked to speak at a conference in Paris in August. It's a paleopathology meeting. I was thinking you could go with me."

"Paris? I've never left the States. That would be amazing! I've always wanted to go there."

His statement was not wholly untrue—the Paleopathology Society was convening its annual meeting in Paris in August, but he was not slated to speak. He had not, in fact, even been approached about speaking. But Sebastien felt confident that this minor detail could be rectified with a phone call to a well-placed colleague in Germany. Tiffany would be none the wiser. To be sure, he was not completely comfortable with the subterfuge, but Sebastien was given to understand that nearly all the most romantic marriage proposals contain an element of trickery.

"That's great to hear. You better clear it with Hank, though. He's already worried about your allotment of vacation days."

Tiffany turned and rested her head on his chest, stroking his side lovingly.

"You can just tell your brother to shove it. I have plenty of time off. Hell, I haven't taken a vacation day in years. Ooh, maybe we can call it a training conference?"

"You don't know what paleopathology is, do you?"

"Fair point. Doesn't matter, though. Like I said. I have plenty of time. And I wouldn't miss a trip to Paris for the world."

"We may as well make a grand trip and visit some other places too, as long as you have the time off."

"Great idea! Where did you have in mind?"

"I don't know. We could go to Bavaria. I've been on the waiting list for the Bayreuth Festival for a long time. This could be my year."

Tiffany looked up at him, scratching his now mature beard.

"That's not an opera thing, is it?"

"Did I say Bavaria? I meant the Riviera—beaches, shops, great food."

Tiffany gave him a tight squeeze across his chest, which provided all the affirmation he needed.

Sebastien looked out at the water, noticing the waves pull back a layer of sand as they retreated into the deep. It was funny how things could be utterly mundane for an entire lifetime, then take on profound meaning at just the right moment. He, too, was feeling the layers being pulled back into the deep layers of insecurity and regret that he hoped would never be washed ashore again.

THE END

ABOUT THE AUTHOR

ABOUT THE AUTHOR

Ryburn Dobbs taught biological anthropology and forensic anthropology at several colleges throughout the San Francisco Bay Area and spent ten years as a forensic anthropologist, working dozens of death investigations. In addition to his anthropological pursuits, Ryburn also worked as an investigative analyst specializing in homicides and unsolved cases.

Where the Blood is Made is the third in the Sebastien Grey series of novels. Visit his Amazon page at https://www.amazon.com/Ryburn-Dobbs/e/B08LN63PC6/.

For more information about Ryburn and updates on new books please visit www.ryburndobbs.com.

CPSIA information can be obtained
at www.ICGtesting.com
Printed in the USA
BVHW031701300922
648400BV00012B/507